Fields of Gold

Fields of Gold

Bridget Kraft

Five Star • Waterville, Maine

First Edition
First Printing: November 2005

Published in 2005 in conjunction with Tekno Books.

Set in 11 pt. Plantin by Christina S. Huff.

Printed in the United States on permanent paper.

Library of Congress Cataloging-in-Publication Data

Kraft, Bridget.
    Fields of gold / by Bridget Kraft.—1st ed.
        p. cm.
      ISBN 1-59414-362-5 (hc : alk. paper)
      1. Swindlers and swindling—Fiction. 2. Real estate
developers—Fiction. 3. Women landowners—Fiction.
4. Women farmers—Fiction. 5. Revenge—Fiction. I. Title.
PS3611.R34F54 2005
    813'.6—dc22   2005024278

Dedication

To Colleen

Acknowledgements

Few writers complete a book without help from other writers. I'd like to thank the members of my critique groups, Megan Chance, Elizabeth DeMatteo, Linda Lee, Jena MacPherson, Melinda McRae, Karen Muir, Joanne Otness, and Sharon Thomas for their editorial suggestions and, more importantly, their friendship.

I'd also like to thank my husband, Paul, for his help researching the Mendocino County hop industry and for his love and continued support.

Chapter 1

Northern California
April, 1882

*. . . can I run the farm alone? If I can't, what will I do? Oh, God, I
wish Father and Mother were here . . .*

Scattered applause and murmured voices pulled
Guinevere Talbot from her grief-stricken thoughts. She
glanced around, momentarily startled to find herself in the
midst of a town meeting. The town used the Methodist
church for its gatherings, and tonight people squeezed into
the unpadded oak pews or stood around the perimeter of the
room. The only other time Guin remembered seeing it this
full was at her parents' funeral a few weeks ago.

Willing back the tears, she stilled her fingers from
kneading her nubby black wool skirt. She felt a hand on her
shoulder and flinched.

"Are you all right, my dear?" Dr. Beauregard Jackson
whispered. A kind smile crossed his deeply lined face. He
shifted his long legs and ran a gnarled hand through his leonine mane of silver hair.

Guin nodded, not knowing what to say. She forced herself
to take a deep breath, and the pungent smell of damp wool
and warm bodies filled her nostrils. The people seated
around her—neighboring farmers and townspeople—listened to the speaker at the front of the room, their faces
bright with excitement.

9

Guin shook off her anguish and tried to concentrate on the tall, black-haired man, Kellen O'Roarke, standing at the oak lectern. "My resort, nestled at the base of your foothills, will bring new prosperity to this valley. People from San Francisco will flock to take the waters."

He gestured broadly to the crowd. "Many of you will find new markets for your farms' produce."

If she still had a farm. Guin's mind again wandered from the speaker's resonating words. Her gaze drifted around the room.

Dr. Jackson patted her hand gently. "It's mighty good you came tonight. Time you started mixin' with other folks again."

She turned away, not wanting to blurt out that she didn't care about mixing with other people. Her whole world had turned upside down in the last month. She wanted her old life back. She wanted her parents alive.

". . . I want what's best for this valley, what's best for you. My hot springs resort is what you need to bring prosperity here. . . ." O'Roarke's baritone voice projected around the crowded assembly. From the back of the room Guin could easily see his expressive features.

Even if it was only from annoyance at having to be here, a spark of life pulled her from her lethargy. For the first time in she couldn't remember how long, the mists of mourning dissipated. She resigned herself to pay attention to the stranger.

Kellen O'Roarke was a smooth-talking promoter if she ever heard one. She listened to people around her murmur their agreement to his plans, but she wanted to make up her own mind. He had a flair with words to excite people like this, but skepticism flickered in her mind, warning her not to believe anyone who promised riches for all.

"What is he talking about?" Guin quietly asked Dr. Jackson.

"Seems this young man bought the old Comstock homestead, the one that's lying fallow in the foothills outside of town past your place. Plans to build himself a fancy resort around those hot springs. They're all the thing with the well-to-do."

"You mean like the resort at Saratoga Springs?"

Dr. Jackson nodded. "But Mr. O'Roarke, he says the springs here are something mighty special, better than anything those folks back east have. He's even had the water analyzed," he added. He raised his eyebrows to emphasize his point.

Dr. Jackson's words intensified her attention, and she glanced sharply toward the lectern. A chill rushed through her at the similarities between this stranger's plan and the disaster that had forced her family to leave New York when she was a child.

She turned to Dr. Jackson, prepared to share her misgivings with him, then paused. Kellen O'Roarke had stopped speaking, and the room sounded suddenly hollow now that his resonant tones no longer filled the air. Scattered applause started, then grew until many in the room clapped to show their vigorous approval of the new resort. A few stood to show their endorsement.

Guin found herself stirred by their excitement, but she hesitated. She didn't want to draw attention to herself by sitting quietly, yet she was reluctant to support the resort.

"Mayor Franklin looks pleased with the response," Dr. Jackson said as he applauded tepidly.

"Mr. Gaspard is smiling too," she said.

"A banker is always pleased when new money comes to town," Dr. Jackson said dryly. "Lawrence is no exception."

11

To her surprise, Guin found herself smiling. The expression felt foreign, reminding her that she'd had nothing to smile about for over a month. Lawrence Gaspard stood next to Mayor Franklin and Mr. O'Roarke, mopping his shiny forehead with a white linen handkerchief.

"Don't you think he's smiling a bit too broadly?" she asked, thinking that the banker always perspired heavily when he was excited or nervous.

"Maybe he's concerned his vault won't be large enough to hold all that money," Dr. Jackson scoffed.

Guin couldn't hold back a small laugh. It sounded rusty, stale from lack of use.

"Come, my dear," Dr. Jackson said. "It's time I escorted you home."

Guin rose from her bench and flicked her skirts to smooth them. "You don't have to. It's not far and I'm perfectly safe." She slipped into her serviceable brown wool coat.

Dr. Jackson straightened her collar. "No gentleman lets a lady go home alone," he admonished.

Guin shook her head, knowing she would never prevail over his southern sense of chivalry. The main door of the church stood wide open and the chattering crowd spilled outside to the grassy yard. Guin eased into the aisle, eager to reach the fresh air.

"Nice to see you, Miss Guin," a neighboring farmer said.

"Sorry about your folks," said the schoolmarm.

Guin had finally started to feel like her old self, but the well-wishers stirred painful reminders of her loss and made her wish she hadn't come. Nodding and murmuring her appreciation for their condolences, Guin wound her way through the crowd, yearning to escape attention. The tears she'd resisted all evening threatened to spill down her cheeks.

12

She shouldn't have come tonight; it was still too soon to be in public again.

As she neared the door, Guin stopped short. Mayor Franklin had started a receiving line. Everyone had to pass Mr. O'Roarke and shake his hand before escaping to the dwindling daylight. She didn't want to meet this man. She wanted to go home.

Inching forward, she watched him. Mr. O'Roarke wore his raven black hair combed back from his freshly-shaven face, revealing a high forehead that she remembered hearing once was a sign of intelligence. Dark eyebrows narrowly framed his eyes, with natural arches at the outer edges. They gave him the appearance of always being interested in what a person had to say. How useful for him. Her distrust grew.

Yes, he was a handsome man, if one liked the charismatic type. She didn't, and she pulled herself from the momentary daze. Her reaction to him bothered her because usually she liked people when she first met them, and overlooked any minor flaws. The only thing she could attribute this evening's reaction to was that her nerves were still too raw to deal with anyone new.

O'Roarke's broad shoulders and chest nearly filled the doorway. Guin eyed the narrow opening left for her to squeeze past. She didn't want to come close to him and his entourage of the mayor and the banker. She didn't want to be forced to talk to them. If only she could slip through unnoticed.

"Miss Talbot, so nice to see you this evening. I didn't expect you to make it." The mayor's voice rang loud and clear through the crisp evening air, catching her by surprise.

Guin winced as people turned their heads to look at them. She liked the mayor, even though he always sounded as if he were on the campaign trail. Her thoughts in disarray, she

13

scrambled to say something suitable for the occasion, something that wouldn't offend him, something that would let her pass by without further delay.

"Thank you, Mayor Franklin. I wouldn't want to miss one of your town meetings. They always give a person so much to think about later," she said softly, praying he wouldn't challenge her.

Instead, the mayor laughed heartily and clapped her on the back. She lurched forward, her hands coming up as she collided with the rock-hard chest of Kellen O'Roarke. She gasped at the strength in his hands as he gripped her shoulders and steadied her.

She caught his clean scent—shaving soap rather than the overpowering cologne she would have expected. He relaxed his hold and stepped away, and she realized that for just an instant, she'd felt safe.

"Are you all right?" His steely blue eyes scanned her face. Shaken by her reaction to him, she heard the mayor fuss over her and apologize, and she knew she should move on before she made a spectacle of herself. But her feet were rooted to the floor. To bolster her original opinion, she looked for something wrong with him and saw with surprise that the skin on O'Roarke's face was smooth and taut. He could not be more than a few years older than Guin herself, thirty at the most. Yet, he projected the confidence of a much older man.

"Yes, I'm f-fine," she finally stammered.

"I'm Kellen O'Roarke. And whom do I have the honor of meeting?" Kellen asked, his deep voice soft, almost a caress.

His tone, the intensity of his gaze, thawed the edges of the icy cold that had enveloped her for so long. He was a dangerous man, she thought with a start. He had drawn her to him like a child to a forbidden object. No wonder he was such a successful promoter.

"This is Guin Talbot," Mayor Franklin said as he patted her shoulder, more gently this time, with his beefy hand. "Her family—I mean, she owns a nice little place outside of town. In your direction, in fact."

Determined to get away, Guin reached out to push her way past the men. Instead, she found her hand clasped in O'Roarke's firm grip.

She looked at her trapped hand, swallowed by his much larger one. She had to get away from this man with eyes that saw to her soul and a voice that could charm the devil. She knew she should be careful, but he made her want to throw caution aside.

Then, she noticed his hands were smooth and callous-free. These were not a working man's hands. How could he understand their lives if he wasn't one of them? Her negative impression restored, Guin tried to ease away. "It's nice to meet you, Mr. O'Roarke. I hope you enjoy your visit."

Kellen O'Roarke continued to hold the woman's hand longer than was entirely proper, but he didn't care. "I'm sure I will, although I plan to stay for longer than just a visit." Through her gloves, Kellen could feel fragile bones, slender fingers, so different from the solid, square hands of the other women he had met this evening.

He had seen her in the crowd while he spoke from the lectern. At least he'd seen the top of her head amidst the sea of shining faces turned toward him, an island of stillness in the applauding crowd. For a moment, he had felt a pang of frustration that he hadn't moved her with his words as he had the others. Then he had finished his oration and the mayor hurried him to the door. When people started to leave, he'd lost sight of her until she approached the door.

"Did you like my speech?" he asked.

"You make a lot of promises, Mr. O'Roarke."

15

He kept his disappointment at her benign response from showing, and wondered why he even bothered with someone such as Miss Guin Talbot. Her shapeless brown coat gave him no clue to her figure. But her face was thin, and her cheekbones defined, so she must be slender.

It was her hair, though, that brought him up short. An ordinary brown and pulled into a tight ball at the back of her head, it made her look like a disapproving old spinster.

"Perhaps we can talk about my promises later," he said, startled to discover that he wanted to seek her out again. Other citizens backed up behind her, and from their chatter, he knew they approved of his plans. So why did this one young woman matter?

She looked at him with unflinching dark eyes and a complete lack of flirtatiousness. He saw the pain she tried to hide, the deep sorrow.

"I'm sure many found your proposal an interesting one, Mr. O'Roarke." Her subdued voice held no promise of future meetings. Guin turned toward the line of people behind her. "I mustn't keep these other fine people waiting. Goodnight, gentlemen." She tugged her hand from his.

Kellen watched her slip away and blend into the crowd gathered on the lawn in the dwindling evening light. The reluctance of one woman on one small farm was not going to affect his plans, Kellen reassured himself. Yet the strange sense of loss lingered.

The mayor clapped his shoulder, and Kellen shook thoughts of the strange young woman from his mind, telling himself she was not worth his time, that he would have nothing more to do with her. Once again, he turned his attention to wooing those who waited to talk with him.

After returning to his hotel room later that evening, Kellen unhooked his tie and tugged it from around his neck, tossing it carelessly into a chair. He unbuttoned the top of his shirt and poured himself a brandy.

"Winfield?" he called to his assistant.

"Yes, sir," a man answered from the next room.

"Join me in a celebratory drink?"

Winfield came through the adjoining doorway. A tall, thin man, he gave Kellen a droll grin. "Certainly, sir."

Kellen poured brandy into another glass, then sank into a well-padded chair and breathed a sigh of relief. As he put his feet on the low table in front of him, he noticed the tie had slithered off the satin upholstery to the floor, but he chose to ignore it.

"To the successful launch of the last step in our plan, Winfield."

"Hear, hear, sir."

The two men clinked glasses, then relaxed to enjoy the imported brandy.

"Winfield, where are my cigars?"

"Those nasty smelling things are in the drawer next to your chair."

Kellen grimaced at the unsolicited commentary. He opened the drawer of the small mahogany table next to him and in a few moments, he was puffing contentedly. He enjoyed a good cigar and a glass of fine brandy after a successful evening, and if he did say so himself, he felt the residents of Spring Valley were greeting his plan with hearty approval.

Winfield coughed in an exaggerated fashion. "Odious things, sir," he said, waving away the smoky air in front of him.

Kellen eyed him with amusement. "For an Englishman, Winfield, you don't seem to understand the need for a man to savor his moments of victory."

"I understand the need, just not why one must foul the air around one, as well. Shall I open a window, sir?"

Kellen knew he would be politely badgered until he agreed. "You may open it a crack, only enough to draw the smoke out."

While his companion tugged at the window, Kellen crossed the room to pour himself another drink.

"It did seem to go smashingly well tonight," Winfield said.

"Yes, it did. Better than I anticipated." Kellen glanced around the room as he reclaimed his chair. "Needless to say, the resort's accommodations will be significantly better than those we've found here in town."

"Spring Valley is rather off the main thoroughfare."

"True. But, that'll change, Winfield." Kellen leaned forward, his elbows resting on his knees. "The railroad will bring San Franciscans here on holiday to enjoy the waters. And I'll be in the middle of them, mingling as if I belonged—and I will belong by then."

"Yes, sir, you will belong."

"Here's to you, Da," Kellen said softly to himself, raising his glass in salute. Soon he'd be in a position to avenge his father's death and bring down the man responsible for it. He finished the remaining brandy in one gulp. "Did you have time to scout the best route between Spring Valley and the resort for the spur line?"

"Yes, sir, I did," Winfield said. "There is a perfect route topographically. Straight and flat. We can build within the budget you have. Barely."

Kellen gave him a sharp look. "Are you sure?"

Winfield shrugged. "We have estimated the costs the best we can. Unless I made a serious error in my calculations, I believe we have enough money."

Kellen scrubbed his hand across his face and mentally ran through the numbers again. Everything he had was tied up in this project. He was mortgaged to the hilt, and couldn't borrow another dollar if his life depended on it. The resort had to open and start making money immediately or he would still lose everything if he could not make the loan repayments on time. Even with his back against the wall, he refused to consider selling shares in the resort. The only way to protect it was for it to be all his.

"I can take you to see it in the morning if that is convenient."

Winfield's words broke through Kellen's worries. Brushing aside his concerns, he smacked his hands and rubbed them together. "Tomorrow should be fine. I don't think the mayor, Franklin, or the banker . . . what's his name again?"

"Lawrence Gaspard, sir."

O'Roarke rued his poor memory for names. Everything else he recalled easily: an itemized bid for a project, the price of a stock five years ago, the sights he'd seen on his many travels. But names escaped him. "Gaspard. That's right. I'll try to remember. It would not do to forget the name of one's banker, now, would it?" Kellen sportily mimicked his companion's voice.

Winfield responded with a chuckle. "No, sir, it would not."

"We'll leave early, right after breakfast. We won't attract as much attention that way."

Winfield shook his head. "I doubt you can go anywhere without being noticed, sir. After tonight's meeting, you will have many eager supporters who will want to discuss their roles in the resort with you. But I will do what I can."

All those eager supporters, Kellen thought. *All except for that one young woman. What was her name?*

When she had fallen against him, he had gripped her delicate shoulders and discovered with surprise that she was firm, not soft. Kellen thought about their brief conversation. No, there didn't appear to be anything soft or enticing about her, and she certainly wasn't the kind of comely, voluptuous woman who normally interested him.

He loved pretty things, and he enjoyed looking at attractive women. When he saw people like that young woman, he wanted to ask why they didn't try to make themselves more appealing. It seemed such a waste to not make the most of whatever one had to work with. Still, there was great sorrow in her eyes, and he had the strangest urge to protect her.

He shook his head irritably. *What the hell was her name, anyway?*

"Do you have time for supper?" Guin asked as she and Dr. Jackson approached her farm. She had not been very good company since they'd left the meeting, and she appreciated his special effort to escort her home. She owed him so much for all the other kindnesses he'd shown her in the past few months. But right now, after being in town for the first time in weeks, she wasn't ready to be alone, and she still felt unsettled about Kellen O'Roarke and his grand scheme.

The elderly man smiled broadly at her. "I always have time to spend with a pretty woman."

Guin brushed aside his compliment with a wave of her hand. "You don't have to say those things to me," she said, turning the wagon down the drive to the farmhouse. She noticed the foreman's cabin was dark; Soledad must be waiting for her at the house.

"I—" A deep throaty bark cut off her words. "Colonel! It's me," Guin called as she stepped from the wagon. A large, bear-like black dog bounded down the front porch steps and gamboled around her. Guin sank her hand into his thick fur and scratched his ruff.

She turned to Dr. Jackson and saw that he had already unharnessed her horse from the wagon and was taking him into the barn. Guin headed for the house, while Colonel romped along beside her.

"Ah, you home again," said Soledad as Guin entered the kitchen. The wise old Pomo woman had been a family friend for years. The day Guin's parents died, Soledad had left her nearby village and quietly moved into the foreman's cabin across the yard. She stoked the fire in the stove and set a pot of stew on to reheat. "I cook dinner."

"Thank you," Guin said. Now that she was home, she was too exhausted to do more than hang up her coat. "Dr. Jackson's joining us."

Soledad mumbled something to herself and started coffee on a rear burner. "I go now. You finish okay?"

"Yes, thank you."

She turned to study Guin with dark button eyes. "You rest."

Guin leaned down to hug the woman. "I will. Thank you," she said again.

After Soledad left, Guin washed her face and hands and glanced around the kitchen. Soledad had cleaned, but they were almost out of wood for the stove. Chopping more kindling was one task she hadn't had time to tackle today. A number of chores had been left unfinished because of that town meeting. But she couldn't blame it all on the meeting. Each day she slipped a little further behind, she thought with annoyance. What was she going to do?

Guin stirred the stew while she considered the meeting. Or rather, the man who'd done the talking tonight. She could still hear his strong voice resonating in the church, and she wondered absently if he had ever chimed in with a choir. She shook the odd notion from her mind as Dr. Jackson joined her.

A little later, Dr. Jackson sat at the kitchen table and stirred the bowl of hot stew Guin set before him. "Have you given some consideration to what you're going to do?" he asked.

"I've thought about it, but I can't decide." Guin took a tentative bite from her steaming spoon. "If I sell the farm and get a good price, I'd have enough to pay off the bank loan Father took out last winter, but I don't know what I would do if I left here."

Dr. Jackson nodded. "You might could find a job in town."

Guin smiled at his southern phrase, then grimaced. "Doing what? My needlework isn't very good, and there isn't enough call for it. Mrs. Bennett would need someone more outgoing than me to work in her store."

She took a couple more bites of her supper. "If I stay, I'm not sure I can do all that Father did to grow the hops and harvest them. But I can't imagine leaving here, Dr. Jackson. This is my home."

Dr. Jackson caught her hand and gave her a solicitous look. "The decision can wait a mite longer. You know I'll help any way I can, my dear."

Guin rose from her seat and threw her arms around his neck. The tears she'd held back all evening flowed freely. "It's so hard without them. Why did they have to die?"

Dr. Jackson patted her gently. "I wish it could have been different, Miss Guin, I surely do. That fever that took your ma and pa was the worst I've seen in many years of doctoring. All we can do is pray they's with the Lord, and keep livin' our lives as best we can."

She eased into her chair and swiped at the tears trickling

down her face. "I know. It's just that Father was so happy here." She smoothed the apron, her hands methodically pressing against the fabric while she thought about her parents.

"Father was one of the New York Talbots," she said. "We weren't the ones with the big money, just cousins. We lived comfortably, but Father wasn't satisfied. He wanted to make a lot of money quickly, and so he invested in a resort project. When the project failed, Father lost everything, and he was too proud to tell anyone. We had no choice, but to come west and start over again."

A look of understanding crossed Dr. Jackson's aged face, and he sat quietly for a moment. "Most all who settled here lost their livelihood or their home, or was looking for a new life. That's nothing to be ashamed of."

"I don't think my parents were embarrassed once they came. They just didn't want to admit to the rest of the family that they'd made a foolhardy mistake."

"So your parents' investing is why you're so ruffled by these plans for a resort?"

"It's the same type of thing, Dr. Jackson. This man, Kellen O'Roarke, comes here with his big plans and everyone gets excited." She crushed the napkin in her lap. "You saw everyone tonight at the meeting. That's all they're going to talk about for weeks. If this is such a wonderful plan, and Mr. O'Roarke is as prosperous as he appears, why does he need to involve everyone else in his schemes? It's like what happened to my father all over again."

"But, you might be wrong. He didn't say nothing about folks investing in his resort. Just that they'd have to be prepared for more business from those rich people coming through." Dr. Jackson studied her for a moment. "Surely you don't begrudge folks hoping to get ahead?"

"At the expense of others, I do." Guin stood and gathered the dirty dishes, relieved to have something to talk about besides her own precarious circumstance.

Dr. Jackson sighed and rose stiffly from his chair. "I should be getting back to town." He gave her a peck on the cheek. "No telling what's waiting for me there. Thank you kindly for the supper, Miss Guin. I enjoyed it immensely."

She eyed him archly. "And the company?"

He laughed at her impertinent question. "I especially enjoyed the company. It's nice to see you jest again, Miss Guin."

He leaned down to pet Colonel, but kept his gaze focused on her. "Don't you be fretting now, you hear? You just take the time you need to decide what you want to do. And don't be taking on the cares of the town. Those fools can fend for themselves."

Chapter 2

Guin followed Dr. Jackson outside and watched him ride down the drive, waving one last time when he turned onto the road and cantered out of sight. She rubbed her arms and shivered in the chill damp of evening. Worries about her future swirled through her mind, forcing her to let go of the past, to stop wishing her life could return to the way it was. If she were to survive, she had to make some decisions about her future. And, quite frankly, the future looked rather bleak. For the first time in weeks, she felt the stirrings of interest in things around her, awareness of something more than her profound grief.

After Guin tidied the kitchen, she went to the parlor to read *The Fair God*. Tonight, the historical novel failed to hold her interest, and she shifted restlessly in her chair.

Feeling ill-prepared to think about her future, Guin again tried to focus on the printed words. This time, her distracted thoughts slipped to the meeting, to Kellen O'Roarke and his big plans to build a resort. No one could deny his charisma and his compelling message. The combination made him a dangerous man. His deep, rich voice had filled the room, and his words had inspired his listeners, exciting them about their new potential. If she hadn't known better, she would have been swayed right along with the others, believed his promises, and been prepared to follow him and to do whatever was necessary to make the dreams come true. She knew better. And still, she had almost fallen under his spell.

Exasperated, she closed the book and rose from her seat. She could not shake the image of Kellen O'Roarke, or the memory of how her breath had caught when the mayor pushed them together in the church doorway. Or how unsettled she felt afterwards.

That sense of breathlessness had caught her by surprise, that rushing in her ears, that loss of awareness of her surroundings. Truth was, she'd never met so handsome a man in her life and wasn't sure she liked how she'd felt. Her life had been a full one, working side by side with her parents, worrying over the young hop vines each spring, coaxing them up the poles, and then savoring the heady rush of satisfaction when the harvest was in.

She'd never been lonely. While she made friends easily, none of the young men in town were interested in her romantically, and she'd felt no desire to change that. Of course, none of them wore clothes that emphasized the breadth of their shoulders. None of them looked at her through determined blue eyes that made her wish, however fleetingly, the interest was for personal, rather than business, reasons. Not one of them had enveloped her hand in his, making her feel dainty. She shook her head, dispelling her wayward thoughts. This man she'd been thinking of was a fantasy. Her fantasy certainly wasn't Kellen O'Roarke.

Moving to the window, she lifted the lacy curtain and looked outside. She'd lived in this house fifteen years, alone for the past month, except for Soledad. Guin seldom saw her, but knowing she was there comforted her and eased the loneliness.

It was late now, and thick layers of clouds blocked the moon's light. Guin rubbed her arms as an apprehensive chill spread through her. The resort would bring strangers to the area, drifters and others looking for work or a way to make a fast dollar. Before this resort scheme, the area held no attraction for troublemakers. Guin worried that the valley's peaceful atmosphere would change. She tried to shake the unsettled feeling, but it wouldn't fade.

She told herself she wasn't troubled by Mr. O'Roarke and his plans, that she wasn't intimidated, didn't feel threatened by him. But since the town meeting, she'd been forced to admit she was on the precipice of change. A change she did not want to face.

In the early morning light, Kellen rode toward the river with Winfield to see the railroad spur line route. He'd tried to think of everything, even ordering special railroad cars to bring guests in style from San Francisco. When the train reached the town, the railroad would disconnect the resort cars from the main train and connect them to Kellen's locomotive, which would bring them on the spur line directly to the resort.

The resort had to be opened on the money he'd saved and already borrowed. It had to succeed. Otherwise, Kellen was ruined. After ten years of hard work and planning, he didn't know if he could start all over again from the bottom.

"This has to work, Winfield. The guests can't be inconvenienced in any way. Otherwise, they'll find someplace else to go on holiday." He would let nothing go wrong with this project.

"Quite true, sir. I am certain we are doing everything possible to avoid those little nuisances."

Kellen stopped his horse and rose in his stirrups to survey the land around them. Trees lined the narrow river's edge, and in between he could see the field on the other side of the bridge. Compared to the new grass and wildflowers along the road and the spring color dusting the surrounding foothills, the farmland struck him as empty. All he saw were furrows and mounds, row upon row of them, with weeds filling the vacant spaces.

"The resort is straight across to that hollow between the hills." Kellen pointed across the barren field toward the foothills.

"Yes, sir. This road follows the property lines of a Miss Talbot and a Mr. Meyer. I propose that our spur line run parallel to the road from town to this point, and then go directly to the resort from here."

His gaze following the direction of Winfield's hand, Kellen frowned. "We can afford that?"

"I believe so, sir, even with the additional expense of a bridge. The land is straight, flat, and easy to build on. Other routes would cost you much more, what with the hilly terrain, the crisscrossing river, and all. I regret that my suggestion does not follow the most scenic of routes."

Kellen smiled at his associate. "Winfield, by the time the guests reach this point, they won't be interested in scenery. They'll be in a hurry to reach the resort and soak in the mineral springs. We'll build on your route."

Kellen surveyed the area again before settling into his saddle. "There's a farmhouse down the road. We can stop today and offer to buy the land from the farmer—what was his name?"

"It is a she, sir. Miss Talbot."

Kellen thought for a moment, then raised his eyebrows speculatively. The image of a plain young woman flashed through his mind. The one who'd looked him straight in the eye, the one who'd held his hand with a steady grip. The one, he reminded himself, he'd thought he wouldn't have to see again.

"Ah, yes. Miss Guin Talbot. I met her last night."

"I understand, sir, that her parents both died from the fever that swept through here less than a month ago."

"She's all alone?" Kellen asked in surprise. That explained the deep sadness he'd seen in her eyes.

Winfield nodded. "Yes, she is quite alone. From what I gather, her parents were rather reclusive, and she has behaved much the same since their passing. Some in town speculate she will lose her farm."

Kellen understood all too well the loss of a parent, but he couldn't help but feel a twinge of guilt, even though his proposal might be well timed. "Well, then, she shouldn't object to making some money on her fallow land, now, should she? Might even agree to sell that strip for a reasonable price."

"If you say so, sir," Winfield responded dutifully.

The two men cantered down the road, then slowed when they came to the drive leading to the house.

"Perhaps you would like me to approach the young lady first?" Winfield offered.

Kellen shook his head. "No, I'll do it. Last night, she didn't seem too thrilled by our plans, but that was before she knew she'd profit from them." Kellen glanced around at the empty fields. "This might be her only opportunity to make some money. She can either keep her place—not that I can understand why she would want to—or leave."

"I am certain she will appreciate how much effort you have put into assisting her with her future."

Kellen caught the amused tone Winfield used when he thought Kellen had overstepped his boundaries. "Don't start acting sanctimonious on me."

"Of course not, sir. I did not mean to suggest that you did not have the young lady's best interests at heart."

A glint of humor was still in Winfield's eyes. Kellen tugged on his vest and ran his hand through his hair to smooth it. "Of course, I do. I'll be back in a few minutes. You ride on ahead and I'll catch up with you."

Kellen urged his horse into a trot down the lane. As he approached the house, he spotted hints of neglect. Yes, he had come at just the right time for Miss Talbot.

A deep growl distracted him from how much Miss Talbot was going to appreciate his offer. He reined his horse to a stop and from a reasonable distance assessed the situation. The beast standing at the bottom of the porch steps appeared huge to Kellen, who'd never been comfortable around dogs. At least, from the growl he thought it was a dog. But then again. . . .

"Nice dog," he said tentatively. "Hello! Anybody home?" he called, reluctant to get down from his horse.

He saw an upstairs curtain move, and after a few moments, the front door opened. Guin Talbot stepped outside and paused at the top of the porch steps. She wore a loose fitting black wrapper, and, again, he felt a twinge of frustration at her shapeless clothes.

"Mr. O'Roarke?"

Her voice drifted to him like a summer breeze over a field. He found himself pleased that she recognized him and remembered his name. Perhaps he'd made more of an impression on her than he'd initially thought. "Yes, ma'am. And, you're Miss Talbot."

She nodded and crossed her arms, her gaze steady, as if waiting for him to take the lead.

"May I talk to you for a few minutes?" He saw her eyes narrow, and he hurried on. "I think you'll find it well worth your while."

Her eyebrows rose as she assessed him, and he sensed from the tilt of her head that he'd come out lacking in her appraisal. That annoyed him. After all, he was here to help her.

She snapped her fingers. The dog quieted and sat next to her like a sentry. "Come in, then."

Kellen climbed from his horse and followed her into the house. He kept a nervous watch on the dog, which padded along behind him.

Once inside, Kellen took a deep breath. The clean, pungent smell of furniture polish mingled with a sweet yeasty aroma from the kitchen reminded him of how nomadic his life had been. For a brief moment, he wondered what it would have been like to grow up in a house like this, living in one place for more than a few months at a time.

Guin shut the door and took his hat, then guided him to the parlor. "Would you like some coffee?"

"That would be very nice, Miss Talbot. But I wouldn't want you to go to any trouble."

"Bringing you coffee isn't going to be the trouble, Mr. O'Roarke."

He watched her leave the room, the slight swaying of her skirt drawing his attention and curiosity. He had the feeling there was considerably more to Miss Guin Talbot than he may have first thought. He glanced around the room, trying to find some clue as to the best way to approach her.

The furnishings were what he'd expected, comfortable, but not fancy. A few family pictures stood on the mantle. He stopped to examine one of a man and woman with a young girl whom he assumed was Guin. Despite the formality of the pose, there was something about the tilt of their heads, a slight leaning toward each other that bespoke closeness. He felt a twinge; the pain from his own loss had faded over the years, but never disappeared. He and his father had cared deeply about each other. They'd traveled the state seeking their fortune. He set the picture back in its place.

At the sound of swishing skirts, he turned to see Miss

Talbot carrying a sterling silver tray laden with a coffee pot, fine china cups and saucers, and plates with cake. The quality of the service intrigued him. This wasn't what he would have expected from a rural farm.

Striding across the room to take it from her, he was surprised she bore its weight with such ease, and followed her to the settee. She poured their coffee and he noticed her hands, the skin soft-looking, the fingers long and tapering, out of place on this woman who must do a lot of rough work.

Kellen glanced at her face as she passed him a plate with a slice of cake and his breath caught. Her eyes, reddish brown, the color of fine imported cognac, were surrounded by long feathery lashes much the same color. Amazed, he realized she had the prettiest eyes he'd ever seen. But then she turned away, and he wondered if he had been mistaken.

He decided he was, for he found nothing attractive as he looked at her more closely in the bright morning light, not her pallid skin or the plain brown hair pulled tightly back from her face. She had nothing to recommend her, yet he found her oddly intriguing. The part of him that loved beautiful things sighed with disappointment, but the part that loved a mystery paid closer attention.

"I made the cake earlier this morning, Mr. O'Roarke. I hope you enjoy it."

"Thank you, Miss Talbot. It's not often I have the opportunity to taste fine homemade sweets."

He took a bite and found the cake delicious. The woman might not be able to run a farm, but she sure could bake. Maybe she'd take the money he offered and open a bakery in town. Should do well. She might even supply the resort. Pleased he had her future secure, he decided the time had come for him to make his pitch.

Watching her closely, Kellen set the cup and saucer carefully on the table in front of him and dabbed his mouth with the fine linen napkin she had provided.

"Miss Talbot, I regret to say that this is not a purely social call." He saw wariness creep into her eyes.

"I never considered it might be, Mr. O'Roarke."

His mouth tightened in irritation at her simple statement. "Actually, I'm here to discuss the resort project and its impact on you."

"If that's so, I'm not sure we have much to say to each other. I'm not concerned with your plans, and I fail to see how they will affect me."

"I'm here to make you an offer. I need to build a railroad spur line from the town's train station to the resort." He paused for a moment, warming to his subject as he always did when he talked about his latest project. "You understand why that's important, don't you?"

He sensed more than saw the shift in her demeanor, the wariness replaced by annoyance. A hint of color touched her cheeks as her gaze sharpened.

"I was at the meeting last night, Mr. O'Roarke. I understand you perfectly," she said.

He heard the edge in her voice and decided a different tack would be in order. "Of course, you understand. I never meant to imply . . . but let me get on to my reason for being here."

"Yes, please do." Despite the natural softness of her voice, there was no mistaking the bite.

"I'm prepared to make you a reasonable offer for the use of some of your farm land."

"Why on earth would you want my land?" Her jaw stiffened so imperceptibly that if he hadn't been watching closely he might never have noticed it. He felt her gathering her strength, and a warning sounded in the back of his mind.

"I need to purchase a right-of-way through your property for my railroad spur line, starting about half a mile from the river, and through to the foothills."

Guin reeled at his words.

Her land.

He wanted to take her land. Not all her property; only a piece. She found it difficult to believe he thought for a moment she would sell a strip that would divide her farm in half, destroying her irrigation furrows and making the land unusable for farming. He must imagine her to be a lady of leisure, someone who did not have to earn a living, someone who did not have to provide for herself.

This was her home.

The realization struck her so hard that she almost recoiled from the blow. This was her home. How had she ever thought she could leave?

"And you propose to make me a fair offer for that right-of-way," she said, still struggling to recover from her shock and not scream at him to get out of her house. She looked at him and saw a flicker of uncertainty cross his face despite his confident smile.

"I'm prepared to make you a good offer that will—"

"I'm sorry, but I'm not interested."

"But this would allow you to do whatever you like," he said, gesturing broadly. "Why, you could do well with a bake shop in town or—"

"No, thank you."

He sat back and his expression suddenly brightened, but Guin thought she saw desperation in his eyes.

"Miss Talbot. I underestimated you. Of course, you don't want to sell the land outright. Tell you what. I'm going to offer you something I haven't offered another living soul. In-

stead of buying that strip of land, I'll give you shares in the resort for that right-of-way so you can profit from its success."

His words were like waving a red flag in front of a bull.
Guin struggled to speak calmly. "I've heard enough, Mr.
O'Roarke. I'm not interested in a baked goods shop or anything else you think would be good for me. This is my farm
and I'm quite happy here." She stood abruptly. "Good day to
you."

His face flushed and his mouth tightened as he stood too.
"Hear me out. As I was saying—"

"I've heard enough, Mr. O'Roarke. Good-bye."

"I need this spur line," he blurted, throwing his hands up
in exasperation.

"That is no concern of mine."

"You must understand, Miss Talbot," he said, placing his
hand on her arm.

When he touched her, when he gripped her arm, he
crossed the boundary. Although he towered above her, she
was not afraid. She refused to be bullied or intimidated by
any man. How dare he use his physical strength to force her to
listen to him. Still lying at her feet, Colonel raised his head
and growled a throaty warning.

Guin looked at Kellen's hand on her arm, then at him, her
expression cold and implacable. "Get out," she said, her
voice low.

"Excuse me?" Kellen heard the quiet anger in her voice
and saw the determination in her eyes. The heated fear of
failure whipped through him as he realized he'd made a
grievous tactical error. Kellen quickly released his grip.

"I said, get out." She strode across the room, grabbed his
hat, and flung it at him.

"But—"

"Get out of my house and get off my land. Now."

He had to salvage something from this disaster. "I can see this is a bad time for you, Miss—"

"Mr. O'Roarke, you are not a dimwit. I should think I've made myself perfectly clear." Guin stepped around the corner and returned with a rifle in her hand. "How much clearer can I be?"

Kellen gulped in surprise. "I, ah, I think you've made your point, Miss Talbot. Perhaps we can discuss this when—"

She flipped the bolt and the sound reverberated in Kellen's ears. He hastily backed out of the house and mounted his horse. As he rode down the drive, he turned to see her standing on the porch, still cradling the rifle, watching him until he reached the main road.

His first impression had been correct: Miss Guin Talbot was one woman he didn't want anything to do with. That prim, mousy little lady was trouble. Usually his projects were well received, but when he encountered problems, it was always because of people like her. People who had a narrow view of the world, people who had never ventured outside their own little community. People who did not want anything to change, even if it meant everyone would benefit.

To think he'd wasted time feeling sorry for her because she'd lost her parents. Why, he'd even offered her something he'd refused to offer anyone else: shares in the resort. Well, he'd talk to Winfield and they'd find another route that would work for them.

A few minutes later, he was still fuming when he caught up with Winfield. "That woman pulled a rifle on me!"

"Sounds as if your usual charm failed you, sir."

"It would take a helluva lot more than charm to get anywhere with Guin Talbot," he snarled. "The woman's a menace, Winfield. She shouldn't be allowed to live without a guard."

"A bad reception, eh, sir?"

"I don't want to talk about it." Kellen scowled and nudged his horse into a gallop in the hopes that a hard ride might improve his disposition before they returned to town. He was in no mood to be pleasant with anyone right now.

Guin sank against the closed front door, her heart pounding. A nervous giggle escaped her lips. She'd always had strong opinions and had never been shy about voicing them. But still, she couldn't believe she'd lost her temper, that she'd actually pulled a rifle on a man. What had possessed her?

But then, what had possessed him to think he could come here with a proposition like that? How could he sit there so calmly while he planned to destroy her farm?

She shook her head and replaced the rifle in its stand. The only moment in their whole encounter she appreciated was the memory of Mr. O'Roarke's apoplectic expression when she'd returned to the parlor carrying the weapon and snapped the bolt shut. He would feel pretty foolish if he knew the gun wasn't loaded.

She'd never been one to rudely insist on her own way, but she had to admit to some satisfaction at seeing this tall, smooth-talking man stammer his way out of her house.

She shook her head. He had to know a farm like hers would be ruined by such a plan. If he didn't, then he should. He ought to know what his grandiose schemes did to people such as her who found themselves run over and lost in the dust. Somebody had to stand up to him.

Now that she had made the decision to stay on her farm, heated energy flowed though her. She had no doubt she would question her judgment later when challenges seemed too great, when obstacles loomed before her. It didn't matter;

the farm was hers and, by God, she would do whatever it took to stay on it.

Guin carried the tray to the kitchen and felt one of her headaches coming on. She didn't have time to be ill, she thought with a groan. She didn't have the luxury of lying down for a day or two until the headache passed. She didn't want to take the powders Dr. Jackson gave her because they made her feel so floaty that she might as well have gone to bed.

Guin massaged her temples and the back of her neck, trying to ease the rhythmic pounding she knew from experience would be hard to dispel. Maybe she'd take a few minutes and rest anyway, anything to ease the intensity of the pain as the headache ran its course.

The pain sharpened rapidly. Rather than negotiate the stairs to her room, she made her way to her parents' room. With a sigh, she eased herself onto the downy quilt. Low clouds blanketed the sky, turning the day dreary, yet still bright enough to bother her eyes. But now that she was lying down, she didn't have the strength to get up and pull the shades. Instead, she covered her eyes with a pillow.

Willing herself to keep her mind clear, Guin strove not to think about O'Roarke's proposal. Each time the idea of him taking her land slipped into the periphery of her thoughts, the pain in her head intensified. Instead, she forced herself to picture more pleasant times in her life. Fishing with Dr. Jackson on a warm spring afternoon. Going to town and finding a new book at the store. Sitting on the porch with her parents at the end of a long, hot day to enjoy the summer sunset.

The pain eased, and she drifted into drowsiness until Colonel quietly woofed once, twice, then stood and growled menacingly as he stalked from the room. She groaned and tried to ignore his warning sounds.

Colonel barked seriously now, and Guin struggled to rise. Her head pounded, but still she forced herself to stagger to the window and peek out. A wagon pulled into the yard and stopped next to the front steps.

She groaned again. "What now, Colonel?" she whispered. For a moment she considered not answering the door. But then, she straightened her dress and smoothed her hair as she followed the dog to the front hall.

She took a deep breath and opened the door.

A sprightly older woman, dressed in black bombazine and carrying an ornately carved walking stick, stepped onto the porch. She looked Guin up and down. "Are you Guinevere Talbot?"

"Yes," Guin said slowly, although she sensed she would regret that admission. The woman's patrician features and sherry-colored eyes looked vaguely familiar, but with the pounding in her head, Guin couldn't gather her thoughts together.

"You look terrible, my dear. Appears I've arrived just in time." The woman turned to the man driving the wagon. "We don't have all day, young man. Take those trunks out of the wagon and bring them in."

Guin gaped at the woman, unable to take in what was happening.

"Tell this young man where to put my bags." The woman tucked the walking stick under her arm and stepped around Guin into the house. Turning to gaze about, she peeled off her gloves. "Now don't you stand there dawdling, too. It's time for tea. Call for the girl to serve us in the parlor."

Guin turned to face her. "Who are you?"

The woman stopped and appeared affronted at Guin's question. "I'm your grandmother, of course. Henrietta Talbot."

"Grandmother?" Guin realized that after fifteen years, it was not surprising she had not recognized the older woman. Incredulous, she asked, "Why are you here?"

"You wired that my son and his wife died, and I couldn't ignore my responsibilities and leave you here alone, unchaperoned. I've come to live with you."

"But . . . but. . . ." Guin stopped. She'd thrown Kellen O'Roarke out of her house without a second thought. But this was her grandmother, who'd dropped everything to come stay with her. Only an ungrateful wretch would send the elderly woman back to town.

"Take the bags to the bedroom at the end of the hall," she said to the wagon driver.

Not caring what her grandmother thought, Guin could no longer ignore the throbbing pain in her head. She headed toward the kitchen to take some of Dr. Jackson's powders. Given the way her day was going, maybe she'd take a double dose.

Chapter 3

"What do you mean you have no girl to serve tea?" Henrietta snapped.

For the second time that day, Guin carried a silver service laden with cups, saucers, and plates of cake, and led the way to the parlor. The stabbing agony in her head had subsided, yet Guin worked to keep the pain at bay. She was still reeling from the idea that her grandmother had come all this way to be with her.

"It's very simple, Grandmother." Guin set the tray on the table. "We didn't have servants when Mother and Father were alive, and I don't need a servant if I'm living alone. I'm quite capable of doing this myself."

"That's not the point, my dear." Henrietta seated herself and fussed with her skirts. "A lady always knows how to do these things and is skillful at doing them herself—but only in the most dire of emergencies, mind you." Henrietta shook her head. "What will people think?"

Guin bit back a response as she poured tea. She thought about the coffee she'd served only a few hours earlier. That encounter, too, had started civilly enough. This one didn't promise to end much better. Guin sensed that if she wavered, this feisty little woman would take over her life. Just as Kellen O'Roarke had threatened to do.

"I don't think people in Spring Valley spend much time worrying about who serves my tea," Guin said finally. She restrained a wry smile at the thought of her friends gossiping

41

about her lack of servants, while they did without themselves.

"But you are a Talbot." Henrietta shook her finger at Guin. "You have a role in the community, a vitally important position to maintain."

"Grandmother." Guin took a deep breath to shake the lingering grip of her headache. "This isn't New York. People don't care who we were. In fact, they don't even know."

Henrietta gasped in horror, her hand covering her mouth. "How can you say that? Everyone knows the New York Talbots."

"Not here. Father didn't tell anyone. All he shared was that we were from the East."

"That's all?"

Guin nodded and watched her grandmother's expression change. The elderly woman seemed to deflate before Guin's eyes; her shoulders sagged, her eyes misted.

"My poor boy." Henrietta fumbled in her pocket for a handkerchief and dabbed her eyes. She sniffed, then turned to Guin. "William took the investment failure harder than I thought. I knew he wanted to get out from under his cousins. They were so difficult to live with. Arrogant brutes, really. Quite spoiled by their mother."

Henrietta's hands shook as she reached for her cup and saucer. "It was such a shame the way the cousins objected to that development," she went on in a sad, small voice. She gazed toward the window. "They were just bored. The resort wouldn't have bothered the family at all."

"Father didn't say much about the family after we moved, and I don't remember his cousins very well."

Henrietta started as if she'd forgotten where she was, and sniffed again. "You were only a child. You haven't missed a thing, believe me." Her words were once again crisp and decisive. "Those boys have only grown worse with age. Thank heavens for my trust fund. If it weren't for that, I might have been at their mercy when your grandfather died."

"I remember him. He was so tall and strong, and he carried me on his shoulders everywhere so I could see better than anyone else." Guin leaned against the settee and smiled at the memory. "You must miss him very much."

Henrietta's eyes hardened and her mouth tightened. "It was that war. That stupid, stupid war against those worthless southerners. We'd have been better off to just let them leave the Union. My Daniel was too good to waste on the battlefields."

Her grandmother's anger jolted Guin, and she reached for Henrietta's hand. "I thought he came home from the war."

"Only the shell of him did. Those army doctors tore the heart and soul out of him when they took his leg. Left him with nothing but indignity, knowing he'd be a burden to everyone when he came home."

"Why didn't you let us know? Father would have helped," Guin said.

"Daniel refused to let me write to your father. There wasn't much he cared about after he returned, but he was adamant that William have a chance to make his own way. After we realized what happened with the investment, it gratified Daniel that his son had acted like a man and not asked for charity from the family. That was one of the few things Daniel had to be proud about."

"I think Father was pleased he did it on his own. He and Mother were very happy."

Henrietta smiled wistfully. "I'm relieved to hear that. I always wondered if his letters were deliberately cheerful so I wouldn't worry. Which I did anyway." Henrietta patted the upholstered arm of the settee. "Well, enough of the past."

She reached for her plate and sampled a piece of cake. "This is very tasty."

"Thank you. You're the second person to comment on it."

Henrietta gaze sharpened. "The second person? Someone else was here? You entertained someone alone?"

"He was no one important," Guin said hastily, wishing she'd kept her mouth shut.

"Guinevere, are you telling me you had a male guest in the house while you were unchaperoned?"

Guin wanted to groan. Instead, she gritted her teeth and forced herself to remain calm. "It wasn't a planned visit, Grandmother. He stopped by unexpectedly to discuss a business proposition. Besides, Soledad is just across the way."

"Who is Soledad?"

"A Pomo wise woman who's lived here since Mother and Father died."

Henrietta gasped. "An Indian? That's not enough. You need someone here, a family member in the house. A Talbot must be respectable at all times. What if someone had seen a man here? Then where would your reputation be?"

Guin stifled her retort. She'd never be able to explain that Soledad was like family. Except, perhaps, less troublesome. Guin slid another piece of cake onto the plate. "Have some more, Grandmother. I made it myself."

"You don't have time to bake cakes, my dear." Henrietta frowned and set the plate down. "Surely you realize you simply cannot continue like this."

Guin snatched up the dishes and escaped to the kitchen before her grandmother criticized her further, and before she said something she might later regret. She set a pan of water on the stove to heat and tried to busy herself. But she knew she couldn't hide forever.

With a sigh, she returned to the parlor. "Grandmother, would you like to unpack and rest?"

"Yes, my dear, that would be nice."

Guin led the way down the hall. "You can use Mother and Father's room. It's on the main floor so you won't have to climb the stairs. Besides," she said with a rueful smile, "it's the only room other than my own that's ready for use."

Henrietta looked slowly around the room. Guin could tell from her tight-lipped expression the accommodations were not what she was accustomed to, but at least she wasn't criticizing the furnishings.

"This will be fine, my dear. I appreciate the trouble you are going to on my behalf."

Guin caught a hint of wistfulness in her grandmother's voice and wondered if there was more to the sudden visit than her grandmother was saying. She realized how vulnerable and frail the white-haired woman really was. She had to admire her for coming all this way alone, regardless of the reason. All at once, Guin recognized how lonely she had been in this house since her parents had died. An unexpected surge of love flowed through her. Impulsively, she crossed the room and hugged her grandmother.

Henrietta took Guin's face between her hands and kissed her cheeks. "You're all grown up now. I wish I'd been here to see it happen," she whispered, her eyes bright with unshed tears.

Guin patted her grandmother's shoulders and nodded. "I wish you'd been here too." She felt suddenly awkward and embarrassed, so she backed out of the room. "I'll be in the kitchen. You call if you need anything."

Henrietta nodded and Guin fled to the safety of her chores. Despite the tender moment they'd just shared, Guin dreaded even contemplating what her grandmother's reaction would be when she learned of Guin's decision to stay on the farm and manage it alone. She'd save that surprise for another day, she decided as she scrubbed dirty dishes. She'd have to break the news soon. The fields already showed signs of neglect. The hop vines had sprouted and needed to be tied to their poles.

Guin couldn't ignore some other issues, either. Her grandmother probably had no idea how thinly stretched Guin's resources were. How would she feed them both when she barely had enough money for her own meager needs? Somehow she had to find a way to absorb this visit. God, she hoped it was just a visit. In the last day, she'd had three visitors, an amazing number for her: Her grandmother, Dr. Jackson, and Mr. O'Roarke. For a moment she wished. . . .

Oh, she wished for a lot of things, but right now, she wished a man like Kellen O'Roarke would visit her for a more personal reason than wanting her land. She hated to admit it, but those Celtic blue eyes flashing with energy had captivated her. She knew he'd draw her under his spell if she didn't remain constantly vigilant.

There was something about the way he moved that spoke to her of illicit rendezvous and of unbridled emotions, things she had never considered before, things she could only guess at. When he'd come to her door, her heart had quickened for a brief moment.

Kellen O'Roarke's ridiculous offer flashed through her mind. She slammed an iron pot on the stove, wrapped herself in a wool shawl, and stepped outside. Colonel followed close at her heels. She breathed in the hint of rain as she left the porch to wander around the yard in the dwindling light, soaking in the security, the sense of belonging the farm gave her.

What kind of a simpleton did Mr. O'Roarke take her for?

She wasn't a foolish woman. She worried, though, that others in the community might not understand this as well as she, others who might be bewitched by the lure of easy riches. Pulling the shawl tighter against the damp twilight breeze, she brooded that he would find a way to force her off the farm. Without her land, she had no way to support herself.

She rubbed her temples, which had begun to ache again. She had no choice, but to continue opposing the resort, to find every argument, legitimate or logical or not, to fight Mr. O'Roarke. She had to convince her friends and neighbors that the resort was a bad idea. Otherwise, they might pressure her to give up her farm.

If that happened, she'd have nothing left.

"I simply cannot understand why you have no one to drive you into town, Guinevere."

"I can drive the wagon myself quite nicely, Grand-mother," Guin said, unable to keep the resigned tone out of her voice. Some days she might agree that extra help would be nice, but today wasn't one of them. "We're only going into town to pick up a few things, something I do on a regular basis. Alone."

Guin snapped the reins, urging the horse to a faster pace. The last two days had been strained, to say the least. She had suggested this trip, thinking that if her grandmother met some of the townspeople, she'd understand they thought differently than people in the East. Her grandmother had to understand the practicalities, the hard realities, dictating life in the west.

Whatever warm feelings she'd felt that first night were long gone. Hopefully, the visit wouldn't last too much longer as Guin was tempted to put her grandmother on the next train.

"Well, it's clear to me that I arrived just in time. We haven't a moment to spare if your reputation is to be salvaged," Henrietta fumed. "My heavens, what would people think? You would be an outcast if the family heard about the way you live. A pariah."

Guin refrained from reminding her grandmother that she already was a pariah to the rest of the family, and had been ever since she and her parents moved to Spring Valley.

"Yes, it's clear we have only one course of action."

Guin stiffened at the finality of the words. "Grandmother—"

Henrietta turned quickly, her eyes shrewd and her mouth set. "Don't think you can beguile me, Guinevere. This situation cannot be ignored any longer. I'm surprised Katherine didn't take her maternal responsibilities more seriously."

"My mother took her responsibilities very seriously," Guin said, bristling at the criticism. "We were very happy on the farm before Mother and Father died."

"That may be, but your parents were extraordinarily remiss by not attending to your marriage arrangements."

Guin gasped in disbelief. The reins slipped through her fingers. She grabbed for them and pulled the horse to a stop. "What marriage arrangements?" she asked stonily.

"Exactly my point." Henrietta stared straight ahead, her hands clasped primly in her lap. "You're twenty-five years old, my dear. Your father and mother neglected the most important part of their parental duty—to see you well married."

Guin snapped the reins and the horse moved forward again. "I have no intention of marrying, Grandmother. There is no one in Spring Valley I'm interested in. Or who is interested in me, for that matter. So just forget that idea. I'm perfectly content with my life the way it is."

Henrietta arched an eyebrow. "Surely there is someone

in this county who is worthy of a Talbot. Although from what I've seen so far. . . ." She whipped a handkerchief from her pocket and dabbed her throat. "Well, if there isn't, we'll simply have to continue looking. We'll go to San Francisco. Farther, if necessary. You may not appreciate my efforts now, but some day, you'll thank me for not neglecting my duty."

Guin chafed with frustration. She owed her grandmother respect. That was all she owed her. She wasn't getting married, wasn't ruining her life to satisfy some out-of-place standard of decorum. Absolutely not. She had a farm to run. She didn't need a man or want one meddling in her life.

Guin stopped the horse in front of the general store and yanked on the brake. After hopping from the wagon, she helped her grandmother climb down.

Henrietta looked around, her nose wrinkling slightly in distaste. "This isn't much of a town, is it?"

"We like it." Guin turned and stepped up to the wooden sidewalk, leaving her grandmother to follow or not, whichever she chose.

"Good morning, Guin!" The voice chimed out the moment Guin pushed through the door of the general store. "It's so nice to see you again."

"Good morning to you, Mrs. Bennett." Guin smiled at the owner, who was stocking the shelves. She glanced around the store and breathed in the varied scents of spices and coffee. She relaxed, suddenly glad she'd come. "I see you have a new shipment of piece goods."

"Yes, finally!" Mrs. Bennett came around from behind the counter. "Let me show you one I thought would look particularly nice on you." She hesitated a moment. "That is . . . I'm sorry. What was I thinking? You're still in mourning."

The bell over the door clanked and Guin turned to see her grandmother, looking every inch a wealthy dame, come inside.

"Good morning, ma'am," Mrs. Bennett said, almost curtseying at Henrietta's regal bearing. "Can I help you with something?"

Henrietta looked around and shook her head imperiously. "It doesn't appear so."

Guin rolled her eyes. "Grandmother, this is Mrs. Bennett."

"Oh, how lovely! Your grandmother's come all this way to visit you," Mrs. Bennett said.

The bell clinked again. Guin breathed a sigh of relief when she saw Dr. Beauregard Jackson enter the store.

"Dr. Jackson," Guin said with a smile.

"Hello, Miss Guin. Mighty fine day for a ride into town." Dr. Jackson spoke in a deep, mellifluous drawl. He glanced at Henrietta, then back at Guin, one eyebrow raised. "I don't believe I've had the privilege of meeting your lovely companion."

Guin heard her grandmother gasp and turned to see the woman's stricken expression, her face washed of its normal color. Instinctively, Guin reached out to steady her. "Grandmother! Are you all right? What's wrong?"

"Oh, my goodness!" Mrs. Bennett fluttered around Henrietta.

"Miss Guin, bring her over here to sit down. Mrs. Bennett, a cold, wet cloth if you would, please," Dr. Jackson said, shedding his usual unhurried manner.

Guin helped her grandmother to the chairs encircling the woodstove in the corner, and wondered what could have triggered the spell. One minute her grandmother was fine, and the next . . .

Dr. Jackson followed and reached to touch Henrietta's cheek.

She recoiled from his hand. "Don't touch me."

"He just wants to feel your face," Guin said soothingly.

"Get that—that person away from me," Henrietta hissed.

Shocked by her grandmother's vehement reaction, Guin glanced at Dr. Jackson and saw his troubled expression. He backed away.

"It's all right, Miss Guin." Dr. Jackson's gaze focused sharply on the older woman.

"Grandmother, this is Dr. Jackson. He's my dear friend, and he's a physician." Guin knelt next to her grandmother. "See? He's leaving."

Henrietta's breathing slowed to a more normal rate. "How can you call that man a friend of yours?" she demanded. She sat ramrod stiff in the chair.

"He was a friend of Mother and Father's. He helped me take care of them when they were so sick with the fever, and he's been very good to me since they died," Guin said. "I don't understand why you're so upset."

"That man is a southerner. And a doctor. It's the fault of men like him that your grandfather was shot and butchered, and died long before his time."

Henrietta's fury stunned Guin, and she scrambled to think of a comforting response. She found none. "The war is over, Grandmother," she said finally, choosing a logical approach. "You can't blame Dr. Jackson for what happened to Grandfather. Dr. Jackson didn't shoot him, and Dr. Jackson didn't amputate his leg. Other men did that."

Henrietta cast a cold, hard look at her, clearly unmoved.

"If nothing else, please be nice to him because he's my friend," Guin said. "He's helped me during the last months. I couldn't have survived without him. Please. For me."

51

Henrietta's expression softened and her eyes shimmered. Guin clasped her grandmother's hand and smiled at the reluctant squeeze she received in return.

Dr. Jackson eased toward them. "I'm sorry if I upset you, ma'am," he said tentatively. "Are you feeling better now?"

Henrietta glared at him, but nodded stiffly when Guin nudged her.

"That's mighty fine, Miz Talbot. I can tell you're a strong woman." He sat gingerly in a nearby chair, never taking his gaze from her. "I'm sorry, too, that you lost your husband in the war. It was a terrible thing, that war. Shouldn't ought to have happened, ma'am."

Henrietta said nothing, but rose from her seat and pointedly avoided looking at him.

Mrs. Bennett hurried toward them. "I brought you a cup of tea, Mrs. Talbot."

Henrietta smiled faintly and took the cup. "Thank you." She sipped the hot brew and glanced at Guin.

Guin couldn't help but wonder if bringing Henrietta into town had been such a good idea after all. So far, Grandmother had offended the first two people she'd met, both of them friends. At least, Guin hoped they would still be friends after her grandmother returned to New York.

She watched Henrietta chat with Mrs. Bennett, although her grandmother did not look happy about it. The smart thing would be to return to the farm before anything else went wrong. She could always run errands another day.

Guin glanced toward the window. The sight of Kellen O'Roarke sent all thoughts flying from her head. The tall man stood outside, looking at the window display, or pretending to. She wasn't fooled; she felt his interest even through the glass.

An uncomfortable wintry feeling settled over Guin. The

last time she'd seen him, she'd run him off with an unloaded rifle. She didn't need another encounter with him. She didn't want to be the focus of his knowing blue-eyed gaze. She didn't want his naturally arched eyebrows raised even higher at something she might say.

No, not now. Not with her grandmother and everyone else standing around watching.

Please let him pass by, she prayed. *Please.*

Kellen O'Roarke paused in front of the store window. He had recovered from his encounter with the gun-toting Miss Guin Talbot. He still found it hard to believe she'd threatened him, and while he was affronted, he had to admire her spunk; spunk he was confident he could manage now that he'd had time to think about it.

He'd been watching her for a few minutes. Then he saw her look in his direction, saw the brief widening of her eyes in recognition, followed by the pointed turning away. He caught the fleeting expression on her face before she resumed her mask of calm, and wondered what was hidden beneath that mask. And what it would take to bring whatever it was out.

His heart pounded and he brushed his strange feelings off as the excitement he always felt when he faced a challenge. He hadn't expected to see her again so soon and wasn't certain he wanted to just yet. But the flare of the challenge reignited inside him, and he knew he could not ignore it.

Winfield approached Kellen and stood next to him. "It would appear there is quite a confabulation inside the mercantile, sir."

Kellen nodded distractedly at Winfield, not shifting his gaze from the people inside the building.

"I see what you mean. Perhaps I should join them. My

thought, Winfield, is to convince Miss Talbot that selling me that strip of land would be the best contribution she could make to mankind." He glanced at his companion for only a moment before refocusing his attention on the group inside the store.

"She could prove to be a strong campaigner, sir."

"Even so, I'm confident I'll prevail. When did you last see me fail?"

"I cannot remember, but if you give me some time, I should be able to recall something before we retire this evening."

Kellen waved aside Winfield's challenge. "Everything else is coming along as planned. Except for the railroad spur. That woman probably has no idea she could ruin the project for everyone in this valley."

"I am certain you will share that perspective with her," Winfield said solemnly.

"Yes. I have to be very careful, though," Kellen said. "It wouldn't do to let her think she has me over a barrel. If she's on her own, she'll need money to start a new life. If she thought she could get away with it, she might ask some ridiculously high price, and then where would I be? No, I have to impress her with how important her contribution is to the community. To her friends and neighbors. I sense she's the kind of person who would respond to that argument."

It would take all his salesmanship to bring her around. Kellen wished she were even moderately pretty. At least, it would make his task more pleasant. He remembered the moment in her parlor, when he'd thought he saw something special in her eyes. But it must have been a trick of the light. Yes, he convinced himself, it had been the light, not the long lashes, not the brown color that reminded him of warm cognac on a cold winter night.

"She should respond to reason. As well as to your incomparable charm," Winfield said.

Kellen grinned at his friend's wry tone before leaving him. The bell clanked as he stepped into the store.

"Oh, Mr. O'Roarke!" Mrs. Bennett bustled toward him. "How nice of you to come to our little store! I can't tell you how excited Mr. Bennett and I are about your resort plans."

"Thank you, ma'am. That's very nice to hear from a prosperous business woman such as yourself," he said, pleased when she seemed to blossom under his compliment. However, she wasn't the one he was interested in. No, it was the woman standing with her back deliberately turned to him, wearing the shapeless black dress. He found her attempts to ignore him mildly amusing, especially when he knew she was aware of his presence and had been since before he'd walked in the door.

Kellen recognized the doctor, but he couldn't place the older woman dressed in black who stood facing him. He caught her unwavering appraisal and decided she was the kind of person who had an opinion on just about everything.

"Good morning, folks." He walked toward the group. Stiffly, Guin turned.

"Oh, my, have you met Dr. Jackson and Miss Guin Talbot?" Mrs. Bennett asked. "And, this is Miss Talbot's grandmother, Mrs. Talbot. From New York!"

Kellen nodded at Mrs. Talbot, shook the doctor's hand, then reached for Guin's. She shot him a penetrating look before slipping her hand into his. Her hand had been gloved when he'd clasped it at the meeting. He'd known it would be slender, but he'd never expected it to be this soft. He remembered having a similar thought when he'd visited her home. He'd thought she was a farmer, but these were the hands of a lady.

"I see you came empty-handed, Miss Talbot." He leaned closer and murmured so only she could hear, "Or, should I say, 'unarmed'?"

A burst of pink colored her cheeks and she withdrew her hand. He smiled broadly, savoring her telltale blush of embarrassment. Perhaps she wasn't as controlled as he'd first thought. Maybe some of her uncompromising attitude was merely a bluff.

"I imagine you enjoy trips to town," Kellen said.

A skeptical frown crossed Guin's face. "Yes," she said slowly. "I enjoy coming to town."

"Must be nice after the isolation of being alone on your farm," he said, thinking the social benefits of selling her land might work.

"Mr. O'Roarke, I am not lonely," she said with disgust. "I have more than enough to keep me busy. Inane chit-chat is for those who don't have anything of value to do with their time."

Her face suddenly flushed again. She hurried away from him and became thoroughly engrossed in examining a pile of colored ribbons. To his surprise, Kellen found himself wondering which ribbon would be the prettiest, which would best bring out the color of her eyes.

He shook his head. This woman always seemed to catch him off guard. She was never what he expected, and despite the problems she caused, she piqued his interest. But he couldn't afford to think about that. He had to concentrate on getting that strip of land.

Mrs. Bennett came up behind him. "I understand Mr. Eldridge is interviewing you for next week's *Sentinel*."

"That's right. I'm meeting him in about an hour." Kellen caught the speculation on the grandmother's face, and he was certain he wouldn't like whatever it was she had in mind.

"Mrs. Bennett, did I hear you say that the newspaper is interviewing Mr. O'Roarke?" Mrs. Talbot casually fingered a bolt of muslin.

"That's right! The editor, Mr. Eldridge, is interviewing Mr. O'Roarke about his plans for a hot springs resort."

"A resort? Here?"

"Oh, yes!" Mrs. Bennett beamed. "We're all very excited."

Kellen's rush of pleasure instantly dimmed at the sight of Guin's set mouth as she approached the group. She may have left the gun at home, but her attitude toward him had not softened.

"How lovely." Henrietta cast an enigmatic look Kellen's way. Her quiet words left him feeling oddly uneasy.

"It's not surprising, Grandmother," Guin said. "Mr. Eldridge usually writes an article about new people in town. He may even do one about you. Last month, he wrote one about Mr. Clarke."

"Mr. Clarke?" Kellen asked.

"That's right. Jonathan Clarke from San Francisco," Guin said. "He bought the old Anderson house on the edge of town and moved in with his daughter. He told Mr. Eldridge he wants to contribute to Spring Valley's cultural life."

Jonathan Clarke. Here. In this small town.

Could there be another Jonathan Clarke? Icy heat flooded through Kellen, and he heard a peculiar roaring in his ears. He tried to shake off his own shock and appear casual. Was it a coincidence? The gnawing in the pit of his stomach told him it wasn't.

Jonathan Clarke.

The one name he would never forget. The name of the man who had stolen their gold mine and ruined his father. The man Kellen had vowed to ruin.

Chapter 4

"Have you met Mr. Clarke?" Kellen studied a cast-iron frying pan, hoping his question sounded like idle curiosity.

"No. I only read about him in the paper." Guin turned to Mrs. Bennett. "Have you met him?"

The shopkeeper shook her head. "Not really. I spoke to him once when he first arrived, but his housekeeper does all the shopping. I'm not sure he's still here."

Kellen wanted to believe Clarke was gone. Perhaps it was a mere coincidence the man had purchased land in Spring Valley. Hopefully Clarke knew nothing about Kellen's plans for the resort. But then again . . .

"I heard tell he's running for the state senate," Dr. Jackson said. "He's supposed to be in San Francisco discussin' his campaign with the party bosses."

"Well, when Mr. Clarke returns, we shall greet him properly and let him know we support his candidacy," Henrietta said brightly. "My goodness. A celebrity in our midst," she continued with a lilting laugh.

Kellen found Henrietta's transformation amazing to watch. No longer disdainful, she seemed to stand taller, her face animated, her laugh cozy and confidential. Once again, he had the unsettling suspicion that Mrs. Talbot was trouble.

"What kind of man is Mr. Clarke?" Henrietta asked Mrs. Bennett.

Mrs. Bennett shrugged. "There's nothing much I can tell

you. He's a very successful businessman. He told Mr. Eldridge he was tired of big-city crime and corruption."

Kellen could have told them Clarke's success was the result of swindling others, and that he didn't for a moment believe Clarke had come to Spring Valley to help the people. But Kellen kept quiet. The time wasn't right. Not yet. Not until he knew the real reason Jonathan Clarke was here.

"I sure hope he's not just bein' a politician," Dr. Jackson chimed in. "I regret that I must take my leave. You take care of yourself, Miss Guin. It was my pleasure to meet you, Miz Talbot, my pleasure."

Henrietta barely acknowledged the doctor as he left. "My dear," she said eagerly to her granddaughter. "We simply must hold a dinner party to honor Mr. Clarke and his daughter. Since the Talbots have resided in the valley for so many years, it's our social obligation to welcome them to our little community."

"But, Grandmother, we . . . I. . . ."

Henrietta brushed Guin's words aside with a wave of her hand. "No arguments, my dear. You may be out of practice entertaining your social peers, but we Talbots know our responsibilities. We will do whatever is necessary to properly receive the Clarkes."

Kellen heard Guin's quiet groan and sympathized with her. He couldn't imagine having an imperious grandmother like Mrs. Talbot, but he had to admire Guin for the respect she continued to show the older woman.

"How thoughtful of you, Mrs. Talbot," Kellen said. "Of course, the Clarkes should be welcomed."

"Thank you, young man. I appreciate your support."

Mrs. Talbot didn't give a damn about his support, Kellen thought grimly. It was suddenly very important to Kellen that Guin not be alone with Clarke. Her refusal to sell part of her land was the biggest threat to the success of his project, and he couldn't ignore the niggling worry that Clarke would find a way to use her. She was as unsophisticated as a babe-in-arms. Kellen had to protect her, and himself, from Clarke at all costs.

"I'd like to make a suggestion, if I may," he said in a rush. "I propose we have your party at the hotel. You'll still be the hostess, of course. Please, I'd consider it a great honor to make the necessary arrangements."

Henrietta looked surprised. "Why, Mr. O'Roarke, what a gracious offer."

"Grandmother, surely we can't accept—"

"Of course we can, my dear. Think how convenient it will be for everyone." Henrietta's smile was a bit too bright, and Kellen wondered if he'd been outmaneuvered.

"But, Grandmother—"

Kellen heard the urgency in Guin's voice.

"Guinevere," Henrietta said in a tone that allowed no further argument.

Guinevere.

So that was her name. It rolled around in Kellen's mind, conjuring up images of kings and knights and passionate trysts. Then he looked at her. At the unadorned, loose-fitting dress, the utilitarian hairstyle, the directness of her gaze. If she had to wear black, he wanted to scold, why couldn't she at least wear a stylish dress instead of that wrapper? Still, something about the lingering sorrow in her eyes made him feel sympathy for her.

He turned to Guin's grandmother. "Mrs. Talbot, tell me when you'd like to have your dinner party, who you'd like to invite, what you want served, and my assistant and I will handle it from there."

"The guest list will be very simple. Mr. Clarke and his

daughter. My granddaughter and myself. And you, of course."

Kellen smiled at how he sounded like an afterthought. Necessary, but still an afterthought.

"And, Dr. Jackson," Guin said. "I'm sure he'd love to come." Kellen caught Guin's determined look, and the urge to gain her support moved him to agree. "That would certainly round out our number. I think that's an excellent suggestion, don't you, Mrs. Talbot?"

Henrietta's mouth opened and then snapped shut. She did not look pleased about including Dr. Jackson on the guest list. Guin was in for a long ride back to the farm.

That wasn't his worry. Instead, he had to consider what to do, now that the man he'd vowed to destroy was in Spring Valley. The same man who would probably relish the opportunity to destroy him. What was the bastard up to? Kellen needed to find out, and quickly.

Kellen and his father, Michael, had prospected for years, finally finding a small gold nugget that promised them riches beyond their wildest dreams. When Michael went to register the claim, he'd met Clarke, who'd convinced the celebrating man he needed a witness when he placed his mark on the deed. Instead, Clarke made sure Michael wrote his "x" in the wrong place, then signed his own name on the deed.

His spirit broken when he realized he'd been swindled, Michael drank himself to death. Kellen had vowed on Michael's grave to protect himself from ever being cheated again and to bring Clarke down. To do that, Kellen had to be wealthy himself. For ten years, he had struggled and clawed his way to the top, working hard and getting some lucky breaks along the way.

The resort would be the last step, providing his smooth entrée into San Francisco's elite society. Then Kellen would divulge how Clarke had cheated and lied to obtain his vast land holdings. Even Clarke wasn't rich enough to save himself from those revelations.

For now, Kellen had to be careful. Deep in his gut, he had the nagging fear that Clarke's presence in Spring Valley was a threat to his plans. He would not lose to Jonathan Clarke again. To beat Clarke, Kellen had to make the resort a success.

Guin sat at the pine kitchen table, taking vicious swipes at the potatoes and carrots she peeled for stew. "I can't believe you're going through with this dinner party."

From across the table, Henrietta looked up from her needlework. "Why would you ever doubt that I would?"

"Because . . . because it's so embarrassing."

Every time she thought about the debacle at the general store, Guin burned with mortification all over again. The knowing look in Kellen O'Roarke's eyes while Henrietta discussed the dinner party for Jonathan Clarke had bothered her. He knew her grandmother thought the only way Guin could find a husband was to be thrown in front of some eligible man.

"Embarrassing? Nonsense," Henrietta said. "We're merely welcoming a new family to the community. It's the gracious thing to do, and as Talbots, it's our responsibility to observe the niceties."

"No one's entertained guests at the hotel before. We should have the dinner here if we have it at all," Guin said. If she was going to be coerced into this, then at least she wanted to be on her own ground. Yet she did not want Kellen O'Roarke in her home again, either.

"Don't be silly," Henrietta said. "You cannot host a dinner party when you have no help. Do you honestly think you can prepare and serve a multi-course meal and then sit at the table looking fresh and lovely and carry on a witty conversation with a prospective suitor? Of course not."

Guin grimaced at the thought of her grandmother's matchmaking efforts. She gouged the eye of the potato and flipped it onto the pile of peelings. "It's ostentatious to have dinner for six at the hotel when I have a large kitchen and a perfectly lovely dining room."

"Then you do agree we should be hosting this dinner."

"No, Grandmother, I do not agree," Guin snapped. She took a deep breath to regain her composure, then sighed deeply. "But I suppose there's no stopping you, now that you're so set on it."

"That's not the attitude I'd expect from a young woman in your situation, my dear. I'd think you would welcome the opportunity to meet Mr. Jonathan Clarke. Lovely name, isn't it? Sounds very solid and trustworthy, don't you think?"

Guin mumbled a response and concentrated on slicing the carrots.

"A handsome widower is just what you need. You're too . . . mature . . . for a young man who hasn't seen the world. Yes, a wealthy widower should do very nicely. And with a lovely young daughter." Henrietta beamed at the thought. "The linkage of two prominent families, securing your children's prosperity for many years to come."

Guin found Henrietta's scenario appalling. "Grandmother, I'm one of the farming Talbots, not one of the New York Talbots. If I were to marry, I'd like to think there was more involved than a simple business merger."

"Don't be foolish. A girl has to be practical about these things when she's waited as long as you have. To be perfectly frank, not many men would consider you, my dear. But you have two advantages in this case. You come from a prominent family and you're old enough to assume the obligations of a motherless child."

"I have enough to do without adding a child to the list," Guin said firmly. "I have a farm to run. And I'm quite content with my life the way it is."

"Of course you are, my dear," Henrietta said. "The farm will be a perfect dowry. The more I think about it, the more I'm quite certain Mr. Clarke will find you most appealing."

The farm as a dowry? Guin hoped she would not explode in the next two days as her grandmother's ideas grew more ludicrous. As she scooped the vegetables into an iron kettle and set it on the stove to simmer, Guin shook her head at the audacity of the whole plan. A dinner party to snag a husband? Ridiculous. And never in her wildest dreams would she have imagined her primly proper grandmother and the upstart Mr. O'Roarke working together.

"I still can't believe you insist on inviting that southern doctor." Henrietta stabbed a needle through a piece of fine linen.

"We've discussed this before. Dr. Jackson's been a friend for a very long time," Guin said patiently. Thank heaven he would be there. At least then she wouldn't feel as if she was being thrust onto the auction block. "The people who settled this valley didn't care about the war. They came to get away from the hate and bitterness. As far as we're concerned, we're all Americans."

"Hmph," Henrietta grunted in response. "That may be, but I don't think I should have to endure his presence."

"We agreed that if I have to attend this dinner, Dr. Jackson is invited." She gave Henrietta a hard look. "If you want to change your mind, I'd be more than happy to cancel the whole thing."

Henrietta scowled. "You're a wicked girl, Guinevere

Talbot, a wicked, wicked girl. You can bargain with the devil."

Guin turned away and smiled grudgingly at the compliment.

"Guinevere, we have yet to discuss what you will wear."

Guin saw through the deceptively mild tone and sighed. She'd managed to avoid the subject for a week. "I'm certain one of my gowns will be fine."

"Which one?" Henrietta said. "I haven't seen anything yet that would be near appropriate."

"I have a number of dresses, Grandmother." Guin hoped her casual tone would be convincing, but the skeptical look on the other woman's face told her she wasn't successful.

"I think we should look at them now, my dear." Henrietta's tone left no room for further argument.

Aggravated from the constant battle of wills, Guin led the way upstairs. When they reached her room, she flung open the wardrobe doors and stood back.

It took only seconds for Henrietta to flip through the choices. "This is absolutely disgraceful," she sputtered. "My servants dressed better than this. These are all old and faded."

She pulled out a mustard yellow dress. "This is a terrible color for you. Gives your complexion a sallow look." She dragged out another one. "This light green would be pretty, if it wasn't so worn. Look at these frayed cuffs, and the elbows are almost gone. We can't even fix it with a little lace!"

Henrietta threw the dress aside and turned to Guin. "If your parents were here, I'd horsewhip them! How dare they do this to you. There's nothing here, and we have no time to make a new dress."

Guin knew her grandmother was outraged on her behalf, but she didn't want to listen to criticisms against her parents.

She'd never given much thought to her clothing; if it was serviceable, then she was satisfied. Looking at her wardrobe through her grandmother's eyes, Guin realized she would embarrass the older woman at the party, and she felt a churning in her stomach.

"I do have one new dress," she said quietly.

"Where is it?" Henrietta asked, her eyes snapping with anger.

Guin left the room and returned a moment later with a muslin garment bag. She opened it and pulled out a black gown, the dress she had worn to her parents' funeral.

Henrietta blanched and hesitantly held the dress up to the light. In a quiet voice, she said, "I'm sorry, Guinevere. I don't mean to criticize."

"I know you don't, Grandmother, but you have to understand. I've had no need for pretty frocks. I don't care about them. I live and work on a farm, and I don't go to town except for supplies and to church," she said.

Henrietta gave her an odd look, one Guin couldn't interpret, and nodded slowly.

"I think I understand, my dear," Henrietta said gently. "You'll look lovely."

Guin glanced sharply at the woman, and could only wonder why she'd acquiesced so quickly. "Fine. That's settled." She slipped from the room before her grandmother could comment further.

The easy agreement about the black dress relieved Guin. She hoped that just maybe her grandmother was beginning to accept her for who she was. At the same time, Guin didn't want to look shabby at the dinner party. Henrietta's words about her clothing hurt. But Guin had always been happy with this life because she believed it was the right one for her. As a child, she had watched her parents' pain and humiliation when they'd lost everything. She'd understood what led to their ruin.

It was greed. They hadn't been satisfied with the modest affluence they'd had, and so they strove for more. Guin remembered how discontented her parents were before moving to California, and how untroubled they seemed after moving West, even when they had barely enough to support themselves from season to season. Happiness had to come from within, she'd learned; from accepting and being satisfied with whom one was.

She'd told her grandmother the truth when she said she didn't need a wardrobe full of colorful gowns. In the past week, her grief had started to fade. The progress she'd made preparing the fields for the new crop pleased her more than any pretty new dress could have done. True, she had to sneak out every morning and listen to her grandmother's harangue when she returned to the house, but it was worth it. At the end of each day, she surveyed the rows of newly planted poles to train the hop vines, and she experienced a sense of accomplishment so new, so breath-taking that she looked forward to each day with growing excitement.

She'd never felt anything like it. Except, perhaps, when she'd encountered Mr. Kellen O'Roarke. He was so different from the young men in Spring Valley. The look of disappointment she'd seen flit across Kellen's face when he entered the store had hurt more than she wanted to admit. His disinterest in her was one thing, but the idea that he might feel sorry for her was almost more than she could bear.

She took a deep breath and released it slowly. If she found herself attracted to a man like Kellen O'Roarke, knowing his only interest was in her land, then she had reason to doubt her judgment. He was a fine example of someone who was never content. He obviously had enough money to live well.

So why did he have to involve the whole town in his schemes, and ruin her life in the process?

As she checked the stew bubbling on the stove and added some dried herbs and salt, Guin resigned herself to respecting her grandmother's wishes. Grandmother could have her way this once. Guin could survive a dinner party. All she had to do was be pleasant for a few hours, and then it would be over. She could return to the life she wanted without any further interference.

But that wasn't true, either. She'd still have Mr. O'Roarke and his land grab to contend with. She hoped he didn't think his new association with Grandmother would help him gain control of her land. He might try, but Guin wasn't about to be persuaded by any of his arguments. Not now. Not ever.

Two days later, Kellen stood in the hotel lobby. He shifted his weight from one foot to the other, adjusted his coat, smoothed back his hair.

"Please stand still, sir," Winfield whispered. "You will draw attention with all that fidgeting."

"Is everything ready?" Kellen asked.

"Yes, sir. Believe me when I say that I dare not err, for I fear Mrs. Talbot would be as ruthless as Alice's Red Queen."

Kellen scowled at his assistant. "I'm not worried about her. It's Clarke we need to be concerned with. Listen to everything tonight, Winfield. Everything." He wiped his hand across his face. "God, I wish this evening was over. If Clarke recognizes me, it's sure to be a complete fiasco."

"I would not be so gloomy. It could prove to be a lively evening with an abundance of scintillating conversation."

"I hope you're right." Kellen fought the urge to run his finger under his tight collar. "Ah, here they come."

"I shall take the ladies' coats, after which I shall check that all the preparations are what they should be. Good luck, sir."

"I need pot-o'-gold luck tonight," Kellen muttered under his breath as he stepped forward to greet Henrietta, taking her hands in his. "Good evening, madam. You look lovely tonight."

"Save your charm for the young girls, Mr. O'Roarke," Henrietta said with a dry chuckle. "It's wasted on me."

"Some women are captivating regardless of their age, Mrs. Talbot." He watched Winfield help Guin with her coat.

"I'm not the one who's to do the captivating tonight," Henrietta said. "This is Guinevere's evening."

Kellen frowned. "Wasn't this dinner planned to welcome Jonathan Clarke?"

"It's the socially correct thing to do. But my real plan is to find my granddaughter a proper husband, and this Jonathan Clarke sounds quite eligible," she whispered conspiratorially.

Kellen wanted to shake the woman. "You want Guin to marry Mr. Clarke?"

"The girl needs to be married." Henrietta looked Kellen up and down. "You are a charmer, but Guin needs someone stable and secure. The farm will make a nice dowry, don't you think?"

A cold fear swept through Kellen. This was worse than he'd imagined. If Guin became involved with Clarke, then Kellen would never get access for his railroad spur line.

Taking a fortifying breath, Kellen stepped across the room toward Guin and his spirits fell. Although her dress was stylish and emphasized her slender form, the black color washed all the color from her face. Her dark brown hair was pulled back, giving her a strained expression. He wished he could find words to flatter her, but he found nothing to com-

69

pliment. He had to admit, however, that her unease might be from her grandmother's plans.

Guinevere.

He wondered if she could work any harder to be so different from her namesake. Still, he worried that Clarke would be interested, not in Guin, but in how she could help him.

"Hello, Miss Talbot. You look lovely this evening."

"Thank you, Mr. O'Roarke." Guin smiled hesitantly, as if she knew he was merely being polite. "I hope this will not be a long evening."

Her candor surprised him. "I think for some of us, it'll be a long night regardless of what the clock says," he said.

She flashed him a puzzled look. "Are you saying you're not looking forward to the party either?"

"Your grandmother has big plans for this evening," he said casually.

"What did she tell you?"

"That she thinks Clarke would be a good husband for you."

Her face blanched. Kellen touched her arm. "It's all right, Miss Talbot. Don't worry."

"How can you say 'don't worry'?" She glared at him as she moved beyond his reach. "You have no idea what I care to worry about."

"You're right, I don't. I'm sorry," he said, suddenly feeling awkward, not knowing what more to say.

Guin tugged at her gloves. "I'm just sorry my grandmother involved you in this."

"I involved myself. I offered, remember?"

Her eyes narrowed. "Why is that, Mr. O'Roarke? Because you think I'll change my mind about selling my land?"

Kellen grinned at the broad challenge in her voice. "I

wasn't thinking about that when I offered to help with the party."

"Oh?" She raised a brow. "What were you thinking about?"

Kellen shrugged and looked away. He didn't want her to see the truth with her penetrating gaze. The last thing he wanted was for her to know he was only protecting his own interests. "It's hard to explain. Just something I felt I could do for you. And your grandmother."

Guin was quiet for a moment, as if sifting through his words to decide if she believed him. Finally she said, "I guess I should thank you, then, for trying to make this less awkward than it already is. And thank you for helping me with the invitation for Dr. Jackson."

The sincerity in her voice caught him off guard. Kellen couldn't remember how long it had been since someone had spoken to him that openly and honestly. Everyone seemed to want something from everyone else, even himself.

"Ah, here comes Dr. Jackson," Kellen said, relieved when the doctor's arrival ended his conversation with Guin. He didn't want to discuss the reasons for this evening's gathering, and he particularly didn't want to share his suspicions with Guin.

"Good evening, ladies, Mr. O'Roarke." Dr. Jackson took Guin's hand and kissed the back of it. "You look lovely this evening, Miss Guin, simply lovely."

Astonished at the faint pink that touched her cheeks and the sparkle in her brown eyes, Kellen stared at Guin. She'd suddenly come alive. Who was she? he wondered with fresh curiosity; who was she, really? She seemed an enigma, obviously coming from a well-bred background, yet living unpretentiously on a farm. He fought the urge to scratch the surface, to find out what lay beneath the austere facade.

71

He wasn't interested in this woman, he reminded himself, except for his resort. Still, his irritation grew. He had complimented her with the same words, and she had barely reacted. She'd kept her hands next to her sides with him, yet offered both to Dr. Jackson. Kellen pushed aside his pique, perplexed that her lack of response bothered him at all.

"Ah, Miz Talbot," Dr. Jackson said to Henrietta. "I am mighty pleased to see you've recovered fully from your spell. I trust you've had no further episodes?"

"I'm quite well, thank you," Henrietta said shortly. "Mr. O'Roarke, perhaps we should go to the dining room to await our other guests." She held out her arm for Kellen to take, then led them through the lobby and into the private room Kellen had reserved.

He turned to see Dr. Jackson escorting Guin, and he watched her take in the room, the dark gold velvet drapes, the silk wallpaper in a lighter gold. The long mahogany table set with gleaming crystal and silver. The soft light from candle sconces, candelabra, and the crystal chandelier that made any woman look lovelier.

Henrietta snapped her fan and glanced around the cozy private dining room. "After the Clarkes arrive, we can all be seated. When the time comes, Mr. O'Roarke, would you be so kind as to sit at the foot of the table?"

He moved in that direction without comment, although he couldn't help but grimly admire her tactical strategies.

"Thank you. Guinevere, you sit there," she continued, pointing to Kellen's right. "You'll be next to Mr. Clarke who will, of course, be seated at my left. We'll put his little girl across from you to give Mr. Clarke a chance to see how well you get along with the child. I'm certain that will be important to him."

Henrietta turned to Dr. Jackson and glowered. "That means you will be on my right."

"I couldn't imagine a nicer place to be, Miz Talbot," Beau said with a lazy smile.

Kellen watched the two older people and wondered what had upset Mrs. Talbot. The doctor was a pleasant fellow, and Kellen couldn't detect anything offensive in his demeanor.

He glanced at Guin. She stood next to the mahogany table. Her face had paled and her slender hands were white from clutching her chair. Even though it could work to his benefit, her obvious distress left him ill at ease.

The door swung open, startling him. Winfield entered the room with a tray laden with glasses and a plate of hors d'oeuvres. Kellen watched Henrietta take a glass of sherry and glance at the grandfather clock in the corner.

"I'm sure they'll be here soon," Kellen said reassuringly.

At his words, a bold knock reverberated in the room. Winfield set down his tray and opened the door.

A confident baritone voice said, "Good evening. I'm Jonathan Clarke."

Chapter 5

Guin swallowed hard as Jonathan Clarke walked into the room. He was nothing like she'd expected. From her grandmother's prattling, she'd envisioned a man slightly older than Kellen. But this man was far older. He stood a little shorter than Kellen and had a heavier build. Thick iron-gray hair accentuated his robust features and sharp gray eyes belied his gregarious smile.

He wore success like a mantle. It wasn't necessarily good breeding that gave him that air, she decided after seeing the size and number of rings on his fingers. It was simply wealth. She found herself suspicious and wary of him in a way she'd never felt with anyone before. Not even with Kellen O'Roarke.

Clarke turned and extended his hand toward the door. A young woman floated into the room, the essence of femininity. "This is my daughter, Julia," he said with a vain smile.

Guin observed the petite blond woman enveloped in ruffles and lace, only a few years younger than herself, and felt dowdy and awkward in comparison. She glanced at her own drab black dress and winced, now wishing she'd had something pretty to wear. Grimly, Guin looked at Jonathan Clarke and saw him approach her.

"So you are Miss Talbot." Jonathan drew her hand to his lips. "I've heard such charming things about you."

Unsure of what to say, Guin nodded. When he turned away, she wanted to wipe the back of her hand to remove the remaining traces of his cold, wet kiss. She watched her grand-mother introduce herself and Dr. Jackson to the Clarkes, and she realized she'd never grow to like these formal social settings.

With an implacable expression, Kellen stepped forward and shook the other man's hand. "Good evening, Mr. Clarke. I'm Kellen O'Roarke."

"Mr. O'Roarke. I've been following your progress for some time." Jonathan's eyes narrowed in speculation. "This resort is quite an ambitious project for someone so young."

Kellen shrugged, his eyes never leaving Clarke's face. "I thrive on challenges."

Puzzled, Guin glanced from Kellen to Jonathan. They acted like adversaries instead of strangers. She had the oddest feeling they already knew each other.

"Gentlemen, let us be seated." Pointing with her fan, Henrietta directed them to their seats. "Winfield, would you?"

"Of course, madam." Winfield bowed slightly before slipping through the door to the kitchen.

Kellen pulled out Julia's chair. Guin saw his frown disappear, replaced by an expression of interest, a softening gaze, a more intimate smile. She could practically see him breathe in Julia's perfume and respond to its alluring fragrance. Julia turned a dazzling smile upon Kellen. Guin watched him melt under the blonde's sparkling charm and velvety laugh. He moved about the room, his confidence apparent in his smooth bearing, and she wished she had half his composure. His well-tailored clothes drew her eyes to his broad shoulders and lean form. He'd even had a haircut since she'd seen him last, making him look quite respectable.

Her parents hadn't given dinner parties, and she was uneasy with the husband-hunter role Henrietta had thrust upon her. She felt alone despite the people around her. Each wanted something from her, wanted her to live the way they thought she should. But what about what she wanted? She resisted the urge to drag her grandmother from the room and race home. Instead, she tried to loosen her grip on her chair; if she had any hope of containing the headache crawling up the back of her neck, she had to force herself to relax.

While Winfield served the soup course, Guin silently bunched her plain black gown between clenched fists. Her headache intensified as she watched Julia's performance. No one could be that simpering naturally. What bothered Guin even more was the enthralled expression on Kellen's face. He chuckled provocatively at some comment Julia had whispered. Guin wondered what it was like to flirt with a young man, to dress to catch his eye.

That wasn't her, she reminded herself. She didn't know how to do those things. Her family had deliberately avoided affairs such as this to avoid pretending to be something they no longer were. Thank heaven she had a purpose to her life, something more important to do than choose a dress for the next social event. Yet, in spite of her mental reassurances, she couldn't help but feel that something was missing from her life.

"I see by your dress that you're in mourning, Miss Talbot."

Guin started at Jonathan's comment. She pulled away when she found him leaning too close to her. On the surface, he behaved in a conventionally polite manner, but something about the speculation in his iron gray eyes made her apprehensive and self-conscious.

"Yes, my parents died from the fever last month."

"It must be difficult for you, a young woman alone."

"Guinevere is not alone, Mr. Clarke. She comes from a

large family," Henrietta said hurriedly. "Surely you've heard of the New York Talbots?"

Guin sank back against her chair, relieved that her grandmother was distracting Jonathan for at least a few minutes.

"We're a proud family," Henrietta continued, "and even if some of us live in unworldly places such as Spring Valley, we follow the dictates of polite society. We did, however, set aside our personal grief to welcome you properly to our community."

Jonathan leaned back in his chair and observed Henrietta, an amused glint in his eye. "Those traditions serve such a useful purpose, don't they? Separating the riffraff from quality."

"Yes, I suppose so," Henrietta said. A frown of annoyance flitted across her face as if she was aware he toyed with her.

Kellen heard the exchange, but continued his pretense of being captivated by Julia. It wasn't hard to pretend. Whenever he shifted position, Julia's delicate floral perfume floated around him. He gazed at her, taking in her satin-smooth shoulders wreathed by the billowing, arctic-blue ruffles of her fashionable silken gown. Honey blond curls cascaded around her face, framing dimpled cheeks and bright blue eyes. Her coquettish smile revealed small, pearly-white teeth.

Kellen glanced at Guin and the difference between the two women was staggering. Guin seemed swaddled by her clothing, her hairstyle, and her demeanor, while Julia floated unfettered. He wished for a moment he could loosen Guin's brown hair, tug a few tendrils free to see if it, too, would shimmer in the gaslight.

He couldn't explain why he even cared.

"It's so nice to meet another visitor to this quaint little town," Julia said.

Her soft purring voice drew Kellen's attention again. He

found himself stirred by Julia's delicate charm, her luxuriant beauty. Here was the kind of lady he'd always dreamed of meeting, the kind of lady who could help him slide into polite society, a lady with every social skill and charm. For a moment, he envisioned a mansion in San Francisco, his first party, and a lovely woman gliding down the stairs to greet their guests . . .

He had to be crazy, he thought, shaking himself out of his reverie as Winfield exchanged his soup bowl for the main course. This was Julia Clarke, daughter of Jonathan Clarke, his sworn enemy, the man Kellen had vowed to destroy just as Clarke had destroyed Kellen's father.

"Tell me about your plans." Julia leaned toward him, enveloping him in a fragrant cloud. "Papa says you're building a resort around some hot springs. I find that fascinating." She cast him a coy glance from beneath long sooty lashes.

"Yes, well . . ." Kellen said with a stalling laugh. He knew Clarke had recognized him, and he suspected the man would use any detailed information he gleaned about Kellen's activities against him. Discussing the details of his business would be sheer suicide. "It's all rather complicated, boring business. Let me tell you about my trip to Nevada—"

He told a rambling story that entertained the others while they ate roast chicken with pear sauce.

Finally, Jonathan laid his silverware down and wiped his mouth with a white linen napkin. "Tell me, O'Roarke, how is that resort of yours coming?" he asked across the table.

Kellen started, uneasy that Jonathan had brought up business during dinner. He swallowed a mouthful of food and shrugged. "I'm still in the preliminary stages, but it's on schedule." He picked up his glass and drained the last of his wine.

"Do you have the letters of agreement you need?"

Clarke's line of questioning irritated Kellen. He swallowed the retort that welled up inside him, stifled the truths he longed to share that would expose Clarke for the crook he was. Instead, Kellen said, "Business is such a boring topic for the ladies. Perhaps we can discuss my plans at another time? Right now, I'm looking forward to this hot apple pie in front of me."

Jonathan smiled, but the predatory gleam in his eyes sent warning prickles up Kellen's spine.

"Of course," Jonathan said smoothly, toying with his wine glass. He turned to Henrietta. "Please accept my apology for forgetting myself, madam."

"That's quite all right, Mr. Clarke. I understand how difficult it is for you successful men to set business aside for even a little while. My Daniel had the same problem."

"You are very gracious," Jonathan said with a polite nod. He turned to look at his daughter.

Kellen didn't miss his frown. He turned his own gaze back to Julia with a new perspective. Her father's only daughter, his precious and cosseted only daughter. Kellen resisted speculating on this new line of thought. Later, when he was alone, he would consider the implications. For now, he continued to listen attentively.

"Don't you just adore the fashions in the new issue of *Godey's*?" Julia said to Guin. "Before we left San Francisco, I ordered five new gowns for the summer season."

"I haven't had a chance to look at it," Guin replied quietly.

"You haven't looked at it?" Julia's voice held shock and amazement. "Why, planning my wardrobe for the summer festivities is the only thing that keeps me from expiring from sheer boredom."

Guin couldn't help but smile wryly. "I have other business to attend to, and I don't get into town very often."

"I can't imagine not living in the city, let alone coming to town only occasionally. Doesn't that sound terribly dull?" Julia said to Kellen.

He heard the veiled challenge in Julia's voice and saw from the tightness around Guin's mouth that she'd heard it too. Despite his suspicions that Julia's wide-eyed, innocent expression was an act, he leaned back in his chair to watch the quiet battle.

"Really, it's not dull at all. I find it most stimulating," Guin said. Kellen saw her chin rise and watched her give Julia the same penetrating gaze that had unnerved him earlier.

"This week I've barely had time to think," she went on. "I love stepping outside at dawn. Dew glistens on the leaves. I can smell the freshness in the air."

Caught up in her words, Kellen stopped himself as he was about to take a deep breath.

". . . the rich earthy smell of the garden when we break its crust and plant new seeds."

His hands clenched and he could feel the dirt sift through his fingers.

"The garden's a rainbow of colors. In the afternoon, we'll relax in the shade with a tangy lemonade . . ."

His mouth watered at the thought of the sour pucker.

". . . pick herbs for drying and fill the house with their pungent aromas . . ."

He remembered that day at her house, the scents of polished furniture and baking bread.

"Oh, then the harvesters arrive with their families. I love the noise. The laughter and shouts of the children. The pickers singing as they strip the hop vines. On Saturday nights, they dance under the stars. When I was young, I used to listen to the fiddlers and imagine myself dancing with—"

Guin stopped, her face flushed as if she suddenly realized she'd become carried away by her subject.

"Fascinating," Kellen whispered, mesmerized by the richness of the life she'd described. He couldn't seem to break away from the spell she'd woven around them. He never could have imagined the poetry of planting and harvesting.

"I understand your place is outside of town, next to the river." Jonathan's words broke the silence.

Kellen saw the hint of a frown cross Guin's forehead and the way she plucked at her napkin.

"That's right." Her voice was soft, reluctant in contrast to the vibrancy she'd displayed only a moment before.

"Isn't that close to the road that leads to Mr. O'Roarke's resort?" Jonathan asked.

Guin's fingers froze above her napkin. Even with her face turned away from him, Kellen felt tension radiating from her. He didn't want Jonathan to know that Guin's land was key to his project. He held his breath, unable to say anything, unable to distract Clarke.

"I don't really know, Mr. Clarke," she said ambivalently. "I haven't paid much attention to plans for the resort since they don't affect me. Do they, Mr. O'Roarke?" she asked, turning to Kellen with a guileless smile.

Her lie astounded him. She knew exactly where her property lay in relation to his resort. He didn't dare raise his hopes that perhaps she was beginning to soften toward his proposal. It was too much to ask for. For now, her fib worked in his favor and he would play out the charade. Somehow, he would find a way to thank her.

"I don't believe they do, Miss Talbot, although I'd have to recheck the plans to be sure." He smiled benevolently at her. Over her shoulder, he saw Jonathan's measured expression as he looked from one to the other.

"There you go again, talking business." Julia laid her hand on Kellen's arm.

Kellen shrugged. "You see how weak we men are? We simply can't resist prying into each other's affairs, can we, Jonathan?" he said, deliberately using the man's first name.

"No, we can't," Jonathan conceded, and then drained his coffee cup.

Before Winfield could move to refill it, Henrietta nodded to her guests. "Mr. Clarke, and Miss Clarke, I have enjoyed having you for dinner, but I must confess I can no longer keep young people's hours. I hope you will excuse me." Winfield hurried to help her with her chair.

Clarke seemed surprised by her abruptness, then pushed his chair back and stood. "This has been a delightful evening, Mrs. Talbot. Thank you. Your warm hospitality is most appreciated."

He turned to Guin and took her hand, kissing it again. "Miss Talbot, it was a pleasure meeting you. I hope we see each other again in the near future. Julia, it's time to go."

Julia scowled at him, but quickly switched the disrespectful expression to one of sassy flirtation as she turned to Kellen.

"I've enjoyed tonight very much. You must come visit us," she said, directing her words only at Kellen. "It's been nice meeting you," she added as her gaze skimmed over the others in the room.

Guin watched them leave, the tension draining from her and leaving her exhausted. Tonight had been the longest, most awkward social event she could ever remember. She'd never felt so unpolished and indelicate as she had sitting across from Julia Clarke. The girl's blatant flirtation with Kellen would have been laughable if he hadn't lapped it up like a pet kitten.

Her gaze lingered on Kellen as he and Winfield left the room to escort the Clarkes to their carriage. She thought about Kellen's hand resting on Julia's, and an icy feeling blanketed her. No man had ever rested his hand over hers. No man had ever touched her at all, not in a personal, intimate way.

She'd never thought about it before, never longed for it. She'd told the truth earlier when she'd said she couldn't imagine living any other life than this one. But maybe that life wasn't enough any longer.

Suddenly, she remembered the soft, whispery sound of his one-word response to her description of farm life. "Fascinating." He had leaned toward her, his head resting on his propped-up hand, seemingly spellbound by her words. The intensity of his blue eyes had held her gaze, sending a spiral of heat through her.

Guin scrunched the napkin resting in her lap and tossed it on the table. He'd meant nothing by it. He was only being polite, nothing more.

Across the room, Dr. Jackson turned to Henrietta. "I'm mighty pleased to see how well you all are doing, Miz Talbot. You appear to be the picture of well-being."

Henrietta acknowledged his compliment with a nod before taking another sip of her tea.

"You are to be commended for rising from your sick bed so soon after your indisposition to put on this lovely celebration. I much admire a woman who puts familial duty before her own comforts."

Henrietta set her cup down and glared at him. "Dr. Jackson, there is nothing wrong with me. I have never been sick a day in my life. I'm not a hothouse flower who wilts at the slightest problem. Perhaps you haven't had much contact with strong women." She stopped, realizing she was about to insult the man again, and her good breeding forbade that.

Dr. Jackson's smile was kind. "I understand. It is clear you loved your husband very deeply. He was a most fortunate man to have someone like you at his side." He patted her hand, letting his hand cover hers for a moment longer than was quite proper.

Henrietta shivered at the long-forgotten warmth of a man's hand touching her but didn't pull away. She heard the kindness and understanding in his words, and despite herself, her attitude toward him softened.

"I did love Daniel more than anything." She cleared her throat.

"If you don't mind my saying, you must care a great deal about Miss Guin too," he said in his deep, drawling voice.

Henrietta looked across the room at her granddaughter, catching her cheeks' pallor and the too-bright smile that had faded into exhaustion as she became lost in her own musings. My, but Guinevere looked washed out, Henrietta thought. Had she been too harsh, too hasty in pushing her granddaughter into attending this dinner? Henrietta's intentions had been the best, but perhaps she should have given Guinevere more time to adjust to her expectations. She was certain of one thing, though: Guinevere would not appear at another social gathering looking as she had tonight, mourning or no mourning.

"I do care about her," she said, turning back to the doctor. "More than you can know."

"This has not been an easy night for her."

"Nor for me," she admitted reluctantly. She had a vague feeling Clarke had toyed with her, but she had not wanted to insult him. He was older than she'd expected, and she had certainly underestimated the age of his daughter, but she brushed those concerns aside. Guin needed a proper husband, and Mr. Clarke still seemed to be an appropriate candidate. Nevertheless, she worried. "Mr. Clarke is not what I expected."

"I agree," Dr. Jackson said. "He seems too shrewd for Miss Guin."

"My granddaughter is not lacking in intelligence," Henrietta retorted. "She can carry on a most astute conversation."

"I didn't mean shrewd as a compliment," Dr. Jackson amended. "I'm not certain I trust him."

"He's a successful businessman who associates with the best people in San Francisco," Henrietta said huffily as she stood up. "Who else in this hamlet is going to be as acceptable a husband as he?"

"It depends, Miz Talbot, on how you define acceptable. Now Miss Guin is a fine young lady. I think we might could find a good husband for her if we study on it real hard, and then let her do the choosing." His disarming southern dialect tempered the severity of his message.

Unamused by his attempted charm, Henrietta snorted in disgust. "That simply shows how little you know about what is best for my granddaughter." She turned on her heel and flounced out of the room.

A grin spread slowly across his face. "She's a fine woman," Dr. Jackson said softly to himself as he watched Henrietta leave the room. "Yes, sir, a mighty fine woman."

Jonathan drove the carriage down the quiet road to his house. Tonight had been most illuminating. Surprisingly, more interesting than he had anticipated. Kellen O'Roarke had grown into an intelligent young man, much more astute than his gullible father. Jonathan had found it incredibly easy to cheat the unsuspecting Irishman and had profited greatly from their one small transaction. He hadn't given a second thought to the O'Roarkes since.

Then Kellen's name had come to his attention. At first, he'd thought nothing of the scrappy young man who wheeled and dealed on a small level. But four years ago, Jonathan realized that Kellen was becoming quite the favorite of California's parvenu circle and that he had aspirations of rising to the top. Tonight had given Jonathan an opportunity to study Kellen O'Roarke up close and to discern that the young man was charismatic in his own right.

It hadn't taken much time or effort, merely a few questions here and there, for Jonathan to learn about Kellen's plans for the hot springs resort. Jonathan reluctantly admitted the idea was sound and should be very successful.

Which meant, of course, he wanted it for himself. He smiled confidently. Despite his daughter's tears and tantrums, he'd uprooted them from their comfortable San Francisco mansion at the end of the winter social season and moved to this drafty house amid farmers and shopkeepers.

After arriving, he'd discovered Spring Valley was the perfect place to launch his political career. No one in the valley came close to his experience and acumen. With a little planning and backing from the right people, he would be the next state senator from this region. After that, who knew how far he could go? He had a few months before the next election. There would be plenty of time to meet people and indirectly campaign until the community clamored for him to serve. Plenty of time to keep tabs on O'Roarke too.

Clarke brought the horse to a stop and carefully assisted Julia from the carriage, holding her arm as they ascended the front steps of their mansion.

"That was an interesting dinner," he said as he tossed his hat negligently onto the entry table.

"The pear sauce was insipid and the vegetables were almost raw." Julia yawned. She slipped off her cloak and draped it neatly on the coat rack, then paused. "I found Mr. O'Roarke very entertaining," she said in a dreamy tone.

Jonathan cast her a sharp glance. "You're to have nothing to do with him." He caught her arm and swung her around to face him. "Understand?"

Julia shrugged out of his grasp. "You don't want me to have anything to do with anyone you aren't in business with."

"There's a reason for that. Partners help you get where you want to go. The others are either a nuisance or an obstacle to be eliminated."

"Mr. O'Roarke could be a partner. He has a lot of money."

Jonathan snorted. "He has money now, but finance is deceptive. One day you have a fortune." He concentrated on lighting a cigar, then, blew out the match. "The next day you have nothing."

"You mean Mr. O'Roarke is going to lose his money?"

"I'm saying that's always a possibility for bright young men who sometimes push too hard too fast." Jonathan smiled fondly at his daughter. "You needn't worry your pretty little head about these things."

"I certainly wouldn't want to be Guin Talbot." Julia grimaced as she approached her father and kissed him on the cheek. "How awful to live in the middle of nowhere. She doesn't even know how to fix herself up. Why, that black dress she wore was absolutely ghastly."

"She has a lot of worries you don't have. I've heard her parents didn't think about the future and left her to fend for herself. I'm taking better care of my little girl."

"I should hope so," Julia said before kissing his cheek again. "Goodnight, Father."

She started up the stairs, then paused and turned to face him, a petulant frown marring her pretty features. "Why was Mr. O'Roarke so interested in her and what she said?"

Jonathan shrugged. "He probably just listened out of politeness. He doesn't matter. Remember that."

Julia didn't look completely convinced. Jonathan hoped she wouldn't argue. He puffed on his cigar and watched until she disappeared at the top of the stairs. He waited until he heard her bedroom door open and softly close before heading for his office to pour himself a brandy.

He found the dark, wood-paneled room warm from the glowing coals in the fireplace. Tonight's dinner had been providential, the first invitation from local people worth knowing. Now he had to find a way to reciprocate, to ingratiate himself not only with those Talbot women, but with the rest of the community as well. What if O'Roarke had political aspirations? No, he had his hands full with that resort.

Jonathan smiled. Subtly, he would promote his candidacy. And set about snatching the resort away from O'Roarke at just the right moment.

Chapter 6

After the Clarkes left the hotel, Kellen insisted on escorting Guin and Henrietta home. Not only was it the gentlemanly thing to do, but he wanted to find out why Guin had lied to Clarke.

Now on the dusty road, he stretched his shoulders to ease the tension as he held the wagon reins. A million stars sparkled in the clear night sky and a bright moon rose from the east. The evening's dinner party had been a long one. He breathed in the crisp, clean air and glanced at Guin.

She sat ramrod straight on the other side of the wagon seat, her hands resting on her lap. Between them, Mrs. Talbot had nodded off, her head resting on Guin's shoulder. Winfield rode his horse a little ahead of them in the darkness.

Guin's coat was buttoned tight and she wore a scarf tied snugly around her neck. Kellen smiled when he noticed a few stray tendrils had escaped her tightly controlled hair, little wisps of hair creating a halo effect in the moonlight. With any other woman, he would have been sorely tempted to tease her about her hair coming loose, but he couldn't bring himself to do that with Guin.

Tonight had taken its toll on her, and he guessed she supported her grandmother's sleeping weight through sheer force of will. She looked at him and smiled back. It surprised him how pretty the smile made her look, softer and more feminine.

He remembered how her face had glowed this evening

when she'd started talking about her farm. She obviously took great pride in what she did. He'd never really talked to someone about living off the land, and he had found himself caught up by her poetic description.

When Guin's smile faded and she turned away, Kellen realized he'd been staring.

"Quite a dinner, wasn't it?" she asked.

"It certainly was," he replied, as surprised by her words as by her smile. He'd thought he would need to initiate any conversation, and had wondered how to bring up the subject of Clarke. Here she'd gone and done it for him.

"Was Mr. Clarke what you expected?" he asked carefully.

"No, he wasn't. Although I don't know what I anticipated, really. Grandmother certainly had strong ideas." She chuckled mirthlessly. "She kept telling me how nice it would be to have a little girl, a ready-made family. Julia is a bit past the little-girl stage."

"She was a surprise. I didn't know he had a daughter," Kellen said.

Julia had been a shock. She'd been a distraction Kellen wasn't prepared for, albeit a stunning one. Julia possessed poise and charm, which Kellen had always considered important qualities in a wife. He'd known all along the proper wife was as important to his success as his financial endeavors, but he'd been too busy to think about it. Until now.

Yes, there was a great deal to think about.

"You seemed quite taken with her."

Guin's insightful comment startled him. "She is a lovely young lady," he said slowly, reluctant to show his interest.

"I'm sure she'll attract all the single men in the county."

Kellen caught the edge in her voice, and he glanced at her. Was she jealous? Somehow, he doubted that. It was hurt he'd heard in her voice, but Kellen did not know how to respond, or if he should even try.

As they crossed the wooden bridge, Henrietta stirred. "Where are we?" she asked, her voice drowsy from sleep.

"Almost home." Guin's relief was apparent.

"That's good. My, what a wonderful dinner party," Henrietta said.

Guin murmured noncommittally, and Kellen smiled at her vague response. "Yes, Mrs. Talbot, it was a delightful party," he said. "You are a charming and most capable hostess."

"Why, thank you, Mr. O'Roarke. I must acknowledge your help. You functioned as an able assistant."

"I was pleased to help."

He pulled the wagon to a stop in front of the house. Colonel pranced around, barking his welcome. Keeping a wary watch on the dog, Kellen jumped from the wagon and then helped Henrietta down. When he came to the other side, he saw Guin had already climbed down. It annoyed him that she hadn't at least waited for him to offer his assistance.

Winfield approached them. "I will take care of Miss Talbot's horse, sir."

"Fine. I'll get the ladies settled." Kellen offered his arm to Henrietta as she negotiated the stairs.

"You're a nice young man, Mr. O'Roarke," Henrietta said. She leaned heavily on him. "Someone raised you well."

Kellen looked up to see Guin standing at the door. She rolled her eyes and he grinned at her before turning a more serious expression back to Henrietta. "Thank you, ma'am. I'm relieved all those hours of deportment lessons weren't wasted."

Henrietta whacked his arm with her gloved hand. "You are a rascal, Mr. O'Roarke, with the Irish gift for blarney."

Then she pulled away and eyed him seriously. "But you're not a shantyman. You've got quality. Use it well."

Her assessment and admonition caught him off guard. "I try, Mrs. Talbot. I may not always succeed, but I try to do what's right."

"I'm sure you do, young man. But remember, success is not always measured by how much you have at the end, but by who you become along the way."

Her words left him feeling strangely ill at ease.

"It's time for bed, Grandmother," Guin said. She opened the door for Henrietta.

Kellen guided Henrietta to the door and clasped her hand as she stepped inside. "Goodnight," he said with a slight bow as he relaxed his hold on her. He did not follow Henrietta. It didn't feel right to enter Guin's home when his business with her was still unresolved. He turned to see Guin leaning against the carved post at the edge of the porch.

Except for those loose tendrils of hair, she looked as stiff and uncompromising as ever. Yet, as she gazed across the yard, there was something about the gentle expression on her face that spoke of an inner contentment. Without thinking, he reached out to touch her, as if somehow he could capture a little of what she held safe inside her. He caught himself barely in time.

That scared him. He didn't want to think of her as someone with hopes, someone who dreamed of a life in opposition to the dream he pursued. He didn't want to feel anything for Miss Guin Talbot, because she had what he wanted, what he needed, to achieve his goal of bringing Clarke down.

He drew away. Nodding brusquely to her, he hurried down the porch steps and across the yard to the barn, where he found Winfield settling the horse. "I'll finish here," Kellen said.

Winfield cast a quizzical look, then nodded. "If you are certain, sir. I will return to the hotel and make preparations to retire."

Much to his disappointment, Kellen made short work of bedding the horse. He needed more time to stop the turmoil in his mind, more time to ease his uncertainty. He left the barn and trudged across the yard toward the house and his horse. He discovered Guin had not moved from the porch, and his steps faltered.

For a little while tonight, riding through the dark silence, they'd shared a bit of companionable conversation. Something about the darkness, the solitude, had encouraged confidences that would otherwise be impossible. Now he felt awkward with her and he could not explain why. He continued on toward the porch.

"Anything else I can do before I leave?"

"No. I appreciate the escort and your help with the horse," Guin said.

"You're welcome." Kellen looked around, suddenly aware of how isolated the farmhouse was. He turned back and saw Guin with new insight. She was a young woman, alone in an often-hostile world. An unfamiliar sense of protectiveness assailed him.

"You shouldn't be out here alone," he said gruffly.

She laughed softly. "I'm not alone; I have Colonel. And I know how to protect myself."

"If you say so." Although she seemed handy with a rifle, he still wasn't convinced. "I'll get some wood for your stove." Before she could object, he strode toward the woodpile around the corner of the house.

Flattered yet flustered, she called after him, "Thank you." His offer had caught her by surprise, and sadness seeped into her as she remembered how her father had done the task each night. The woodpile was under her bedroom window, and in the cool of the dusky evening, she'd hear her father's rhythmic chopping. When he finished, he would light his pipe, the smoke rising to her window. If she sat along the sill, she could see the glow of his pipe as he puffed. That time seemed so very long ago.

Suddenly she felt lonely. Only moments before, she'd been drained by the evening, yet now she had to admit she didn't want the night to end. Not now. Not while she felt so alone.

When Kellen returned, she blurted, "Would you like some coffee before you go back to town?"

Kellen hesitated before answering. "I don't want to put you to any trouble."

"It's no trouble." She pointed toward the kitchen. "Please. Stay a few more minutes."

Kellen followed her to the kitchen and sat at the table while Guin stoked the fire and set the coffee pot on the stove. While the coffee was perking, she set slices of bread and a crock of butter on the table. "Chopping wood always worked up a hunger in my father."

"Did for me too. Thanks."

Guin watched him slather butter on a thick slice of bread, so common a motion, yet it stirred unfamiliar longings as she watched his long fingers maneuver the knife, the faint dusting of dark hair on the back of his hand glinting in the lamp light. He took a large bite and she saw again his even white teeth. She swallowed hard.

When he glanced at her through dark lashes and caught her staring, she quickly looked away, suddenly warmed by her awareness of him, by the ludicrous vision of him sitting across from her every evening.

"You must be tired."

Guin's head snapped back and she caught the gentle look on Kellen's face, so different from his usual alert expressions.

"I suppose I am," she admitted, then laughed wistfully. "I don't care for those little parties. They seem so pointless."

Kellen nodded in agreement. "Sometimes, and sometimes an amazing amount of business is conducted at functions like that." He took another sip of coffee, his forehead furrowed in deep thought. Finally, he said, "Why did you lie to Clarke about the location of your farm?"

The question hit her hard, and she wasn't sure how to answer. "I don't know," she said. "I . . . I guess something about him bothered me. I felt as if he was trying to use me to get to you, and I didn't want to be caught in the middle." Guin saw Kellen's face relax, the tension leave the set of his jaw. Puzzled, she cocked her head. "You and Mr. Clarke already knew each other."

Kellen threw her a sharp look, then seemed entranced with the dregs in his cup. When he faced her again, his eyes were shuttered, his expression closed. "We've never met, but we know of each other."

Guin sensed he was not going to tell her anything more than that. The air between them sharpened, the warm coziness of the kitchen turned crisp with an undercurrent of tension.

"I should thank you," he said, "for hedging with him."

"Are you afraid he'll hurt your project?"

Kellen hesitated. "Let's just say I think you showed good judgment by staying out of it. You should continue to stay out."

"This isn't some harmless game, Mr. O'Roarke," she replied angrily. "You may think this maneuvering is fun in a big city like San Francisco, but what you do in a small town like Spring Valley can ruin the community."

"Don't you think I know that?" he shot back. "This isn't a game to me, Miss Talbot. This is serious business. I'm mortgaged to the hilt. Every penny I have is tied up in this project. If it fails, I'm ruined."

"I don't understand why you'd risk everything. You're obviously successful, so why not be satisfied with that? My family was happier here, on this farm, than we ever were when we lived in New York."

Kellen laughed derisively. "You call this success? You're barely running this farm by yourself. How do you know you'll survive? How do you know you'll still be here two years from now? If you have one bad year," he said, shaking his finger at her, "you're ruined. You have nothing to fall back on. Nothing."

He rose from his chair and took two steps away from the table before turning to her, his expression dark and forbidding. "I'm not going to spend my life always worrying about how I'm going to live," he said. "I'm not going to lose everything I have because some bank suddenly decides my credit's no good and forecloses on me. Success means not living in fear; it means being able to protect what you have from those who'd do anything to steal it from you."

"I won't lose my land," Guin said. "This is a farming community. I'll always be able to borrow money from the bank, or use my credit at the Bennetts' store until the next season."

"How can you be so naive? It was different for your father. He was a man. You're a woman, a woman alone with no resources to fall back on. Without money in the bank, without other assets besides this farm, you're defenseless against anyone who has the money to snatch this place out from under you." Kellen began pacing the room. "Don't you understand? You can't be complacent. You have to keep accumulating more so they can't take it away from you."

Guin shook her head. "There is no 'they.' No one here wants my farm but you."

"I can assure you, Guinevere Talbot, I won't be the last." He leaned across the table, his hands splayed in front of her. "With the railroad coming through, this valley is prime for the plucking."

"Is that what you're trying to do? Pluck my farm out from under me? Leave me with nothing?"

He felt as if she'd slapped him, then he slowly straightened. "No, Guin," he said in a low voice. "I only want to use part of your land, and I'm willing to pay a fair price for that use."

Kellen jerked his coat from the chair and threw it over his arm. "I've stayed too long. Goodnight." He turned on his heel and left through the back door, closing it quietly, but firmly, behind him.

Guin sat stone still until she heard his horse gallop down the drive, then the tension from their argument fell away from her. Shutting her mind to his words, she rinsed the dishes and banked the woodstove coals. Despite the comfort of the familiar tasks, she couldn't shake the unsettled feeling lingering from the evening, from Kellen O'Roarke and his stinging words. Their discussion bothered her more than she wanted to admit.

For a short time this evening, she'd forgotten his real purpose. She'd been distracted by how dashing he was, by the depth of his blue-eyed gaze. The directness of his look had warmed her, made her feel she held all his attention, and made her want to reach out and bring it back whenever he turned away.

She was being foolish, she knew. She had trouble reconciling the man he undoubtedly was with the man she wished him to be. She still had to worry about protecting her farm and herself from Kellen. He'd made it clear she was about to be a pawn in a game far too sophisticated for her. Her land lay in the heart of the battlefield. That was all he was interested in, her land. Even his warnings about Mr. Clarke were not so much about protecting her as about protecting her land for his own advantage.

She sighed heavily as she extinguished the last light before going upstairs to her room. What would a man like Kellen O'Roarke possibly find interesting about a woman like her? Except for her land, nothing.

Two weeks later at the resort construction site, Kellen finished his lunch and leaned against a tree. Exhausted from the long hours he'd been putting in, he was in no hurry to return to work. Thick layers of clouds covered the sky, graying the valley. The day's heavy heat weighed him down, matching his mood. Preparations for building the resort had filled his time during the last weeks as he supervised the layout of the buildings, ordered supplies, and hired workers. He did not want to acknowledge that he'd used these activities as excuses for not seeing Guin Talbot. Yet, as much as he dreaded a confrontation with her, it could not wait much longer. The spur line had to be started soon.

When he saw the man in charge of the resort's construction workers walk across the flat, cleared land, Kellen pushed himself up. "Harry," he called out. "I went over the supply order. Anything you want to add?"

"I think we got enough for now." Harry turned and walked to the middle of a marked-off area. "This here's the main house. We got your kitchen and common dining room there and there. Rooms for the manager are at the back." He walked to the far side of the clearing. "Here's where we'll build the fireplace for the sitting room. You sure it needs to be this big?"

"Yes, I'm sure," Kellen said. "Do we have enough river rock?"

"We was getting there, and then the fellow I told to get more didn't come back this week. Don't go worrying about it just yet. We got time."

"I won't worry. Yet." Kellen looked at the bare hillside. "What about the cabins?"

"Like you wanted, we got spaces cleared for the big ones for families and the smaller ones scattered up the way toward the grotto."

Kellen nodded. "Good. If you haven't got anything to add, I'll take the list with me into town. If you think of something else, I'll be at the grotto."

Kellen made his way up the hillside path between brush and trees. He reached the grotto and paused, filled with the same excitement as the first time he'd seen it. The grotto was the center of the hot springs activity. The natural cavern opened for the water to bubble through the rock to the surface. Months ago, when he'd stepped into the water to test it, the effervescent fizz had both relaxed and stimulated him, leaving him with the feeling that all his cares had been washed away and he could conquer the world.

Hot, soothing water was not going to help solve his problems with Guin Talbot, however. His enthusiasm and confidence slipped as he again considered how to obtain her consent to use her land. Without that spur line across her property, all his other efforts would be futile. How was he going to win her agreement?

As he made his way down the hill, Kellen wondered at the differences he had seen in her. Which Guin Talbot should he approach? The fierce protector of her property? The naive idealist? Or the shy, plain wallflower? And what about the radiant enthusiast who worked the land? He shook his head and realized he had never seen a woman with so many aspects to her personality. Who was the real Guinevere Talbot? He shook his head again. In the end, he guessed, it didn't matter. Whoever she was, he couldn't put off talking to her any longer.

He mounted his horse and galloped down the road, reaching the outskirts of Guin's farm sooner than he was ready.

From across the river, he caught a glimpse of the field. It looked different than it had when he'd come by the farm months before. Then it had been barren, with mounds and furrows filling with weeds. Now the weeds were gone, and bright green vines lushly twined their way up the towering trellises, blocking a clear view of the field. The difference surprised Kellen. How had Guin done so much in such a short time? He paused, stricken by the sudden awareness that she posed a more formidable challenge than he'd previously thought.

Kellen pursed his lips, deep in thought as he followed the road and crossed the bridge. As he crested the rise that separated the hop fields from the house and outbuildings, he saw three people hoeing weeds in the field, two men and one woman. When he recognized Guin, he grinned, hoping to catch her off guard. Colonel barked, announcing his arrival, and Kellen saw Guin stop working and watch as he approached.

She eyed him from beneath a broad-brimmed hat. "What brings you out here?"

Kellen saw the tiny beads of perspiration on her brow and at the base of her throat where her shirt parted. Her skin glowed from her exertions, her eyes shone brightly, and she radiated a vitality he found curiously attractive. Beneath the wariness he saw in her eyes, he sensed her confidence. He found the smattering of new freckles across her cheekbones provocatively enticing. "I see you've been working hard since I was here last."

Guin smiled cautiously. "This is a farm, and farms require a lot of work."

"Yes, well, perhaps you could take a break and we could talk?"

"I have a lot of work to do. Besides, I can't think of anything we have to talk about," she said with finality.

"I won't take much time. Hear me out, please."

Guin hesitated, then nodded and laid down her hoe before leading him across the field. She pulled a basket out from under the trees that edged the river. After taking off her gloves and pouring buttermilk into two cups, she handed one to Kellen. She sat down, removed her hat, and patted her face with a cotton cloth.

Kellen looked at her worn dress and sturdy shoes, so different from his fine linen shirt and quality leather boots. He felt a twinge of embarrassment. Given their last discussion, she could have no doubt that this was not a social call. She was gazing at the field, a soft smile tugging at her lips. Kellen felt the contentment he'd sensed in her before.

She fanned herself with her hat. "I'll have a good crop this year, God willing. The vines came back from last year, and we've opened the irrigation furrows and set up the training wires."

"I imagine your grandmother's not pleased you're working out here."

Guin turned to face him and shrugged. "The vines need a lot of care. My father worked with them every day to keep them growing up the trellises. Now, I'm doing it." She turned away from him and looked out over her field. "There's nothing wrong with honest labor."

He heard a touch of pride in her voice. She looked secure and happy, Kellen decided, as if she belonged here, as if she fervently believed everything she'd said the last time he saw her. Doubt crept into his thoughts, but he brushed it aside. He wasn't taking the land away from her, he reminded himself. He was only asking to use a small piece of it. She could continue to grow her precious little plants and profit from the shares in his resort.

His confidence was restored by the time she turned to him, a questioning look on her face.

"You didn't come here to discuss my hop vines, did you?"

"I wondered if you'd given any thought to my offer to use part of your land." He saw the shuttered look in her eyes, felt her imperceptibly pulling back.

She picked up a small stick and poked at the ground with it. "I've thought about it. I haven't changed my mind."

"It's a good deal for you. You can still use the rest of your farm and have a small interest in the resort. You can even sell some of your produce to the resort. I plan to pay top price for the freshest food I can find."

Guin shook her head, and her expression hardened as she looked across the field. "My father grew hops, Mr. O'Roarke. Now I do. Not vegetables. Not fruit. The flowers I grow are for my own enjoyment. I grow hops and sell them to the brewers."

Her response irritated Kellen. She was the only person he knew who could annoy him this quickly. "Okay, grow your hops. You don't have to plant vegetables. It was just an idea."

"There are only a few places where hops grow well," Guin continued, as if he had not spoken. "This valley is one of them. I don't want to change, and I don't plan to."

"I'm not asking you to change, Miss Talbot," Kellen said,

his frustration rising. He only wanted one small section of her land, for God's sake.

Guin finished her buttermilk and put her cup down. "Follow me," she said.

Noting the no-nonsense tone of her voice, Kellen dropped his cup and hurried after her. She strode across the field, lifting her skirt to keep it from dragging across the mounds, stepping only in the furrows and ducking between trellises, while he stumbled along behind her.

Finally, she stopped. "Look over there. That's the river." She turned and pointed in the opposite direction. "There's the road."

"I know."

"Your railroad spur will follow the road to this point, isn't that right?"

"Yes," Kellen said.

"You want the spur to turn here and cut through my land, cross the river, and go straight to your resort."

"Yes," he said, unable to keep impatience out of his voice.

"Look at my field. Look at it closely."

Kellen followed her command and stared at the field, at the mounds and furrows and trellised vines. He shrugged. "So?"

"Look at the direction of the rows."

"They run parallel between the road and the river."

"That's right. They do that for a reason, Mr. O'Roarke." She said his name as if it were an obscenity. "We have irrigation set up at the end of the field. Water's drawn from the river into the irrigation canal on the high side, and then the water runs down the length of the furrows. If you put your railroad through my field, I can't water my crops. If I can't water my crops, they'll die."

She turned and marched across the field to where she'd

left her hoe and began working without so much as a backward glance in his direction.

Kellen remained where he stood, frozen by the implication of her words. He scanned the field again, then paced the length and width of it. He walked between the rows, checked the road, the river, the route he'd chosen for his spur line.

A wave of heat flowed through him. Damn! She was right. The spur line would devastate her irrigation system. Which would ruin her farm.

He felt the flicker of failure, the fear that his plans were destroyed. Not by someone else's chicanery, but by his own unwavering scruples. When he had vowed on his father's deathbed to never again be the victim of someone else's treachery and to ruin Jonathan Clarke for what he'd done, Kellen had also vowed he would never hurt innocent people. Which meant he couldn't hurt Guin. He couldn't destroy her farm, even if it was the only way he could succeed.

What was he going to do? Everything he owned was mortgaged to raise money for the resort; he'd taken out loans that had to be repaid. If the resort didn't open on schedule, the loans would be in default. He'd be penniless.

All because he had vowed to hurt no one. Not even one little hop grower.

Not even Guinevere Talbot.

Chapter 7

Dr. Jackson reined in his horse in front of the Talbot house and climbed from the wagon. The yard was quiet. Frowning slightly, he grabbed a small bag, made his way up the steps and knocked on the front door.

Time passed interminably until the door opened. Beau couldn't stop the smile from spreading across his face. "Good afternoon, Miz Talbot. Mighty fine day out."

Henrietta looked him up and down suspiciously. "I suppose it is a nice day. Guinevere's not here."

Beau nodded. "I didn't suppose she would be. I came to see you, Miz Talbot."

Henrietta's face tightened. "I don't need any doctoring, sir. I'm feeling quiet well."

"You look the picture of health, ma'am. I didn't come for that either. I thought you might like some penny candy. Arrived fresh this week at Miz Bennett's store."

Beau held up the small bag. A blush of pleasure lit Henrietta's face, then her frown returned. "Do you like horehound?" he asked.

Henrietta hesitated, then, she said, "I love horehound. Come in, Dr. Jackson."

Beau chuckled to himself as she opened the door wide enough for him to enter and led him to the parlor. He sat in the high-backed chair she directed him to, although he would have preferred sitting next to her on the sofa. Maybe next time.

"I'll get a dish for the candy. Would you like some coffee, Dr. Jackson?"

"That'd be mighty fine, Miz Talbot, mighty fine. But don't you be going to any trouble on account of me."

"It's no trouble."

Beau watched her sail out of the room, and he chuckled again. It warmed his heart to see a handsome woman get all fluttery when an admirer came to call. Not that he thought he stood much chance with Miz Henrietta Talbot. After all, she was a Yankee through and through and wouldn't want any part of someone like him. Still, there weren't many women his age in Spring Valley, and none other was refined as Miz Talbot. Yes, sir, she was a mighty fine lady.

"Here we are, Dr. Jackson." Henrietta entered the room, carrying a laden tray.

Beau jumped up to help her, and his fingers brushed against hers. Henrietta pulled away so quickly he almost dropped the tray. Perhaps the little lady from New York was not all that impervious to his charm after all.

"Are you enjoying your visit?" Beau asked as he stirred three spoonfuls of sugar into his cup.

At first, Henrietta did not respond. Her lips were pursed as she poured coffee into a fine porcelain cup. Finally, she said, "I came to Spring Valley to be with my granddaughter. Guinevere is a fine young woman, but I'm afraid my son and his wife did not do their duty by her."

Beau could tell from the way she spoke in a rush that this was difficult for her. "What might you mean by that?"

"They were happy with their new life. Perhaps too happy, because they ignored Guinevere's future. She should be married by now and have her own family. They did nothing to expose her to potential suitors, they dressed her in near rags, and worst of all, they left her with this farm. She's out

106

there now, working in the field with the hired help. It's deplorable."

Beau nodded. "I see what you mean, Miz Talbot. William and Katherine were very happy together. To watch them, a body would think they had no need for anyone else. They came to town to shop and to attend church, but I can't say as I remember them at any of the socials. Miss Guin always seemed a shy little thing, except with her daddy. She followed him everywhere. He taught her everything he knew, and she's doing right well from what I can see."

"But, it isn't right," Henrietta insisted. "It doesn't matter if she's doing it well or not. The point is she shouldn't be doing it at all."

"Have you talked to Miss Guin about that?"

"I'd get farther talking to that beast of hers."

Beau nodded. "Ah, yes. Colonel."

"That's the most ridiculous name I've ever heard for a dog."

"It sure did seem good at the time. Miss Guin, she found herself this little black puppy, and he always sat straight and tall, never moving, except with his little brown eyes following her around the yard. I think it was William who said he looked like a military man standing at attention, and Miss Guin, she decided he should be an officer."

"That sounds like something William and Guinevere would come up with." Henrietta sipped her coffee. "How can I get through to my granddaughter, Dr. Jackson? You know her better than I."

Beau was surprised by Henrietta's question. She must be desperate to ask for his help. "Have you asked Miss Guin how she feels about it?"

"I try, but she always dreams up another chore she must do right away."

"Well, Miz Talbot, I don't think you're going to like what

I have to say. I think if Miss Guin's happy, then she should be left alone."

"Shows how much you know!" Henrietta said. "My granddaughter must behave in a socially acceptable manner. Working in the fields is not acceptable."

"I'm not sure what help I can be to you." Beau set his cup on the table. "I did come calling for another reason."

"What's that?"

"Appears Mr. Clarke, he's planned a big party for the town, and I'm supposed to let those who live around these parts know about it."

Henrietta's eyes brightened. "A party? What kind?"

"From what I gather, he's hiring some fiddlers for a dance. There'll be a light supper."

Henrietta sniffed indignantly. "It would have been nice if he'd sent us a personal invitation after the trouble we went to for that dinner party in his honor. When is it going to be?"

"Two weeks from Saturday."

Henrietta took a deep breath and from her scrunched expression, she looked as if she was making a distasteful decision. "Dr. Jackson, I need your assistance. It's important for Guinevere. Will you help me?"

Beau hesitated for a moment, unwilling to pressure Guin. But the opportunity to be on Miz Talbot's good side was a strong temptation. As long as Miss Guin wasn't hurt, that is. "Yes, Miz Talbot. I'd be honored to be at your service."

"You must promise to keep this a secret," Henrietta warned with a wag of her finger.

Beau grinned, enjoying the chance to be part of an intrigue. "I promise, Miz Talbot, I won't tell a soul."

Two weeks later, Guin returned to the house from the field, tired but pleased with her progress with the hops. Since it was a Saturday, she'd spent only the morning working outside. After a bite to eat, some house cleaning was in order, and if any daylight remained, she planned to tackle the flowerbeds that had run amuck. Her grandmother tried to help with the cooking, and Soledad worked the garden, but the bulk of the responsibility for the house fell on Guin's shoulders. She hadn't been to town for weeks, and they were running low on supplies.

She took a deep breath and savored the scent of wildflowers floating through the warm air. So far she had faced all the challenges of growing hops. Now was the maintenance time of the season, keeping the vines irrigated and twining, hoeing the weeds back. Unless the weather turned soggy, a bad windstorm blew in close to harvest, or the price of hops fell, she would have a successful season. Maybe.

Despite her bravado with Kellen, terror still struck her heart when she considered the bank loan she had to pay off after the harvest, but so far her crop appeared to be flourishing. Besides, she knew from listening to her father that the banker, Lawrence Gaspard, was good about rolling loan principles over to the following year if the interest was paid.

Yet pride made her eager to pay off the loan completely so that foreclosure would no longer be a threat. Kellen had frightened her with his warnings that someone might try to take her farm. There was always the possibility the bank's policies could change, especially since she was a woman alone and had not yet proven she could manage the farm successfully. She sighed heavily. So much depended on this year, on her ability to take control of her life.

Guin paused and looked around at the farm, at her farm, and smiled. She couldn't imagine giving this up in search of something better. She pulled off her heavy gloves and set them on the railing. Her hands were still relatively unscathed by the heavy work only because of the gloves she wore religiously. Each night, she smoothed lotion into the skin so her hands stayed soft. For that her grandmother should be grateful, she thought with a grimace. The freckles across her nose and the light darkening of her skin despite a broad-brimmed hat were another matter Guin heard about with irritating frequency.

She found a few chores around the yard that needed doing, anything to delay entering the house. The front door swung opened, startling Guin from her thoughts.

"Guinevere?" Henrietta called.

"Yes?" Guin frowned. Henrietta had bustled around the house these last two weeks, humming little ditties to herself and wearing a small, most-pleased-with-herself smile. That only meant trouble.

"Please come in now, Guinevere." Henrietta's tone left no room for discussion.

Guin reluctantly crossed the yard. Her grandmother was up to something; she just knew it. The last time her grandmother had acted this way was when she planned that disastrous dinner party. Guin hated to think about that night. She shied away from remembering the time she'd spent later that evening talking to Kellen because it always left her with an uncomfortable, frustrated emptiness.

"There you are, dear, finally," Henrietta said, hovering around Guin as she stepped inside the house.

Guin found herself swept up by her grandmother's orders to bathe and wash her hair. The copper tub waited for her in the kitchen, already filled with steaming water, and Guin smelled her grandmother's rose-scented oil wafting through the air.

"Thank you, Grandmother," she said, eagerly shedding her clothes. "This is a special treat."

"I thought you deserved something nice after all your hard work."

Guin eyed Henrietta suspiciously, but decided to enjoy the bath before she asked too many questions. She'd learn soon enough what her grandmother was up to.

Henrietta did not disappoint her. Later, as Guin sat on the porch and brushed her hair dry, her grandmother made her next move.

"Guinevere, dear," Henrietta said in a cozy tone. "I have the most exciting news."

Guin stifled the groan that rose in her throat. The news had to be hideous for Henrietta to act this cheery.

"There's going to be a party in town tonight, a dance. Isn't that thrilling?"

Desperation swept through Guin, and she felt beads of nervous perspiration on her skin. Henrietta would not coerce her into another one of those situations again. Absolutely not.

"I'm sure the townspeople will enjoy it very much," Guin said as blandly as possible.

"But it's for everyone, my dear. Mr. Clarke has invited everyone in the valley. That's what Dr. Jackson told me."

Guin turned sharply toward her grandmother. "Dr. Jackson? When have you seen him?"

"He came by one day while you were working." Henrietta waved her handkerchief in the general direction of the field.

"Why didn't you let me know he was here? I would've liked to have seen him."

"You know how it is with doctors, my dear. He has so many patients he didn't have time to sit around and visit."

Guin frowned, wondering why Henrietta was deliberately being vague. She hoped Henrietta had not been rude to Dr. Jackson, but she couldn't bring herself to ask the question without appearing impertinent.

"We don't have much time to dress," Henrietta continued, "and you'll probably want something to eat before we start."

"I'm not going, Grandmother."

"But, Guinevere—"

"No. I'm not making a fool of myself again. Last time was bad enough when there were only six of us. I won't embarrass myself in front of the whole valley."

"I understand, my dear," Henrietta said quietly. "I know you are not fond of these occasions." She glanced at Guin and seemed to pause when she caught Guin's raised eyebrow. "All right," she said matter-of-factly. "You hate parties. But these are people you know. They're your neighbors and the people you went to school with."

"I don't feel comfortable."

"Is it because you don't have a pretty dress to wear?"

Guin shrank from the truth in Henrietta's words. She remembered the pretty frocks she'd worn daily as a small child, the parties she'd attended with her parents, and she remembered how that had all changed when they moved west.

"That's part of it," she said softly as she turned to look out the window again.

"Is the other part of it that you don't know how to dance?"

Guin gasped and whirled around to see the sympathetic expression on her grandmother's face. "How did you know?"

Henrietta shrugged and brushed an invisible speck of lint from her dress. "Your father had two left feet despite years of dancing lessons. Your mother was always content to sit quietly at his side rather than glide across the floor in the arms of another man, even though she was a beautiful dancer." Henrietta shook her head. "Your mother was so graceful. I think that's the first thing your father noticed about her, that and her beautiful chestnut hair." Henrietta stepped closer and lifted Guin's hair, letting the long strands flow through her fingers. "You have your mother's hair," she said with a smile.

Guin refrained from contradicting her grandmother. Her mother's hair had been beautiful, and Guin knew her own was a drab brown, but she wasn't about to argue with Henrietta.

"So it's all right that I don't go?" Guin asked, hoping she'd convinced Henrietta of the folly of her attending.

"Of course not," Henrietta said, her sprightly manner returning. "Come with me. I have something I think will change your mind."

Guin doubted Henrietta could do anything to alter her determination to avoid the dance, but she agreed to wait in the parlor. Henrietta returned in a moment carrying a gown. Guin gasped when she saw the dark green sateen shimmer in the afternoon light. She couldn't help but reach for the dress and hold it against her. She stood in front of the parlor mirror and took in the slim-fitting bodice edged with lace, the narrow sleeves, the gently draped skirt.

She turned to face her grandmother again, still clutching the dress. "How . . . can I . . . what about our mourning?" she stammered.

Henrietta's gaze softened. "I don't think your parents would want you to shut off your life. Besides, the dress is a dark color, and Mrs. Bennett assured me no one would criticize you for not wearing black."

Guin gulped and nodded, unable to say anything for a moment. "Thank you. Thank you so very much, Grandmother. The gown is beautiful, the most beautiful I've ever owned."

"You better get dressed now. I have another surprise for you."

"I'm afraid to ask what it is," she said with a nervous laugh.

"I think you'll be pleased." Henrietta took the gown from Guin and smoothed some of its wrinkles. "Dr. Jackson's coming early to give you dancing lessons."

"Dancing lessons?" Guin's cheeks flushed with embarrassment. Why was her grandmother so insistent? Still, it might be fun. "You're teasing."

Henrietta shook her head. "No, my dear, I'm not. Dr. Jackson graciously agreed to teach you the rudiments of dancing. I would do it, but I think it's better to practice with a man, not with a short old woman like me."

Guin looked hard at her grandmother. She was up to something; Guin just knew it. Still, the new dress was so beautiful. Finally, she said, "All right, I'll go. But I'm not throwing myself at every unmarried man there."

"Of course not, dear." Henrietta patted Guin's arm. "I wouldn't force you to do anything you don't want to do. Now get dressed so you'll be ready for Dr. Jackson."

Without another word, Guin went up the stairs, her earlier trepidation giving way to anticipation. She knew she'd given in to her grandmother's scheming, but just this once couldn't hurt. She'd be strong the next time.

Kellen raised his hand to ease the tight collar around his neck and then remembered Winfield's reprimand about nervous gestures. He slowly lowered his arm while he scanned the crowded room. The empty warehouse next to the train depot would soon be filled with the valley's bounty. The rest of the year it stood empty, except for occasions like this.

The setting was ideal to talk about his resort in general terms. He needed to keep people excited and feeling involved, in case Clarke started to talk against the resort. The reception he'd received this evening from the locals had been most promising, but he had to remain vigilant. Once again, uneasy prickles slithered down his neck, and he worried what Clarke was up to. It could only mean trouble. He glanced around and spotted a farmer he needed to talk to about supplying food for the resort and started toward him.

"Mr. O'Roarke! There you are."

Kellen turned to see Julia Clarke gliding toward him from across the room. She was beautiful, no doubt about it. Her blond hair enhanced her fair complexion, and her silk dress emphasized her ample feminine curves. He admired her attractiveness, and for a moment he was flattered that she'd sought him out. She looked like a fairy princess come to life . . . until . . . until he looked into her eyes and recognized a calculating mind behind the pretty facade. Yes, up close Julia Clarke appeared to be very much her father's daughter, a woman to approach cautiously. The question was, could she be a weakness in Clarke's armor, something Kellen could take advantage of? If he found exactly how to use that weakness, would he? That remained the biggest question of all. He'd sworn he would not sink to Clarke's level in his efforts to bring the man down, but it sure was hard to overlook this potential opportunity.

"Miss Clarke, it's nice to see you again," Kellen said evenly, determined to mask his inner turmoil and indecision.

"You must call me Julia. May I call you Kellen?" Julia flashed a brilliant smile while she slipped her arm through his.

Kellen chuckled congenially. "I'm not sure your father would approve of that informality, Miss Clarke."

"Oh, pooh," she said, patting his arm. "Father won't care."

Kellen suspected Julia and her father had discussed him.

Did that mean she was working for her father or against him? "I certainly wouldn't want to offend your father or lead him to believe I was taking improper liberties."

Julia laughed, apparently amused at the thought. "That would be rather difficult, wouldn't it, Kellen, since I haven't seen you since that little dinner party."

"Yes, that's a shame isn't it?" Kellen had deliberately avoided the Clarkes in the last few weeks, even going so far as to duck into doorways when he saw Julia in town.

"Perhaps we can go riding together," Julia suggested. "I'd love to see your resort. It sounds idyllic."

He just bet she'd love to see the resort. So she could run right home and tell her father all about it. "I'd surely love to, Miss Clarke, but I'm not a wealthy man of leisure like your father. I'm working all the time. This dance is the first time I've stopped to socialize since the dinner party."

Julia pouted prettily, and Kellen had no doubt she practiced the expression to perfection before her mirror. "Now, don't mar that pretty face of yours with a frown," he said, tapping her nose. "I promise I'll try to come see you soon."

From the skepticism in her eyes, Kellen figured she was trying to decide if he was telling her the truth or just placating her. "Would you like some punch?" he said in an effort to distract her.

"That would be delightful." Her radiant smile lighted her face, but stopped short of reaching her eyes.

"I'll be right back," he promised and stepped away, relieved to have escaped, if only for a few minutes. He reached the punch table, picked up two filled cups, and started to return to Julia when a commotion at the door caught his attention.

At first, he saw only Dr. Jackson, whose leonine silver mane always distinguished him in a crowd. Then Mrs. Talbot stepped past the cluster of people at the door. Kellen felt his heart beat a little faster in anticipation, but he couldn't define what he was waiting for. When he saw Guin, his breath caught in his throat. He could not ignore the quickening in the pit of his stomach.

She looked stunning. Her hair was up, but in a soft, feminine style, the auburn highlights glinting under the oil lamps. The dark green dress she wore draped gracefully over her slender figure, her gentle curves no longer disguised. Her brown eyes were wide, almost like those of a startled fawn, and he could tell from her fidgeting hands that she was nervous. Still she radiated understated elegance, making Julia's dazzle seem garish by comparison.

Her unexpected beauty stunned him. How could he have missed it? Kellen set the punch cups down and headed toward Guin. The music started again, and he had to weave his way through the dancers. His impatience grew, his pace increased, until finally he reached her.

She turned from Mrs. Bennett and her mouth curved into a hesitant smile.

"May I have this dance?" Kellen asked. Without waiting for a response, he took her hand and led her away.

Chapter 8

Guin floated around the room in Kellen's arms. The intensity of his blue eyes stilled anything she might have said. She'd seen him cross the hall and shivered at his relentless approach, at the determined set of his jaw, the untamed gleam in his eyes. When he'd taken her hand and drawn her onto the dance floor, her breath had caught and her heart had pounded so hard she'd thought it would explode. She tried to relax and follow his lead.

"You look beautiful tonight," Kellen said as he maneuvered them between two other couples without missing a step.

His warm expression said he wasn't merely being polite, and she felt a blush heat her face. "Thank you, Mr. O'Roarke. It was nice of you to ask me to dance. Especially after our last conversation."

"That was business, Miss Guin. This is pleasure." Kellen smiled benignly at her. "I try not to confuse the two. Nice crowd tonight."

Guin returned the smile. "Yes, isn't it. Lovely evening too."

"The weather has been mild. Is it unusually so?"

Guin shook her head. It was as if they'd declared a truce for tonight. This was not the time, not the place to renew their disputes. She would not ask about his resort; he would not ask about her farm.

He led her through another narrow passage between other

dancers, and she marveled at the smoothness of his movements. "You're a wonderful dancer," she said.

"It's one of the few ways for a fellow to hold a girl in his arms," he said with a wide grin. Then, his expression turned more serious. "Your eyes really are the color of cognac. Rich and warm."

His voice had trailed off to a whisper, and Guin listened hard to hear his last words. She stared at him in disbelief; no one had ever told her she was pretty. No one except her grandmother, but Guin had discounted that. Yet from the intensity of his gaze, she could not disregard his comment. Her delight grew; she felt feminine and attractive, and all those things she had never had time to feel.

Unable to respond, wanting only to savor the glorious moment, she lapsed into silence as the music continued. When it stopped, she joined the other dancers in applauding the fiddlers, and dared hope Kellen would ask her to be his partner again. But another man approached and asked for the next dance, and then another, and before the musicians started playing, the dance card her grandmother insisted she carry was full.

"This is my dance, Guin," a thin blond man said. George Johnston, a former schoolmate, smiled broadly, exposing uneven teeth stained from chewing tobacco.

The music started and she circled the room with George. Guin had to concentrate harder on her dancing, for he wasn't as accomplished as Kellen. His jacket did not fit as smoothly as Kellen's, and the fabric felt coarse under her fingers. And although George was tall, his shoulders weren't as broad as Kellen's.

Guin realized with annoyance that she was comparing George to Kellen, and that wasn't fair. George was a good man, a man who ran his farm on the other side of town. A man who was content to take care of what he had and not push for more. Someone she should be delighted to talk to.

"How're your hops doing this season?" George asked.

"Fine," Guin said absently. Still she searched the room for Kellen.

"That's good. You know, I started raising sheep last year. Wool's a good cash crop, and sheep grow even if the weather's bad."

"Yes, I suppose they do." Guin tried to appear attentive.

She spotted Kellen leaning against a pillar, his gaze on her, his expression inscrutable. Then he disappeared from view. "Yeah, sheep are good," George said. "So's fruit. I heard some fellows plan to grow fruit trees on the lower foothills. 'Course everyone's excited about selling to Mr. O'Roarke's resort when it opens. Growing anything different means we won't all be competing against each other."

Guin glanced at George's broad grin, so honest and open. Yet it did nothing for her, stirring only the barest memories of friendship from their childhood. Unlike Kellen's smile, which assaulted her with a heated rush from her cheeks to her toes. She looked for Kellen again. Julia Clarke was with him now and was chattering away. He looked directly at Guin, then he took Julia's hand and led her onto the dance floor.

Guin struggled to hide her disappointment. She couldn't blame Kellen for asking someone else to dance. Despite the truce during their one dance, they had no reason to come together for anything but business.

Still, why did he have to ask Julia? Of all the other young women standing in small clusters or sitting with their families, why her? Just because she wore a dress that probably cost more than all the others' combined? Just because her father was rich and Kellen wanted to be rich too?

Guin's irritation shifted to herself. She shouldn't be paying so much attention to Kellen. As the evening wore on, though, it seemed to Guin that they played hide-and-go-seek. Despite the attentions of her dance partners, she felt a spark of delight whenever Kellen came into view, and a dash of disappointment when he disappeared again.

Henrietta tapped her foot to the music and searched the room for Jonathan Clarke. Guin would be wise to make time for him this evening. Although Henrietta had some concerns about the man and was no longer completely convinced he would be a good catch for Guin, she did not want her granddaughter to overlook the possibilities of such a match.

Yet she could not miss the simmering tension between Guin and Kellen when she'd watched them dance. They'd made such a graceful picture, Guin in her stylish new dress and hair done up all pretty and soft, and Kellen in his perfectly tailored black suit and crisp white shirt. She was engrossed in possibilities when Dr. Jackson tapped her shoulder.

Henrietta looked up at him. "Yes?" she asked, annoyed at the interruption.

Dr. Jackson smiled. "I was wondering if you would grace the dance floor on my arm, ma'am."

The invitation surprised her. "No, thank you. Not now. Perhaps later," she added to soften the rejection. She moved away from him, as if looking for someone, even though she knew no one else in the community except Mrs. Bennett.

"Miss Guin looks much happier than she did at the dinner party. You must be pleased that your plans worked so well this time."

Henrietta started. Dr. Jackson was persistent; she would give him that. She turned to face him. "Of course, I am. I

121

want only what's best for Guinevere." She continued to move on, hoping he would end his shadowing.

"She sure is a pretty little thing. Hard to believe she's all grown up."

She stopped. "Are you following me?"

Dr. Jackson smiled as if pleased with himself. "Why, ma'am, a gentleman never abandons the lady he's escorted to a soiree."

"Don't worry about that, Dr. Jackson. It isn't as if you are my official escort this evening. Please don't let me keep you. Surely there is someone you're looking forward to dancing with tonight."

"There is," he said with a twinkle in his eye. "But she's not interested in dancing right now."

Henrietta looked at him, baffled for a moment until she realized what he was saying. "Now Dr. Jackson—"

"Call me Beau, please."

"Dr. Jackson, I appreciate all you've done to help Guinevere these last two weeks. I could never have arranged for the dress if you hadn't agreed to be my go-between with Mrs. Bennett. I greatly appreciate your taking time this afternoon to help Guinevere learn some dance steps."

"It was my pleasure, Miz Talbot, my pleasure entirely. Miss Guin needs to get out more, and I was happy to help."

"I am already indebted to you, sir. And I do not wish to be more so by monopolizing your time. Surely there are others you wish to talk with this evening," Henrietta said, not masking the encouragement in her voice.

"I'm perfectly content to wait until you are rested enough to dance before I visit with others." Dr. Jackson clasped his hands behind his back and rocked slowly on his heels as he watched the dancers.

Henrietta pursed her lips. She was not interested in this

man, not in any man. She still loved her Daniel. Besides, she wasn't accustomed to being coerced like this, and she did not care for it. At this point, though, she saw no gracious way around him. "All right, Dr. Jackson, I'll dance with you," she said.

"I wouldn't want to be forcing my attentions on you, Miz Talbot. But I sure would be pleased to have you in my arms." He quickly clasped her hand and pulled her amidst the other dancers before she could voice any more objections.

Henrietta remained stiff and unyielding as they circled the room. She did not want to relax, did not want to once again feel the pleasure of being held by a man. It had been so long. So very, very long. Thoughts of Daniel filled her with sadness, and with outrage that a good man had been taken from her long before his time, long before she was ready to let him go. It was that war, that damned war. Henrietta glanced up at Dr. Jackson and she wanted to hate him for being one of those southerners.

Yet, she couldn't hate him. He'd done nothing, except show her the greatest consideration since her arrival. He clearly had a deep fondness for Guin, to be watching over her after her parents' death, encouraging her to go on with her life despite her tragic loss.

Henrietta grimaced and realized it was another thing she had to be angry about. Dr. Jackson supported Guin in her plans to keep the farm. That idea should be short-lived.

"That's right, you just loosen up and let me do the leading, Miz Talbot."

Dr. Jackson's words broke into Henrietta's thoughts, bringing her back to the present. She realized she had relaxed despite herself, and although she found the doctor's silly grin rather pathetic, it also had an endearing quality she couldn't easily dismiss. Looking around the room, she spotted Guin dancing with a man she didn't know. "Who's that with Guinevere?"

Following her gaze, Dr. Jackson said, "Ah, that's George. Nice fellow."

"Tell me about him."

Dr. Jackson chuckled. "He owns a farm on the other side of town from you folks. Good, stable man. Industrious and hard working. Doesn't drink too much and doesn't chase women. 'Course he doesn't have much time for that foolishness. His wife died last fall in childbirth, leaving him with four young'uns and a new babe. Sure could use a wife to help out."

He'd told her a whole lot more than she'd wanted to know, but Henrietta quickly crossed this George fellow off her list of prospects. The last thing her Guinevere needed was a ready-made family and a man who didn't know when to keep his trousers buttoned.

The music stopped, and Henrietta stepped away. "Thank you for the dance. You needn't feel obliged to attend to me further."

Dr. Jackson chuckled. "I'd be delighted to bring you some punch, Miz Talbot. I have a powerful thirst, what with all the dancing Miss Guin and I did at the house, and the long ride into town. We've been here quite a spell and—"

"Punch would be fine, Dr. Jackson," Henrietta snapped. Anything to keep him from a long, rambling explanation. He certainly was not a man of few words.

In minutes he returned, and she sipped the cool drink gratefully, suddenly aware of how hot the room had become. She put her punch cup down, feeling faint. She tried to take a deep breath, but couldn't.

"Miz Talbot, we should step outside."

She heard Dr. Jackson's voice, as if coming through a tunnel. His strong arm supported her as he guided her out the door into the cool of the evening. Away from the press of people, once again able to draw a breath, she realized she'd started to swoon.

"My goodness," she said softly. "This is most embarrassing."

"Don't you be thinking a thing of it." He guided her to a bench and settled her onto it. "If you're feeling dizzy, bend your head down to your knees for a moment."

"Dr. Jackson, that is an impossibility. I can barely sit down."

Alarm crossed his face and he squatted next to her, grasping her arm to take her pulse. "Are you in pain, Miz Talbot? Should I call for Miss Guin?"

"Oh, no, Dr. Jackson." Henrietta tried to take a deep breath, but failed again. "It's just my . . . my corset is so tight." Even in the dim light, she could see his chagrin as he jerked back. "Come now, you can't be embarrassed. You're a doctor."

"That doesn't mean I'm not a man. That I'm impervious to a woman's charms," he said, his voice thick with emotion.

His admission surprised her, and she struggled to find the words to respond.

He sighed heavily and cradled her hand between his. "You needn't fret, Miz Talbot. I didn't mean to upset you. I've known all along how you're feeling about me. I'm getting older and can't be wasting time. Carpe diem! I have to tell you, I'm hoping you'll change your mind."

"I'm sorry, but I can't," she said in a quiet voice.

"I thought a relation to Guin and her daddy would judge a person for who he is." He shook his head sadly. "It's not me you dislike, Miz Talbot, it's where I come from. I'm sorry, but that's not right. It's not fair. But, don't you be worrying. I won't be bothering you any more."

Henrietta watched as he walked toward the door, his shoulders sagging, then he stopped. She held her breath as he returned to her.

"If you're feeling better, I'll escort you back inside," he said, his voice devoid of its usual charm and congeniality.

She was ashamed of herself. Even after she'd treated him so badly, he did not ignore his responsibilities as a gentleman. "I am feeling better," she said, rising to her feet.

She rested her hand gently on his offered arm and walked into the hall with him. Once inside, he bowed stiffly and left her. Henrietta felt the loss of his nearness, but she quickly brushed aside the sentiment and looked for Guin. Instead, she saw Dr. Jackson dance by with a grand-motherly woman in his arms, smiling up at him. He bent his head as if to hear the woman better, then the two laughed uproariously. Henrietta felt a tightening around her heart, a loneliness she'd ignored for many years. Watching was the worst thing she could do. She moved toward Mrs. Bennett.

As she made her way through the crowd, Henrietta finally spotted Guin. She'd been dancing with a local man, but Jonathan Clarke had approached the couple. The sight pleased her at first, but then, she noticed the tension around Guin's mouth, the flat look in her eyes. And she noticed a coldness in Clarke's mien that she did not care for. She tapped her fingers against her lips. Jonathan Clarke wasn't the best man for her granddaughter after all.

"I believe this waltz is mine."

Guin saw Jonathan Clarke cast a steely look at her partner, who stammered and backed away.

Her skin prickled as Jonathan took her hand and guided her onto the dance floor.

"How is your farm, Miss Talbot?"

"This is a busy time."

"I'm sure it is. Farmers are very important to the life of this community. We have to protect them from encroachment."

Guin sensed he was leading up to a discussion about Kellen's resort and the spur line. She might share her feelings with her grandmother or with Dr. Jackson, but Jonathan Clarke was the last person she would talk to about it. "I'm enjoying your dance very much," she said to change the subject. "It was nice of you to sponsor it for the town."

Jonathan chuckled humorlessly. "This seemed a good way for people to meet me."

"I'd heard you were planning to enter politics," Guin said to make idle conversation.

"I haven't made up my mind yet, Miss Talbot. It's a big responsibility, representing the best interests of this community," Jonathan said.

But the momentary tightening of Jonathan's grip on her hand, the sharp glint that flashed through his eyes, made her think that perhaps there was more going on here than a seat in the state legislature. Why would he attempt to deceive her? His actions recalled once again how she'd been put off from the moment she'd met him.

At last, the dance was over. Guin thanked Jonathan and inched her way to the side of the room. She prayed the musicians would stop for a few minutes so she could rest her weary feet. But no, the music started up again. She picked up her dance card, but before she could glance at it, Kellen stood before her and held out his hand.

At this point, she didn't care if it wasn't really his turn.

Her spirits lifted as he took her into his arms. The weariness that had plagued her melted away and the delight she'd experienced during their first dance together returned.

"You've had a busy evening, Miss Guin."

She blushed at his teasing grin. "It has been a grand evening, Mr. O'Roarke, a perfectly splendid evening."

Kellen took in the flushed dewiness of her face, the radiant glow in her eyes. He glanced around and guided them toward the open door at back of the room. He waltzed Guin into the cool evening air, and caught the little "oh" she gasped when she realized where he had taken her.

"I thought you'd like some fresh air," he said. He wished it was a star-lit garden, not the outside of a train station.

Guin stepped away from him and breathed in deeply. "This is wonderful." She touched her hair, starting to tuck away the few tendrils that had fallen free.

Kellen caught her hand. "Leave them."

She looked at him, startled, and he was relieved she was not afraid of him. Kellen reached up and touched the soft loose curls, silky and shimmering in the moonlight. "I never realized how pretty your hair was until tonight," he murmured.

Guin smiled and looked away. "I think you must be over-tired."

"I'm tired, but not too tired to recognize a beautiful woman." Kellen took hold of her shoulders and closed the gap between them. He saw uncertainty in her eyes, but still no fear.

"I'm going to kiss you, Guinevere Talbot," he whispered. He lowered his head until his lips met hers. Soft, so very soft. Like the petals of a rose. He felt a frisson of surprise course through his veins, followed by the heat of desire.

Kellen deepened the kiss, stroking Guin's lips with his, savoring the heady scent of her, pulling her closely into his arms. When she placed her hands on his shoulders, he felt the thrill of knowing he'd ignited the fire within her. He heard her gentle moan, felt her sway against him. Over the years he'd kissed many women, but none had left him feeling this way, invincible, yet protective. None had left him wanting so much more, yet being noble enough to keep from taking it.

For a moment, for one glorious moment, as he molded her body to his, he forgot his plans to destroy Clarke, his resort, his need for Guin's land. All too soon reality filtered into his mind, dampening the fire burning inside him. Slowly, reluctantly, he eased away from Guin.

She was breathing hard, her eyes heavy with desire, her lips swollen from his kisses. He almost threw off sensibility and kissed her again. Yet he held back, knowing he had no right to touch her at all.

Finally, her breathing eased and her eyes brightened with a new awareness. "I'd thought dancing was all you did well," she said with a shy smile.

Kellen fought the ache, the longing, brought on by her words. "I think you're supposed to slap me for being a rogue," he said smiling. Guin laughed, and the tension fell away from him. "I should apologize, but I won't."

"I'd be disappointed if you did," Guin said. "But perhaps we should go inside."

"I suppose we should." Kellen ran his thumb gently across her lips. The puffiness had receded, but there was something about the glow of her skin, the shining in her eyes that still made her appear as though she'd been thoroughly kissed. He listened for a moment and heard the musicians stop for a rest. "We can go in now." Kellen quickly guided her into the room before others pushed toward the door for a breath of fresh air.

Guin found herself somewhat dazed, and she was sure it wasn't from the bright lights. No, her disorientation had more to do with the jumbled emotions swirling inside her.

She glanced around and realized Mrs. Bennett and her husband had claimed Kellen's attention. For a moment, she felt bereft. That was nonsense, she chided herself. He was wise to separate himself from her, especially since they were not supposed to be friendly. Still, she wondered if the changes she felt inside showed on her face. Suddenly very thirsty, she wandered toward the refreshment table.

Her first kiss. Something every girl dreamed about. How many were fortunate enough to have it with a very handsome man who obviously knew what he was doing? Guin sighed as she picked up a punch cup and let the cool liquid sooth her burning lips. She'd almost swooned, right there in his arms. With embarrassment, she realized she'd responded like a brazen hussy, not like a lady, a woman with responsibilities.

All the reasons she should have nothing to do with Kellen O'Roarke came rushing back. She even wondered if he might have kissed her as another way to pursue his campaign to gain access to her land. She didn't want to think so. She wanted to believe his kisses were real. Yet, she couldn't deny that he was smooth, and he was relentless in pursuing what he wanted.

The musicians resumed their places on the dais and tuned their fiddles. A former classmate of Guin's approached, and she knew without looking at her dance card that he was her new partner. As she followed Henry onto the dance floor, she spotted Kellen across the room talking to Julia.

Guin remembered her reactions to Kellen when she'd first seen him at the town meeting. Even then, she'd recognized his glib tongue that could sweet-talk everyone. Had she fallen victim to that charm? Perhaps a little. She wasn't about to let him have her land, however, no matter how nicely he talked to her, no matter how thoroughly he kissed her. She would remain strong. She had no other choice.

Chapter 9

Kellen stared at the ledgers lying on the desk in front of him. He threw his pen down in frustration. Everything cost so damn much. Supplies, transporting the supplies, labor—it all added up.

He rubbed his hands across his face. He'd known before he started this project that the resort would take all his resources, every cent he had and every cent he could borrow. It would all be worth it, if the resort was financially successful and if it gave him access to the right people. He needed both those things to expose Jonathan Clarke. Kellen had been working ten years to achieve this.

Scanning the numbers again, he confirmed that he had no margin for error, no leeway for unexpected expenses. Panic fluttered in his stomach; he quickly squelched his fear of failure. Yet failure remained a possibility as long as the funds for the railroad spur sat untouched in the bank. They would stay untouched until he found a way to cross Guin's land without harming it, without destroying her farm, as he'd promised. So far he hadn't found one.

Kellen leaned back in his chair and gazed out the window. He squinted at the mid-day glare, his thoughts drifting to the previous week's dance, as they had many times. Guin had surprised him. In his mind's eye, he again held her in his arms and danced around the room, while the auburn highlights in her hair shone under the lights and her eyes sparkled. Most of all, he remembered her lips, petal soft and pliant under his kiss. At the memory, his body responded and Kellen shifted position, unable to remember the last time simply thinking about a woman had affected him so much.

"Good afternoon, sir."

Kellen started at Winfield's voice. "I didn't hear you come in."

"I trust your accounts are in order?"

"They're as good as they're going to be until we open the resort." Kellen turned to face his assistant and caught the sober look on Winfield's face. "What's wrong?"

Winfield shook his head. "You always do go straight to the problem, sir. Are you not supposed to offer me a cup of tea, or perhaps a drink? Remember the niceties."

"Winfield, my good man. I know it's early, but perhaps you would care to join me in a libation?" Kellen hopped up from his seat and strode to the cut crystal decanters filled with their favorite blends. He turned to face Winfield, a wide grin on his face. "How's that?"

Winfield rolled his eyes. "I do not know what I am to do with you, sir. You are correct. It is early. However, a small glass of sherry might be in order."

Kellen frowned as he poured two drinks, sherry for Winfield and a stiff whiskey for himself. He crossed the room and handed the drink to Winfield. To anyone else, Winfield would have appeared tranquil and at ease as he sipped his drink. Kellen knew him too well. Whatever Winfield had to tell him was not good. Kellen's gut churned, and a flicker of panic returned.

When he couldn't stand it any longer, Kellen asked, "What's the matter, Winfield?"

Winfield raised one eyebrow, then sighed. "I do believe we have a minor problem. At least at this point it is minor, but if the trend continues, we could be in for a time of it."

"What are you taking about?"

"It has to do with the resort, sir."

"I gathered that." Kellen wanted to shake his friend.

"It is difficult to explain because it could be a simple co-incidence. Or it could be a trend. I am not sure which yet."

"What may be a coincidence or a trend?"

Winfield's brow furrowed. "It started last week. The local farmer who promised to supply us with food for the laborers has now said he cannot do so. When I asked him why he must break his contract with us, he mumbled some nonsense about running short for his own farm workers."

"That sounds reasonable," Kellen said with a shrug.

"Yes, except I had specifically asked him about that potentiality when I contracted with him, and he assured me he had abundant capacity." Winfield looked affronted that the farmer might have lied to him.

"Is there more?"

"Yes, sir, there is. I had also contacted a number of farmers, and then contracted with their laborers to work on the resort until they are needed for harvest. These were the farmers' sons and seasonal workers. Yesterday, two of the men approached me and said they could not continue to work for us. Their reasons were unsatisfactorily vague. I offered to pay them more money, but they were not interested."

Kellen winced at the thought of paying money they did not have to keep the work going. "I suppose it's possible the farmers misjudged how long they could get by without those men."

"I seriously doubt that, sir. These are experienced farmers we are dealing with, and the laborers have worked their crops for years. They know precisely when the laborers are needed and when they are not."

Kellen tossed back his whiskey. "What do you think is going on?"

"It strikes me as peculiar that these incidents should all occur within a week of last week's social event."

"Clarke's dance?" Kellen's attention sharpened. "You think Clarke is behind this?" When Winfield shrugged, Kellen said, "Work on that. Quietly, of course. We don't want to arouse any suspicion, or let on that we know something is afoot."

"I quite agree. We do not want to show our hand too early. Yet we must not ignore the possibility that Mr. Clarke is involved in some skullduggery."

"A man like him doesn't pick a town like Spring Valley at random to live. We have to find out what he's up to, Winfield. We can't afford to lose time or money."

"I will be more vigilant and ask subtle questions. No one will speculate that I am searching for specific information."

"Good. Keep me informed. I assume we can find someone else to supply the camp's food?"

"I am looking into alternate arrangements, but nothing is yet confirmed."

Kellen nodded. "Keep on it. Can we get by without those workers?"

"It will be most difficult. The supervisor is a competent man and assured me he will do whatever he can to finish on schedule. However . . ."

Kellen looked at him keenly. "However what?"

"There is the possibility we will lose more workers."

"I'm not about to let that happen, Winfield. I'm counting on you to get to the bottom of this. If your suspicions are correct, then we'll take action."

"Very good, sir."

Kellen waited until Winfield left their suite before he

swore and smacked the leaded crystal glass on the table. What was Clarke up to? Kellen knew the man too well to believe that these setbacks were pure coincidence. These subtle, seemingly unrelated incidents could undermine Kellen's whole project unless he figured out what was going on and stopped it.

Scarcely able to believe she was attending another social event in town, Guin perched on the wagon seat and clicked the horse's reins. She scanned the landscape surrounding her farm, flat terrain ringed by undulating hills, a patchwork of cultivated greens and natural browns. Breathing deeply of the sweet, clean air, she felt a warmth envelope her. This was her land, her home; it was where she belonged.

"You seem quite pleased with yourself."

Henrietta's words broke into Guin's train of thought, and she grinned. "I have every reason to be pleased. This is the first Fourth-of-July celebration I've been to. You bought me another pretty dress," she said, smoothing the skirt with one hand. "And we're each bringing a basket for the box social."

"I certainly hope we brought enough food," Henrietta fretted.

Guin laughed easily. "I don't think you need to worry about that. Instead, you should be worried about how you're going to get your basket to the tent, it's so heavy."

Shrugging off Guin's concerns, Henrietta asked, "Are we late?"

"Not really. Mrs. Bennett told me last week that the festivities don't start until after noon. The band marches through town to the pergola, then the mayor gives his speech, the band plays again, more town dignitaries speak, and after all that is the church-sponsored box social raffle."

"I can't believe I let you talk me into fixing a dinner for the raffle."

"I was already making a basket to bring, so it wasn't hard to make enough for two. Who knows, Grandmother, maybe you'll meet some handsome man who'll be so overwhelmed by your cooking that he'll fall to his knees and beg you to marry him on the spot."

"Guin!"

Guin laughed at her grandmother's horrified expression. "That's happened before."

"Well, I never." Henrietta harrumphed and resettled herself on the wagon seat.

"Maybe you don't want just anyone bidding on your box lunch," Guin said slowly. "Maybe you've already picked someone out. . . ."

Henrietta blushed furiously. "Don't be ridiculous," she snapped. "I'm only doing this to help the church raise money. I couldn't care less about who buys it."

Guin grinned and decided not to tease her grandmother any further. After all, she didn't want much scrutiny herself. While she'd browned flour-coated chicken in a sizzling frying pan, she'd conjured up an image of the man who would share her meal. A tall man with broad shoulders dressed in citified clothes. A man with knowing blue eyes, with lips that still reminded her of a searing kiss the two of them had shared. A kiss that told her more about what went on between a man and a woman than she'd ever imagined.

A man named Kellen O'Roarke.

She had to acknowledge that Kellen threatened more than her farm. He threatened her equanimity, her focus on who she was and what she wanted. The land she worked was part of her; it nourished her spirit to watch the plants she cultivated for both their beauty and their usefulness.

Guin guided the wagon to a large flat area near the church and hobbled her horse. After helping Henrietta from the wagon, she said, "You wait here while I take the baskets to the tent." Guin hauled the two heavy baskets from the wagon bed and carried them to the already crowded table inside the tent. When she returned to her grandmother, she asked, "Can you hear the band?"

"Sounds like a wounded animal in its death throes."

Guin laughed to see the pained look on her grandmother's face. "They'll sound better when they're all tuned up. I hope."

The rest of the afternoon flew by for Guin. She and her grandmother stood on the wooden sidewalk in front of the Bennetts' store and waved their tiny flags as the band marched by, a few brass and a drummer who more than made up for their lack of numbers in volume and energy.

Sipping tart lemonade, they listened to the mayor, Matthew Franklin, and the banker, Lawrence Gaspard, extol the country's virtues and exclaim over how proud all the listeners should be to live in a community with a wonderful future like Spring Valley.

As the applause faded, Guin cupped her grandmother's elbow. "Let's go to the tent. The raffle begins soon."

"I'm in no hurry," Henrietta said, her mouth forming a tight, thin line.

"I know." Guin patted her grandmother's arm. "But I am."

"Do you think Jonathan Clarke will bid on your basket?" Henrietta asked.

Guin considered the question before answering. "I doubt he'll bid on anyone's basket," she said.

"Perhaps you have someone else in mind to share your meal?" Henrietta hinted slyly.

Guin wished she could quell the heated flush that crept into her cheeks. "I'm only interested in helping the church raise money for the new bell." She figured if that excuse worked for her grandmother, it should work for her.

"Of course, you are, my dear." Henrietta laughed.

"Miss Talbot! Miss Talbot!"

Guin turned and frowned when she saw Julia Clarke hurrying toward her. Julia wore a porcelain-blue percale dress decorated with tiny sprigs of embroidered white flowers. The dress emphasized her fair complexion and generous curves. Her loveliness intimidated Guin less than before, since she knew that her own dress of pale pink muslin suited her.

"I'm so glad I finally found you." Julia gasped to catch her breath.

"Is something wrong?"

"Oh heavens, no. It's just that the woman who owns the general store, oh, what's her name?"

"Mrs. Bennett?" Guin offered. Julia looked all around, but never directly at her.

"Yes, that's it. Mrs. Bennett. She asked me to tell you she'd like your help for a few minutes."

"My help? I thought the store was closed today."

"It is, but she needs to bring some things here for the social, and she thought you'd help her."

Julia clasped and unclasped her hands in agitation.

Guin glanced at the tent, saw all the baskets sitting on the table in front, and the mayor heading toward them. This was her first box social and she did not want to miss a minute of the excitement. Her heart skipped a beat when she spotted Kellen and Winfield off to the side in deep conversation, but Kellen didn't seem to see her. She sighed and tried to reassure herself that a few minutes wouldn't hurt. She hesitated. Still, Mrs. Bennett had been so nice to help Grandmother with the dresses, Guin felt she owed her thanks. She turned to face Julia.

"All right. I'll go." Guin thought she saw a satisfied gleam in Julia's eyes. That was ridiculous, of course. "Grandmother, find a seat and I'll join you in a few minutes."

"But Guinevere, the raffle—"

"I'll be back in plenty of time." Guin hurried toward the main street of town, wishing Mrs. Bennett had discovered earlier that she needed help.

"Ah, Miss Talbot," Lawrence Gaspard greeted her in front of the bank. "How are you this day?"

"I'm fine, and I enjoyed your speech," she said politely. "I'm surprised you're working today."

Gaspard paused from unlocking the bank's door. "Just a few minor things I have to check." He looked around furtively. "I was wondering if you had a few minutes to discuss that loan of yours."

Guin's stomach clenched in fear. "Is there a problem? The payment's not due until after the hops are harvested."

"Everything's fine, just fine," Gaspard said.

"Oh, good. You had me worried," Guin said. "If there's no problem, can we talk about it later? Mrs. Bennett is waiting for me at the store."

"That would be fine, Miss Talbot. Just fine. We can talk about it later."

Still uneasy, Guin left him. When she reached the Bennetts' store, she tried the door, but it was securely locked. Guin peered into the window, shielding her eyes from the glaring afternoon sunlight. The store appeared empty. She glanced up and down the street and saw a few stragglers. Most of the community, not just the single men and women, had gathered at the tent to watch the raffle.

Guin tapped her feet impatiently. She'd heard about the

social over the years, but her parents had never attended, saying they were too busy or not interested. Yet Guin found she'd enjoyed herself so far today, and she wanted to savor every minute, to experience it all so she could relive it later in her mind.

Finally, she went around to the back, thinking Mrs. Bennett had used the storeroom entrance, but that was locked too. Perplexed, wondering if perhaps Julia had misunderstood the message, Guin returned to the front of the store.

Tobias Eldridge, the newspaper editor, strolled down the street. "Hello, Miss Guin," he called, his voice full of cheer.

"Mr. Eldridge, have you seen Mrs. Bennett?"

"Sure have. I just left Mrs. Bennett and the mister near the trees. They're laughing and talking with some other folks about how Doc Jackson outbid old man Whitaker for your grandmother's basket." Tobias chuckled. "She looked angrier than a irritated wasp looking for someone to sting. What's going on with those two?"

"It's a long story. Is the raffle over already?"

"Oh, there're some baskets left, but they're going quickly."

Guin didn't want to be rude, but she didn't want to talk any longer. Julia must have misunderstood Mrs. Bennett. "I'd better check on Dr. Jackson and make sure my grandmother isn't harassing him too badly."

Eldridge called after her, "I wouldn't be surprised if I publish a few engagement announcements before harvest time."

She hurried toward the tent. Scanning the open area she quickly spotted her grandmother and Dr. Jackson sitting on the church steps in a shady spot. She grinned at the self-satisfied look on Dr. Jackson's face as he finished a piece of chicken, and her grandmother's rigid posture and stiff expression. At least not all their efforts had gone to waste.

Guin ducked into the tent. On a table sat a few remaining baskets. Frowning, she looked outside. The mayor was on the pergola holding up another girl's basket, the blushing girl standing beside him while several young men called out offers.

The crowd had thinned and Guin didn't see anyone who might be interested in bidding on her basket. All that work for nothing. Disheartened, Guin slipped unnoticed from the tent with her basket and carried it back to her wagon. She flipped it open and stepped back in surprise. Inside lay a white linen tablecloth with matching napkins. They weren't hers. Guin flipped through the contents. She snapped the lid shut. This basket looked like hers, but it wasn't. So where was hers?

Then she remembered. Julia's odd look, her anxious movements. Had Julia deliberately lured her away from the tent? There was only one way to find out.

Grimly, Guin made her way through the clusters of people, her gaze concentrated on finding her basket, and whoever had it. At last, she recognized Julia sitting at one of the tables. Guin had no trouble identifying Julia's companion, even if his broad-shouldered back was to her.

Then she noticed the wicker basket on the ground next to them, similar to the one she'd picked up in the tent. The bright yellow and white gingham liner spilled over the sides. It all became very clear.

From the panicked look on Julia's face when she looked up, Guin knew her conclusions were accurate.

"Hello, Julia. Kellen."

"Guin!" Kellen sprang to his feet with a pleased smile. "I wondered if you were here, but I hadn't seen you."

"I had some things to do, but they've all been taken care of." Guin's gaze fixed on Julia, who didn't even have the decency to look away. Did she plan to brazen her way through this?

"Please join us," Kellen urged.

"Kellen, dear, don't you think—"

"Don't worry, Julia. From the weight of your basket, I'm sure you made plenty." Kellen hesitated, then looked at Guin. "I guess you didn't bring a basket."

He sounded almost disappointed, and Guin could not help but thrill at the thought that Kellen might have bid on her basket. "Actually, I—"

Julia interrupted. "We really don't want to keep you from your other friends, Guin."

That did it. Guin wasn't going to slink away simply because Julia wanted to be alone with Kellen. That was her basket and her food they were about to eat. Guin wasn't going to sit idly by and let someone else take credit for the hours of preparation she'd spent in a hot kitchen in the middle of a heat wave.

"I'd love to join you, Julia," Guin said as she sat next to Kellen. She tried to ignore the fact that by forcing Julia's hand, she would also be calling attention to herself, attention from Kellen she wasn't sure she wanted. She'd come too far to back down now.

"I wonder what delicacies you've fixed," Guin said, striving to keep a taunting edge out of her voice. She set her arms on the table and clasped her hands together. "You do know the rules, don't you? Everything has to be made by the woman herself." Guin cocked her head to one side. "Let me see. I'll bet you made some fried chicken. Nicely seasoned with a crisply golden crust."

Kellen set the basket on the table and started poking through the contents. He looked up and grinned at them both. "Good guess, Guin. Here's the chicken," he said as he set it on the table.

"And, some strawberries, fresh picked this morning."

Kellen pulled out a tin, opened it, and breathed deeply. "I love fresh strawberries."

"I shouldn't take all the fun out of it for you, Julia. You should tell Kellen yourself what you made for your box lunch."

Julia glared at her. "It's nothing special, just the usual things."

"Some potato salad, perhaps? Do you prefer the kind with eggs and pickles? Or the kind with a vinegar marinade? What about rolls? Are they drop biscuits or rolled?" Guin glanced at Kellen and saw his growing puzzled expression. "Which do you like better, Kellen?"

"I don't really care." He looked uncertainly from one woman to the other. "Everything smells wonderful and I'm hungry."

"Tell me, Julia, do you prefer your Dover cake with or without raisins and currants?"

Julia's face turned crimson. She stood up and swayed against the table. "Please excuse me. I'm feeling quite poorly all of a sudden."

Kellen slowly rose to his feet. "You shouldn't go alone if you're not well. I'll take you home. Wait here while I get a carriage." Frowning, he nodded to Guin, then strode toward the horses.

Julia turned to Guin, her misery replaced by smug confidence. "Keep the basket, Guin. I've got what I wanted."

As Julia walked away, Guin sat in stunned silence. How had she lost? Kellen was escorting Julia home, while Guin was left with a delicious box lunch and no one to share it with.

Chapter 10

Evening had settled over the valley by the time Kellen pulled in front of the Talbot house. He spotted Dr. Jackson's horse in the corral with Guin's. Reassured that he wasn't stopping by too late, he started up the front stairs. He heard Colonel's bark from the kitchen, so he went around the house to that door and knocked.

Guin opened the door cautiously. "Kellen! What're you doing here?"

"May I come in?"

"Of course." Guin stepped aside and gestured for him to sit at the table. "I'm afraid the parlor's already occupied," she said with a wry grin.

"I saw Dr. Jackson's horse in the corral. You ladies do keep late visiting hours."

"Actually, Dr. Jackson escorted us home and Grandmother is entertaining him." She looked tired, but there was a wariness about her too.

"Well, I won't stay," Kellen said, but he didn't move toward the door.

Guin looked at him with a puzzled frown. "You've come a long way to step inside the kitchen and then leave."

"The truth is, I wanted to apologize for leaving you so suddenly at the picnic."

"You don't need to apologize." Guin turned from him and started fussing with a dishtowel. "You had your hands full."

"Julia said she was sick, and her face was so red, like she

145

had a fever or something. . . ." Kellen stared at the cake sitting on the kitchen table.

"What's the matter?" Guin asked.

He pointed at the cake. "What kind is that?"

"It's a Dover cake. With currants and raisins." She looked at him with defiance in her eyes.

It took him only a moment to figure it out. "That was your basket, wasn't it? That's how you knew what was in it. But how did she—then you—" He burst out laughing and collapsed into the nearest chair. For a moment, Guin looked angry, then she was laughing with him.

"What in the world's going on out here?" Henrietta demanded from the doorway. She carried a tray with small plates and cups to the sink.

Kellen's laughter faded and he watched Guin wipe her eyes as she continued to laugh.

"It's a long story, Grandmother." She glanced at Kellen and began to giggle again.

"I hope you don't mind my coming by so late, Mrs. Talbot."

"Nonsense, young man. In New York, I would have been appalled, but Guin keeps telling me things are different out here." She shook her head. "As long as you don't stay long, I suppose it's all right. Just remember, tomorrow is a work day. For some of us, anyway." Henrietta spun on her heel and returned to the parlor.

A giggle slipped out, and Kellen saw a glimpse of Guin he might easily have missed. Her eyes sparkled and her hair wisped softly around her head, giving her a playful appearance.

"I took the 'ailing' Miss Clarke home," he said, "and she seemed to make a miraculous recovery, but she wasn't the least bit hungry. I never did get fed."

"You poor man." Her tone was mockingly sympathetic.

"I don't suppose you might have. . . ."

She stared at him expectantly. She wasn't going to make him grovel, was she?

"You know, any leftovers?"

"Oh," she said in mock dismay. "You want me to feed you."

She laughed, but before Kellen knew it, she had set a plate for him. "Is this what I missed earlier? Fried chicken, nicely seasoned with a crisply golden crust? Potato salad in a vinegar marinade? Drop biscuits and freshly picked strawberries?"

She nodded. "Seems a shame you didn't get to eat any of it. Particularly since you paid for it."

She had a good point, and any guilt he'd felt quickly faded. Especially when he bit into the chicken. He finished eating and licked his fingers. "Miss Talbot, you do have a way with food. A man would never stray far from your kitchen for fear he'd miss some delight."

Guin looked away, but not before Kellen spotted the blush of pleasure cross her cheeks. He chided himself. He had no business saying things like that to her.

"Would you like more tea?" she asked.

"Sure, and a piece of that cake, if you don't mind," he said, more for the pleasure of watching her move across the room than because he was hungry. He liked the way her skirts swayed, the way the soft lantern light profiled her subtle curves as she turned, the way her constrained hair had loosened after the long day. When she leaned over to pour the tea, his fingers itched to ease the pins from her hair and watch the thick chestnut tresses tumble around her face.

She finished pouring and sat down across from him. "Did you get your money's worth?" she said with a shy smile.

He took a bite of cake and moaned. He swallowed, then

147

said, "Yes. Definitely. What I didn't know was that I was going to have to wait so long, or come so far, to enjoy it. What happened?"

"Oh, that's not important," Guin said.

He smiled to himself. She could have told him a wild tale, but instead, she chose not to. She knew that he knew Julia had pulled a stunt and then had tried to get away with it. He had to admire Guin's restraint.

Instead, she drew him into a summary of the day's festivities, the mayor's speech, the parade, the large crowd. At last, they exhausted that topic and fell silent.

Guin glanced at Kellen over her cup. His gaze held hers, and he saw in her questioning eyes, in her satin-soft skin, in her moist lips, all the things a man should want, all that should make a man content. He'd missed that in his life, the gentleness and sense of belonging only a good woman could give a man. He breathed in the scent of her. She smelled sweet and womanly, and part of him longed for what she might offer.

"I have to go." He didn't like the hurt that flashed across Guin's face as he leaped from the chair.

"It is late," she agreed. "Tomorrow morning will come early."

He felt her awkwardness and knew what she was thinking. Why had he come all this way so late? Would he touch her, kiss her before he left?

He steeled himself to resist the temptation, knowing that if he took her in his arms, he would not be able to let her go. He owed her more than that. She was a decent woman. She deserved someone . . . different from him. Not necessarily better, just different.

What she offered wasn't for him, he reminded himself. He was striving for something more than that which would satisfy other men. He looked away. She'd felt the pull between them too; he could tell from the nervous clatter of the dishes she gathered and set to soak, the way she avoided looking directly at him. For a moment, for a fleeting second, he regretted not following his yearnings. For the first time, he questioned the course he had chosen for his life.

He took a deep breath and pushed his uncertainty away. He had no time for such foolishness, no time to regret what might have been if Clarke had never entered his life years ago and ruined his father.

"Say goodnight to your grandmother for me." He picked up his hat and hastened out the door.

Guin nodded and followed him outside. The moon bathed the yard in silvery light. When Kellen climbed onto his horse and turned to tip his hat in farewell, she felt his turmoil. Why had he come all this way to her farm? She hated to think he was motivated by some misguided sense of duty. Instead, her fanciful side, the feminine side that had blossomed since the night of the dance when she'd worn a pretty new dress and been kissed in the moonlight, wanted to believe he had come because of his interest in her. Interest in her as a woman, not as the owner of land he wanted.

Yet that was foolishness. A man like Kellen would never be attracted to a woman like her. They were too different; they wanted different things and viewed the world in different ways. He was merely being nice because he wanted something from her. That was all. She shouldn't read anything more into it.

She sighed with regret as reality squashed her momentary illusions, and she stepped back inside the house.

A few days later, Guin rode her horse across the meadows at the base of the foothills. She savored the fragrance of ripening summer crops and flowers filling the dry, early evening air. Work had been hard that day, the sun beating mercilessly on her and her workers, the vines growing longer and more difficult to restrain without damaging the hop burrs. In the softening light, she relished the cooling breeze on her face. She urged the mare across the grassy field, then guided her up the road that followed the edge of the foothills and let the horse take the lead.

Lost in thought, she almost missed the faint sound. She stopped and listened intently, then slid quietly from her horse and stepped away from it. The road ran along the crest of a foothill overlooking the river and her farm.

She heard it again: a moan; she was sure of it. Guin hurried to the edge of the cliff and peered over the side. In the dusky light she had difficulty seeing. The scrubby bushes, dry grass, and rocks all looked alike. Finally, she thought she spotted a bit of blue amid an outcropping of brush below her.

"Hold on!" she called. Clutching at scrubby bushes and exposed rock, Guin slipped and slid down the hill until she reached the ledge. She carefully turned the man over and gasped. "Mr. Somerset!"

"Help me," the man whispered before losing consciousness.

Guin brushed dried blood from his temple and looked around. There was no way she could drag him up to the road. Going down wasn't a choice either; she'd barely kept herself from falling when she'd come this far.

"I'm going for help." She pushed Winfield as far from the edge of the rock outcrop as she could and scrambled to the road. When she reached the top, she ran to her horse and marked the place in her mind before galloping down the road toward the flat land. Her workers' cabins were closest. Pedro and Joel had lived on the farm and worked for her father for years. Both dark-haired, Pedro was stocky and quiet, while Joel was wiry and loquacious. She'd been relieved when they'd told her they would stay and work for her after her father's death. Now, she routed them into action.

"Hurry," she urged. "We must get back before the light's gone."

Without a word, Pedro hooked a cart to her horse and piled in blankets and ropes.

Joel gathered the tools they might need. "I'm thinking a shovel'd be a good thing to have. Maybe an axe. Don't think we need a hammer."

Guin wanted to hustle him along, but Joel had his own ways, and any interference would only slow him down. When everything was loaded in the cart, she drove ahead while they followed rapidly on foot. In a few minutes, they joined her at the base of the hill.

"He's up there," Guin said, pointing to an outcropping of brush halfway up the hillside.

"You wait here, Miss Talbot," Joel said, handing a scythe to Pedro and grabbing a blanket. "We'll bring him down."

Guin chafed at being left behind. "Be careful. We don't know how badly he's hurt."

She waited, pacing back and forth. Looking over her shoulder at the horizon, she gauged there was only an hour left before daylight disappeared completely. She peered at the hillside and tried to determine how much farther Pedro and Joel had to climb. She heard voices, and from the sounds drifting down she could tell they'd found Winfield. Still she worried.

Finally, Pedro and Joel returned, carrying the injured man hammocked in a blanket. She rushed to meet them as they cleared the brush.

"Here we are, Miss Talbot," Joel said. "We'll get him in the cart, then cushion him with blankets."

"It's going to be uncomfortable no matter what we do," Guin said grimly. She quickly checked for any obviously broken bones and heavy bleeding. When she found none, she shoved another blanket under Winfield.

"Meadow faster," Pedro said.

"You're right, Pedro. He's unconscious, so the faster the better," Guin said. She guided her horse across the flat land. The cart jostled and bounced, but Winfield seemed oblivious to the rough ride.

Somewhat relieved when they reached the house, she slid from the horse and turned to Pedro and Joel. "Unhook the cart."

When the task was finished, she said, "Joel, take my horse into town and get Dr. Jackson. Then, find Mr. O'Roarke at the hotel and tell him Mr. Somerset is here. Grandmother!"

"Yes, ma'am." Joel mounted the horse and galloped toward town.

Henrietta opened the door and stepped onto the porch. "Guinevere, where have you—good heavens, what happened?"

She rushed down the porch steps and gasped when she saw the unconscious man in the cart. "Oh! It's Mr. O'Roarke's friend. Bring him inside. To my room." She hurried into the house.

Guin gripped two corners of the blanket. Carefully, she and Pedro eased Winfield from the cart. Guin's arms ached as they carried the injured man between them into the house, but she did not weaken for fear she would drop Winfield. Her work in the fields had left her strong enough.

Instead, she worried about Winfield. What had he been doing in the foothills at this time of day? How had he hurt himself, and where was his horse? The questions tumbled through her mind as she and Pedro hoisted him onto her grandmother's bed and removed his torn and dusty jacket.

"Guinevere, you should leave now," Henrietta said. "Pedro and I will handle the rest."

Guin looked at her in surprise.

"It's not appropriate for an unmarried young lady to undress a man. Pedro and I will do it."

If Henrietta had not been so serious, Guin might have laughed at the idea of protecting her sensibilities. This was Winfield Somerset they were talking about, a man old enough to be Guin's grandfather. Who did her grandmother think cared for Guin's parents while they lay dying from the fever?

This wasn't the time to argue. Guin closed the bedroom door and hurried to the kitchen. She stoked the fire and set a pot of water on the stove to heat, along with a fresh pot of coffee. At this point, all she could do was wait for her grandmother and Pedro to finish with Winfield. Wait for Dr. Jackson to arrive. Wait for Kellen to come.

In the vacuum of the moment, she felt suspended. A year ago, if she'd heard that moan coming from the bushes, she would have rushed home and turned everything over to her father to handle. He wasn't here anymore, so she'd had to do it alone.

She had not panicked. Instead, she'd organized a rescue party, brought Winfield safely home, and, except for her grandmother, she had directed others. How far she'd come in such a short time. Maybe she really could make it on her own. Maybe she could manage the farm. For the first time, she felt it was a real possibility, and the discovery brought with it a heady feeling.

Her thoughts were disrupted by the sound of a horse's

hooves in the yard. Footsteps clattered up the steps. She rushed to the door and flung it open as Kellen burst through.

"Where is he?" The wild look in his eye frightened Guin.

"At the end of the hall." She pointed the way.

Kellen brushed past her. In a moment, she heard voices, Kellen's raised, Henrietta's calm and soothing. Guin started to close the back door when she heard a buggy racketing down the road. She waited for Dr. Jackson. He stepped from the buggy and grabbed his black bag before joining her.

"Joel said you found an injured man."

Guin nodded. "Winfield Somerset, Kellen's friend."

"Where is he?"

"In Mother and Father's old room." Guin followed Dr. Jackson as he hurried down the hall.

"Tell me what you know," he called over his shoulder.

Guin briefly recounted how she'd found Winfield and had him brought to the house. She bumped into the doctor as he stopped inside the room, which was crowded with Henrietta, Pedro, and Kellen.

"Everyone out," Dr. Jackson ordered. "Everyone," he added sternly when Kellen opened his mouth to protest.

"Kellen, come have a cup of coffee while Dr. Jackson examines Winfield." Guin plucked at his sleeve, and he reluctantly took a step toward her. She noticed Dr. Jackson signal her grandmother to stay behind.

After she'd given them her profuse thanks, Pedro and Joel left for their cabins. Kellen slumped in a chair, his face buried in his hands. His air of devastation was so different from his usual confidence that it frightened Guin.

"Kellen?" she whispered.

Slowly, he turned toward her, his face so ravaged with grief that she gasped. Without thinking, she threw her arms around him and eased his head onto her shoulder. He collapsed against her and she was surprised at how nice it felt to be needed. By him.

"He'll be all right," she soothed. "Dr. Jackson is a good doctor. He'll take good care of Winfield."

"You don't understand," Kellen said in a ragged voice. "I can't lose Winfield. He's all the family I have."

His words confused Guin. Winfield wasn't related to Kellen, she was sure of it. "What do you mean?" She eased away so she could look at him. "Tell me about him."

Kellen drew a deep breath as if driving himself to regain control. "I met Winfield in a mining town." A sad smile crossed his face. "I was twenty at the time, as rough and uncouth as they come."

"Where was your family?" Guin asked quietly.

Kellen shrugged. "Dead. Ma died when I was very young, and Da died a year before I met Winfield."

She quietly poured him another cup of coffee and sat across the table from him.

Kellen sipped his coffee. "Winfield was as out of place in that town as a newborn babe. He was stranded when the man he worked for was robbed and murdered," Kellen said. "A bunch of rowdies started harassing him—you know, shoving him back and forth, making cracks about his city clothes and proper manners." He shrugged again. "It didn't seem right, so I rescued him."

"How did you do that?"

"I beat them up," he said. "Of course, it wasn't too hard since they were all drunk."

"But still, you took on several men to help someone else. He must have been grateful."

"I guess so. At first, he tagged along with me. A regular nuisance. Always cleaning my clothes and correcting my grammar." Kellen shook his head. "I kept telling him to stop, to go away, to find someone else, but he insisted it was his duty to make me into a gentleman. Finally, I stopped fighting him and started listening. He taught me everything I needed to know, how to dress, how to act, how to talk."

Kellen hesitated, then shook his head. "That man in there," he said, pointing down the hall, "was my teacher, and he became my business associate. What's most important is that he is my best friend. I trust him with my life."

Guin sat quietly, deeply moved by the emotion in Kellen's words. She had many of the same kinds of feelings about Dr. Jackson.

Kellen stood and paced the room. "Do you have any idea how he was hurt?"

Guin shook her head. "I was riding along the ridge of the foothills and I heard a noise. When I looked over the side of the cliff, I saw him."

"You didn't see anyone else? Or, hear anything?"

She shook her head again. "Nothing. I assume he was riding a horse, but it was gone."

Kellen hunkered down in front of her and took her hands. "Did he say anything after you found him? Or, when you brought him here?"

His piercing gaze probed deep into her soul, and she wished she could give him whatever answers he so desperately wanted. "He was moaning when I found him. If he hadn't been, I wouldn't have known he was there. He moaned again when we set him in the cart, but he must have been unconscious, because he didn't respond to my questions."

Kellen rose again. "I hope to God it's not because—"

"The patient is resting nicely." Dr. Jackson said as he walked into the room. "Bad bump on the head, a few scratches from tumbling down the hillside, but nothing

156

broken. He'll need to stay here for a couple of days, at least until we know he's out of danger. Miz Talbot's bringing her things upstairs for the duration."

"Can I see him?" Kellen asked.

"Not now, son. He's sleeping and he needs his rest. You might could see him later."

"Can I at least sit with him? I won't disturb him."

Dr. Jackson pursed his lips as he looked intently at Kellen. At last, he nodded. "You can sit with him for a few minutes. Then, go to your hotel and get a good night's sleep."

"But—"

"You can ride with me back to town." Dr. Jackson's tone left no room for argument, and Kellen raced down the hall.

"Dr. Jackson?" Guin asked. "Is Winfield really going to be all right?"

The doctor turned toward her, his face sagging with worry. "I didn't want to worry the boy. His friend had a bad blow to the head. I can't say he'll get over it, but I'm praying to the good Lord that I'm wrong."

"What do you mean?"

"You never can tell about these injuries. A person can pull through just fine. But sometimes. . . ." He shook his head. "We just have to wait."

"You don't think he's going to die, do you?" Guin asked.

"He's an old man like me, but he's strong and healthy. So if he doesn't bleed inside his brain, I don't think he's going to be dying."

"But he may not be the same?"

Dr. Jackson nodded slowly. "Like I was saying, we can only pray for him."

The news tore at Guin. She liked Winfield, and he was important to Kellen. But all they could do was wait.

She shivered as cold fear enveloped her. This was so like

when her parents had caught the fever. She'd cared for them as best she could, making them comfortable, cooling them with damp cloths, but in the end, waiting was the only thing she could do.

She hoped for Kellen's sake that Winfield recovered soon. She didn't think Kellen was the patient type. If Winfield was here, Kellen would be here. She didn't want to watch him pacing the floor, sitting with his friend, commanding Winfield to be well.

Dr. Jackson left the room and returned in a few minutes with Kellen, who argued all the way.

"I won't be a bother," Kellen insisted.

"I'm sure you won't, son. But these ladies are quite capable of tending to his needs. You'll be more good to him if you're alert when he wakes up."

"He will wake up, won't he?"

The fear she heard in Kellen's voice tugged at Guin's heart. She wanted to take him in her arms, reassure him that all would be well, that his only friend would be all right soon.

"I don't have room here, but Soledad's visiting her people. You can stay in her cabin, behind the barn," she said.

"Thanks." Kellen's relief was palpable. He followed the doctor down the steps, then turned back to her. "You'll let me know if anything changes?"

"Of course."

He nodded, somewhat pacified, but Guin sensed the turmoil burning inside him as he strode across the yard.

Chapter 11

Reluctant and worried, Kellen made his way down the hall. Winfield had looked so horrible the night before, his face drawn and ashen, caked blood in his hair and on his clothes. Kellen had wanted to shake himself awake from this nightmare. But there was no escape.

He hesitated at the closed door, then tapped softly and stepped inside. Winfield was lying in the bed, his eyes closed and his arms stretched comfortably at his sides. Guin and Henrietta had washed away the blood and dirt, and put him in a clean nightshirt. Kellen crossed the room and sat gingerly on the edge of the bed.

"Good morning, Winfield," he said softly.

Winfield opened his eyes and smiled weakly. "Hello, sir."

At least Winfield's standard greeting hadn't changed. Maybe he'd be okay after all. "You had us worried last night. I was afraid you were dead."

"I regret that I caused you distress, sir." Winfield looked at Kellen quizzically. "Begging your pardon, sir, but do I know you?"

Kellen's breath caught at the question. "What?"

Winfield shook his head. "Have I . . . have I met you, sir? I do not believe I have laid eyes on you before this moment."

Kellen rose to his feet, his gaze never leaving Winfield's face. "If you'll excuse me." He turned and fled the room.

When Kellen barged through the kitchen door, Guin

looked up. "What's wrong?" She set her bowl down and quickly dried her hands on a towel. "Is Winfield worse?"

"He's awake, but he doesn't know who I am."

"What do you mean, he doesn't know you?" Guin asked.

Kellen looked at her in exasperation. "Just what I said. He was awake and we started talking. Then, he asked who I was and said he'd never seen me before."

She gasped. Her hands flew to her cheeks. "That's terrible. I'll send Joel for Dr. Jackson."

Kellen waited impatiently while Guin left the kitchen to call for her worker. When she returned, she said, "Joel's on his way to town. Here. Sit down and tell me what happened."

"I . . . well . . . Winfield's very calm. He doesn't seem to be hurting anywhere. But he doesn't know me," he repeated.

Guin nodded slowly. "Dr. Jackson did mention last night that injuries to the head can be difficult."

Kellen looked at her sharply. "What else did the fine doctor tell you? What else did he say while I was out of the room?" Guin sighed. He could see reluctance in her expression. "What else?" he demanded again.

Slowly, she said, "Dr. Jackson said these injuries are unpredictable, that no one can tell how bad they'll be."

"Did he say anything about how long it takes to get over them?"

Guin met his gaze, her eyes sad.

"I see," he said. "Either he doesn't know, or Winfield may not recover at all."

"We can only pray he'll be all right." Guin laid her hand gently on his arm. "In a few days, he could be fine."

Kellen shrank from her grasp. "How the hell can you say that when Dr. Jackson doesn't know? Winfield could be like this forever."

Fear and despair filled him as he stormed from the

kitchen. He paced back and forth across the yard, thinking of Winfield and his past. Winfield was all Kellen had left, the only person he felt close enough to call family. The older man was important to him, for far more than his assistance with business. Together, they had worked so hard for so many years. Winfield was a good person, without a spiteful bone in his body.

He heard Guin cross the porch and come down the steps toward him.

"I thought you might like something to drink," she said.

Kellen took the glass of lemonade she offered. He downed it quickly, then followed her into the kitchen.

"Tell me again where you found him," Kellen said.

Guin refilled his glass and repeated her story.

"How could Winfield have fallen and hurt himself like that? He's a careful person. He hates high places," Kellen said.

"I don't think his horse threw him," Guin said. "I can't see him falling down the hill if he was on the road."

"What brought him to the edge of the road?" Kellen asked again. "I can't think of any business he could have been conducting there."

"Could he have stopped to enjoy the view?" Guin asked.

"That's not like Winfield. He doesn't waste time like that." Kellen deliberated for a moment as a terrible thought came to him. "Guin, what if Winfield's fall wasn't an accident?"

"What do you mean?"

"What if someone pushed Winfield. On purpose. If that's what happened, then as long as he's still alive, Winfield is still in danger."

"Why would someone do that?"

"I don't know."

"Who would do such a thing? No one could possibly wish that dear man any harm."

"Maybe he wasn't the real target. Maybe someone hurt him to get at me."

"That's awful," Guin said. "What are we going to do?"

The idea that someone might have deliberately set out to kill Winfield seared Kellen's mind. If this was attempted murder, and not an accident, then his troubles were greater than he'd first believed.

"Are you going to tell the sheriff that you don't think it was an accident?"

Startled, he looked up at Guin. "Maybe later." Maybe later, when he'd figured out how to prove what had happened, and who had done it.

He watched her as she moved around the kitchen. She wore her hair the way she normally did, all pulled up and rolled into a knot, but it didn't look so tight this morning. When she glanced at him, her warm brown eyes held only tenderness and concern. His throat tightened and he swallowed several times to clear it.

"Dr. Jackson should be here soon," she said. "Will you tell him you think Mr. Somerset was deliberately hurt?"

"I don't know." He did know, but he wanted to question the doctor alone. He brooded about Winfield's lack of memory. He needed to know what had happened and why. He was sure Winfield's fall had been no accident. Now he had to do everything in his power to protect Winfield from another attack, and protect Guin and Henrietta from being innocent victims from the danger he'd brought to this small farm.

His path now clear in his mind, Kellen watched Guin ladle oatmeal into a bowl. His stomach growled in response. "Is that for Winfield?"

Guin nodded as she set the bowl on a tray. "Dr. Jackson said he could eat a little cereal, until we know for sure he can keep it down."

Kellen rose from his seat. It was time to face Winfield again. "I'll take it to him."

He proceeded down the hall. Outside the door, he took a deep breath, knocked softly and pushed the door open. "Hello, Winfield. Sorry about rushing out before. I had . . . um . . . are you feeling any better?"

"Oh, hello. I feel rather sore. My bones seem to have experienced a rather bruising ordeal. And my head aches, especially when I press this spot here." Winfield raised his hand and touched his head gingerly.

"Then, don't do it, Winfield. I'll take your word for it." Kellen paused, his lips pursed, while he thought about how close he'd come to losing his friend.

Winfield shifted to a sitting position, rustling his bedclothes as he straightened them. The sound distracted Kellen and he refocused his attention on Winfield's immediate needs. "Are you hungry?"

"Quite. I have listened hopefully to the sounds emanating from the kitchen for some time now."

Always the gentleman. Kellen smiled and said, "Guin's made you some hot cereal."

"I suppose I can make do with that, although I had hoped for heartier fare."

Kellen set the tray on Winfield's lap, then took a chair to wait until his friend was ready to talk. He wasn't sure what to ask, or if he was ready to hear the answers.

"Are you troubled, sir?"

Startled, Kellen looked at Winfield. "I'm worried about you. Are you sure you don't remember who I am?"

"I believe I share some of that worry. I cannot say that I

recognize any of you fine people who have attended to my needs. I am not even certain who I am, except that you call me Winfield, and so I must assume that is my name."

Kellen was appalled by Winfield's confession. He had not even considered the possibility that Winfield did not know his own name. The situation was worse than he'd thought, much worse. "You're Winfield Somerset. Do you remember the accident?"

"The accident?"

"Yes, when you fell off the cliff and banged your head?" Winfield shook his head, and Kellen sighed heavily. "Do you remember why you were on that road, or if you were with anyone?"

Winfield looked thoughtful for a moment, then winced. "I do not recall. Regrettably, the act of thinking about it causes my brain to hurt."

"All right. Stop thinking then. I won't ask any more questions. Your name is Winfield Somerset. I'm Kellen O'Roarke, and we've been friends and . . . we've been friends for a long time. This house belongs to Guin Talbot. She and her grandmother, Henrietta Talbot, are taking care of you. Dr. Jackson examined you last night, and he'll be back in a little while to check on you."

"I am most appreciative of that information, sir, and am relieved to know we are friends. I sensed I had a fondness for you."

Kellen left the room, torn between relief that Winfield was physically well and worries about Winfield's mental condition. What if he never regained his memory? Kellen had come to depend on Winfield to watch his backside, and he would miss that help. For now, though, he would put up a good front.

When he reached the kitchen, he realized Guin had been

busy in his absence. His stomach growled again at the tantalizing smells.

Guin turned from the stove and gestured for him to sit at the table. "How is he?"

"Except for not remembering anything, he seems normal." He winced. "I introduced myself. That was difficult."

She slid a plate of fried ham and eggs and a bowl of hot cereal in front of him. "I'm sure it was. Does he remember anything?"

"Nothing." He picked up his fork and a new thought struck him. Frowning, Kellen hesitated before taking his first bite, and set his fork on the plate. "You can't keep feeding all of us like this. I'll pay for whatever Winfield, Dr. Jackson, and I eat. And I'll get you some help from town. You and your grandmother shouldn't do all this work alone. You have your farm to take care of."

Some of the tension eased from her face. "I'm glad to help Winfield."

"It's not right that you should bear the extra expense and his care alone."

She pulled out the chair across from him and sat in it. "Grandmother helps some with the house, and she's a good nurse for Winfield. But, you're right. I can't work the farm and be here too."

She looked at him in that direct way he'd at first found so unnerving, but now found captivating. He wanted to take comfort in her quiet resilience. Instead, he said, "I'll ask Mrs. Bennett to find someone, and I'll pay the wages." After she nodded in agreement, he returned to his breakfast while Guin got up and set a place for Dr. Jackson.

Guin left the room to do some chore or other, leaving Kellen with time to think while he ate. He poured himself more coffee, noting how at home he felt in this kitchen with its scarred wood table and yellow gingham curtains, how his sense of belonging felt stronger here than anywhere else he could remember. He took a deep breath and wondered if perhaps Guin's arguments about belonging somewhere had some validity. Maybe someday, after the resort was completed and he'd had his revenge, maybe then he'd settle down, have a place to call home.

The whir and clop of a horse and buggy came from outside. Dr. Jackson stepped onto the porch as Kellen opened the door.

"We need to talk, alone, as soon as possible," Kellen said in a hushed voice.

Dr. Jackson raised a questioning eyebrow, then nodded. "Let me examine Winfield first."

After what seemed an eternity, Dr. Jackson returned to the kitchen. He motioned for Kellen to step outside. The two men walked to the barn in silence.

Kellen turned to face the doctor. "How is he?"

Dr. Jackson smiled softly at Kellen's bluntness. "His body is fine. He'll be sore for a spell from those bruises, but the scratches are healing nicely. No infection there."

"What about his memory?"

Dr. Jackson paused, then sighed deeply. "That's a might trickier to answer. I've had some experience with this sort of thing, from the war."

"And?" Kellen prompted when Dr. Jackson hesitated.

"I'm gonna be blunt with you, son. Your friend's hurt. A blow to the head like that ought to have killed the man. But Winfield, he seems a sturdy sort. If he's not bleeding inside his head, then he might could be okay."

Kellen didn't know whether he should be reassured or not. He kicked at the straw lying on the barn floor. Without looking up, he asked, "What about his memory?"

166

"That's an even trickier question to answer." Dr. Jackson turned and paced in a circle. "You see, son, the mind is a strange thing. It sometimes blocks out what it don't want to remember. Sometimes the memory, it comes back on its own, gradual-like or all at once. Sometimes it comes back in pieces."

"Dr. Jackson, I don't think this was an accident."

The doctor looked bewildered. "What might you be getting at?"

"I mean, I think someone deliberately tried to kill Winfield."

"Why's that?"

"Guin told me about the place where she found him, and an accident there doesn't make sense."

"We should go to this place where Winfield fell and see if it tells us anything."

"Do you have time?"

Dr. Jackson glanced across the yard at the house and his mouth tightened in a grim line. "Winfield is going to be staying here for a spell. If we need to know something to protect him and those fine ladies in there, then we must make time."

His words struck Kellen hard, giving voice to his own unspoken worry that if someone had tried to murder Winfield, then Guin and Henrietta could be in danger while caring for him.

"I'll tell Guin we're leaving," Kellen said.

He hurried to the house, and met her on the porch where she was busily tying the ribbons on her broad-brimmed sun hat. "Dr. Jackson and I are going to the hill. Can you tell us where you found Winfield?"

Guin stepped into the yard and shielded her eyes from the bright sun as she scanned the rolling foothills to the east. "It was up there," she said, pointing. "Where the road follows the natural curve in the hillside."

Kellen looked in the same direction, but the hills all appeared the same to him. "Is it the third ridge from the oak tree, or the fourth one?" he asked, attempting to narrow it down.

"Why don't I just go with you?"

"You don't need to do that. We can find it."

"But I know the exact spot."

He wanted to argue with her, wanted to tell her they didn't need her help. But the truth was, it would save him and Dr. Jackson a lot of time. "All right," he said reluctantly. "You can show us the spot, and then we'll take it from there."

"You're serious, aren't you?" Guin stared at him. "You really believe this wasn't an accident."

Kellen took a deep breath. "I'll tell you after we check the area where you found Winfield. Agreed?"

"Agreed." Her tone indicated he would be hard-pressed to put her off.

"Let's go."

Dr. Jackson stood by his horse and buggy. He handed Guin up to the seat and Kellen climbed in back. Within a short time, they were climbing into foothills covered with low-lying brush with an occasional oak tree growing here and there.

Guin watched the road intently. She grabbed Dr. Jackson's arm. "This is it."

Kellen jumped from the buggy. "Stay here. I don't want to stir the ground any more than we have to. Where did you find Winfield?"

"Just below the edge over there." She pointed to a place where the road widened away from the hill. "I stopped when I heard a noise. It was Winfield moaning. I don't know what you're going to find now. I slid down the hill to him, then climbed back up to my horse. When I came back with Pedro and Joel, they climbed up to Winfield from the bottom."

Kellen walked gingerly to the spot, examining the ground intently. "How frequently is this road traveled?"

"Not often, this time of year," Guin said. "If they leave the valley at all, most people go south to Hopland or north to Willits during the summer, not east."

Kellen looked at the valley sprawled before him, the variegated green and brown patchwork of cultivated fields, orchards, and fallow land.

He walked back to Guin and checked the tracks her horse left on the dry road, then returned to the cliff's edge. "It looks as if there were two other horses here yesterday besides yours." Kellen hunkered down and pointed. "Dr. Jackson, what do you think about these footprints?"

Dr. Jackson leaned over Kellen's shoulder to examine the stirred tracks. "Appears there're three different shoes. Miss Guin's, now hers is easy to tell because she wears those small shoes. These other two looks to be men's prints."

Kellen approached the cliff and looked over the edge. He saw the outcrop of brush that had caught Winfield, and he shivered at the thought of what would have happened if Winfield had fallen a few feet to either side. It was a good hundred-foot drop to hard ground. A coldness swept through him that had nothing to do with the dry breeze blowing through the valley.

He turned back. "There might have been a struggle here." He pointed to the ground around him. "This set of footprints leads to those hoofprints and disappears."

Dr. Jackson nodded. "I'll notify the sheriff when I get back to town."

Kellen raised his hand. "No, not yet." He gazed intently at

169

Guin and Dr. Jackson. "In fact, I'd just as soon not tell anyone about Winfield's accident for a while. I don't want it known that he's staying at the farm, or that he's lost his memory."

"Do you think we can do that?" Guin asked.

"There are only six of us who know, the three of us, Mrs. Talbot, and your two workers."

"They won't say anything if I ask them not to," Guin said. "I'm sure Grandmother can keep the secret."

"I didn't tell anybody in town about it," Dr. Jackson said.

"It'll be safer for everyone if we keep this quiet," Kellen said. "Whoever pushed Winfield probably thinks he's dead. We don't want that person coming to your farm to finish the job. And it'll give me a chance to nose around and see what I can learn."

"Then my grandmother and I will keep Winfield at my place until you're satisfied it's safe. Don't talk to Mrs. Bennett or anyone else about coming out here," Guin said. The two men nodded their agreement.

"I'd be happy to talk to your grandmother about the patient's needs, Miss Guin," Dr. Jackson said.

She gave him a knowing look. "I'm sure you would, Dr. Jackson. Go ahead, and I'll talk to Joel and Pedro. Anything else?"

"Keep your eyes and ears open for anything unusual or out of the ordinary," Kellen cautioned.

If he had his way, she would stay inside her house with the doors bolted, safe, until he solved the puzzle. The reality was that she had a farm to run, just as he had a resort to build.

They returned to the buggy and started down the winding road and crossed the bridge. When they returned to Guin's farm, she headed toward her fields and Dr. Jackson went inside talk to Henrietta.

As he rode his horse back to town, Kellen wondered how he could discover if Winfield's accident was really attempted murder. Could it be related to Winfield looking into the problems threatening the resort?

He wiped his hand across his face. God, he wished Winfield was healthy and safe. Kellen's heart tightened at the thought of how close he had come to losing Winfield. That was something he could not bear. Winfield had turned a scruffy boy into a gentleman. Kellen knew he owed Winfield more than he could ever repay. If that meant work on the resort was delayed because Kellen had to find Winfield's attacker, so be it.

When Kellen reached town, he headed straight for the hotel to review Winfield's papers and notes in hopes of finding something—anything—that would indicate what was going on.

Five hours later, Kellen had to admit defeat. He'd pawed through every scrap of paper he could find in Winfield's room and on the desk the two of them shared. He had found nothing but financial estimates for the resort and a list of investment activities over the past eighteen months. The list struck him as somewhat odd, but then Winfield liked to dabble in stocks. Kellen assumed the figures had something to do with that. He hoped Winfield hadn't invested heavily, because the list showed some distressing losses.

Tired and disgruntled, Kellen went downstairs for a solitary dinner in the dining room, and then a brandy and cigar in the salon. He sorely missed Winfield's witty banter, and knew his bad mood lingered because Winfield was not there to provoke him into better spirits.

The grandfather clock in the hotel lobby struck midnight as Kellen made his way to the stairs, tired but still angry.

"Oh, good evening, Mr. O'Roarke."

Kellen turned to see the desk clerk. "Hello, James." He started toward the stairs again.

"I hope Mr. Somerset is feeling better after his accident."

The words sent chills racing down Kellen's back. He swung around to face the clerk. "He's all right," he said slowly.

"I'm pleased to hear that." James' pleasant smile confirmed his words. "I was concerned yesterday when Miss Talbot's man came to get you yesterday. I heard him tell you Mr. Somerset had been in some kind of accident."

Kellen relaxed. "Yes. An accident."

"I hope he wasn't hurt too badly."

"Not too badly," Kellen said. "I'll tell Winfield you asked about him." He turned and hurried up the stairs before the desk clerk could ask any more questions.

Damn it all. His plans to keep Winfield's location and condition a secret were ruined. He had no time at all now. He had to find Winfield's attacker, and soon.

Chapter 12

At the end of the week, Guin drove to town early in the morning for supplies. Dr. Jackson had come to the farm to check on Winfield and had nearly fallen over himself offering to stay with her grandmother until she returned.

When Guin entered the general store, the little bell over the door clinked to announce her arrival. The smells of coffee and spices, yard goods and farming tool oil blended together. "Hello, Mrs. Bennett."

"Oh, hello, Guin." Mrs. Bennett rose from a chair by the woodstove, still reading the newspaper she held.

"That must be an interesting issue of *The Sentinel*."

"You wouldn't believe it. The whole town—the whole valley—is all abuzz over Mr. Eldridge's editorial."

"What's it about?" Guin asked absently as she withdrew her shopping list from her pocket.

"It's about Mr. Somerset and Mr. O'Roarke's resort and how it's maybe bringing the wrong kind of people to Spring Valley."

"Let me see that." Guin snatched the paper from Mrs. Bennett's hands and read the editorial.

Tobias Eldridge had written about Winfield's accident. She gasped at the questions he raised as to whether or not it really was an accident. He concluded by noting that this was the only violence to have happened in the valley since it had been settled and advocating that the community rethink its support of the resort if it meant bringing big-city problems along with greater prosperity.

She crushed the paper. "That's the most ridiculous thing I've seen in a long time. How can he get away with implying the resort is bringing crime to Spring Valley? Mr. Eldridge should be ashamed of himself."

"It's not that ridiculous." Mrs. Bennett's eyes widened. "We don't know for sure how the accident happened. Mr. Somerset hasn't been seen since he was hurt."

"I've seen him," Guin snapped. "So has Dr. Jackson and so has my grandmother." She stopped, realizing she had said more than she'd intended.

"We came here to get away from the cities and their problems," Mrs. Bennett said as if she hadn't heard Guin's blunder. She shivered. "I can't tell you how afraid I was in the city. It wasn't safe for a woman to walk alone on the streets. We want to live where we know everyone and where it's safe. The resort will bring a lot of strangers to Spring Valley. That might not be good."

Guin opened her mouth to argue, then halted. Hadn't she been opposed to the resort since the very beginning? *The Sentinel*'s editorial merely echoed what she had thought all along, that the resort was not in the valley's best interest. Her opinion had softened over time. She still wasn't convinced they needed the resort, but she wasn't as vehemently opposed as she had been.

She handed her lengthy shopping list to Mrs. Bennett. "My goodness," the shopkeeper said with a laugh. "Looks like you plan to feed an army."

Relieved that Mrs. Bennett had apparently not caught her slip about Winfield's location, Guin shrugged. "Joel and Pedro are hungry after a hard day's work, and Grandmother has decided I don't keep enough supplies on hand. She still thinks people will come calling like they do in the city." She held her breath and hoped Mrs. Bennett would accept the lie.

"I guess those city ways are hard for some folks to give up," Mrs. Bennett said as she filled Guin's order. "Might be nice to try that life, if the work didn't pile up while we pretended to be genteel ladies."

Guin laughed at the way Mrs. Bennett sashayed through the store, imitating what the shopkeeper thought was the way wealthy city people walked. "I think we're much better off the way we are. Although on these hot summer days, I wouldn't mind sitting under a tall shade tree, sipping lemonade, instead of tending the hops."

"How's your farm doing?"

"So far, it looks good. If the weather holds, I should have a bumper crop."

Mrs. Bennett set a box of supplies on the counter. "Some of the other farmers have said the same thing." She sighed and shook her head. "Now they're all worried that prices will fall because everyone's going to have a good harvest. This is the darnedest way to make a living."

Guin nodded in agreement. "I'm hoping to make enough to clear my account with you and pay off the bank loan Father took out last winter. It'd be nice to have something left over so I don't have to start next year in debt."

"I'm really glad you're making a go of it, Guin. It's not easy being a woman on her own, but everyone believes you can do it."

Guin blushed at the words. "You mean people around here talk about me?"

Mrs. Bennett laughed. "Of course, they do. Everybody talks about everybody else, you know that. But it's nice talk. And everyone's real glad you've started coming to town more."

Guin was not sure how she felt about people in the community discussing her plight. As Mrs. Bennett said, though, that was part of living in a small community. Since the dance and the Independence Day celebration, she'd realized how isolated her family had been. While she did not fault her parents for the choices they had made, she had come to realize that she needed and wanted something different for herself.

"I think that's all of it." Mrs. Bennett plunked a brown-paper-wrapped package of sugar on the counter. "I'll just put it on your account." She smiled broadly. "Sure is nice to know you're getting along well. Bring your grandmother with you next time. She's such a delightful lady."

Guin's eyebrow rose skeptically. "I'll see what I can do," she said.

"Do you want some help carrying these to your wagon?"

"No, I'll just make several trips." Guin picked up a box and headed for the door. Before she could reach it, Kellen came through the door.

"Guin! What are you doing here?" Kellen asked.

"I'm getting supplies," she said, shifting the box in her hands.

"I'll take that."

Before she could stop him, Kellen swept the box from her, his hands skimming along her arms. She felt a heated shiver radiate along the trail left by his touch. "I'll get the others," she said, flustered.

In the last few days, Kellen had become a fixture at her house, arriving before she left in the morning, and still there when she returned at night. He spent most of each evening with Winfield, but still she was aware of his presence in her home, of the low rumble of his laughter in Winfield's room, of his sudden sporadic appearances in the kitchen for more coffee or something for Winfield to eat. So why did his presence cause this flutter in her now?

Before she figured out the answer, they had all her purchases loaded in the wagon. "Have you seen *The Sentinel*?" she asked him.

Kellen frowned. "No. Why?"

"There's something you should read. Wait here." Guin went back into the store and returned with a copy of the newspaper, which she'd smoothed and folded under her arm. "Come with me."

She walked him down to the river. Tables were still scattered under the oak trees from the Independence Day celebrations.

"What's this all about?" Kellen asked.

"Read the editorial, inside back page."

Kellen flipped the newspaper open and rapidly scanned the article, scowling as he read. He crumpled the paper when he finished. "Damn." He took several long strides away from her, then turned, his expression inscrutable. "Are you pleased about this?"

Puzzled, Guin shook her head. "Why would you ask a question like that?"

"Because . . . because . . . you've been opposed to my resort from the very beginning."

"Well, yes. I mean, I was," she stammered. "I mean—"

"If you found a way, you'd try to stop me, wouldn't you?"

His accusation hurt. "I've never done anything to hurt your resort."

"Except to deny me the access I need to make it work."

"What? And destroy my farm in the process? What a stupid thing to expect of me." Guin looked at him with fire in her eyes. "So that's how it is. I'm good enough to take care of your friend, and put my grandmother and myself at risk. But at the first sign of trouble, you turn on me."

"I didn't mean—"

"Yes, you did, Kellen O'Roarke. You are an ungrateful, miserable man."

She left him then, and Kellen said nothing as he watched her go. He didn't need this right now. He had enough problems to deal with. Two more men had reported they could no longer work on construction of the resort. Supplies took longer than they should to arrive, and Kellen seriously worried that a delay in opening the resort would push him past the deadline for making his first loan payments. Winfield's amnesia and the need to protect him from another attack were crippling Kellen's ability to get the resort finished on time. He scrubbed his hand over his face, as if the gesture would erase his problems.

It didn't.

As he strode toward the hotel, Kellen considered what step he should take next. Tobias Eldridge seemed like such a reasonable, intelligent man. Why would he write such a column? How could Eldridge have learned that Winfield's "accident" might have been something more than an accident? Why would Eldridge take such an antagonistic stance to the resort, other than to create controversy where there was none? Kellen's first impulse was to confront Eldridge, but he decided that wasn't the best strategy. Better to remain calm and optimistic, appear to brush aside the harmful comments as idle prattling. He probably should bring Winfield back to town to prove he was still alive. That would go far to quell any rumors.

Kellen clenched his teeth and decided that until he returned Winfield to the hotel, pretending he didn't care about the editorial was the best approach. It would be the most difficult acting job he'd ever attempted. Perhaps he would write a response to Eldridge's editorial after he'd had time to think. He returned to town and strolled down the street as if he hadn't a worry in the world.

"Mr. O'Roarke! Kellen!"

He turned to face the female calling him and groaned inside. Just what he didn't need. Julia Clarke. He forced himself to smile. She was a lovely young lady who knew how to amplify her assets to the greatest advantage, but she was the last person he wanted to see.

"Miss Clarke, what a pleasure."

She slipped her arm through his and encouraged him to walk with her. "It's been such a long time. Why, if I didn't know better, I'd think you were avoiding me."

"Not at all," Kellen said. "I've been very busy."

"How awful about your friend. Is it true that he's dead?" she whispered in horror. He shook his head. "Thank goodness. But still, you must be so worried."

She clutched his arm to the soft undercurve of her breast and looked tearfully up at him. "Do you think there's a madman loose in the valley? I'm so afraid about who he'll attack next."

Kellen pulled his arm away and patted her hand before releasing it. "I wouldn't worry about that. Winfield had an accident, that's all."

"But I thought . . ."

"You thought what?"

Julia faltered and glanced nervously around. "I thought someone tried to murder him," she whispered.

"You can't believe everything you read in the newspaper."

She frowned at him. "What newspaper? I don't know what you're talking about."

"You didn't read the editorial in the paper? Then where did you hear someone tried to murder Winfield?"

"I must have heard people talking about it. Let's not waste time talking about that unpleasantness," Julia urged with a delicate shiver. She gazed dreamily into Kellen's eyes. "Let's talk about when you're coming to dinner."

"It's difficult to plan with all the work I have."

"Surely you must eat."

Dare he walk into the enemy's lair? "You're right," he said with a smile. "I do need to eat. When would you like me to come?"

Julia clapped her gloved hands with delight. "Tomorrow night would be wonderful."

"I'll be there." Kellen's stomach clenched, and he knew without a doubt he had been manipulated by a scheming woman masquerading as a charming young lady. The evening wouldn't be boring; he was sure of it.

"Winfield asked again when he can get out of bed," Henrietta said, returning to the kitchen.

Dr. Jackson watched her enter the room with an empty tray. "I'm not surprised he is suffering from his confinement. Man like him stays busy all the time, but until he gets some of his memory back, I'm not inclined to let him roam freely. Besides," he said with a low, rumbling chuckle, "I'm not so sure I like the idea of another man having the opportunity to flirt with you."

Henrietta's eyes widened in surprise, then narrowed as she pursed her lips. "Sometimes, Dr. Jackson—"

"Beauregard."

"Dr. Jackson," she repeated firmly. "Sometimes you come up with the most ridiculous ideas. Winfield would never behave indecorously with me. Why he's . . . it just wouldn't be proper." She busied herself setting the dishes in a tub of soapy water.

Dr. Jackson knew what she'd almost said and was encouraged by the change in attitude. At least she'd stopped before she'd stated her belief in the class differences between herself and Winfield. If she thought of Winfield as an employee, so be it. He certainly wasn't going to tell her that Winfield was no more a simple working man than he was.

He sat quietly, puffing his pipe and watching Henrietta bustle around the kitchen. "You know, Miz Talbot, when I met you, I thought you were a fine lady."

She turned to him, one eyebrow raised in skepticism. "You no longer think I'm a lady?"

He chuckled at the edge in her voice. "Oh, I still think you're a lady. I also think you're a mighty fine woman."

"I don't have any idea what you're talking about," she said, her eyes narrowing with suspicion.

Dr. Jackson rose slowly from his chair and approached her, wishing his old joints didn't creak so loudly. He didn't want her to think of him as an old man. "What I'm trying to say, Miz Talbot, is there's a lot more to you than stuffy city ways. You're a strong woman who cares deeply for those around you."

"I don't understand what you're getting at." Henrietta stepped around him to wipe the table with a damp cloth.

He took a deep breath and decided to plunge ahead. "I think you could be a bit nicer if you didn't worry so much about what people might be thinking."

She stopped and scowled at him. "What you mean is, I should be nicer to you."

"It would be mighty fine if you weren't quite so prickly all the time."

"Dr. Jackson, you are here to take care of your patient. I am here to live with my granddaughter. We can do nothing about the fact that we must be in the same place most of the day. Which reminds me, don't you have other patients who need attention?"

"Not much business this time of year. I left a note on my door where they could find me, and so far, no one's needed me. Except Winfield. And you."

She scoffed at him. "That's ridiculous. I'm not sick, never have been. Only needed a doctor once in my life, and that was when William was born. Only the doctor was late and my housekeeper had to take care of everything."

Dr. Jackson nodded slowly. "So a doctor let you down."

"That's right."

His heart quickened. He knew he had to go on. "Then came the war. Your husband, he had battlefield surgery." Henrietta nodded, and Beau caught the glistening in her eyes before she turned away. "You've had no use for doctors ever since."

"What are you trying to get at in that convoluted logic of yours?"

"I think, Miz Talbot—Henrietta—that my being a doctor is what's causing the problem here. For a minute, just for a minute, forget that I'm a doctor. Forget that I'm a southerner. Think of me as a man."

He laid his hands on her shoulders and gently, ever so tenderly, turned her around and pulled her towards him. Her eyes widened, her mouth opened in surprise, but she didn't protest. He lowered his mouth to her cheek, kissing her softly, so very softly, and when he felt her sigh, his blood stirred as it hadn't done in years. Unwilling to tempt fate, he eased away from her, gratified to see that her eyes were still closed.

She opened her eyes, and he saw the bewilderment in them. Now was the time to retreat. "I should oughta go into town and be sure there's no other patients needing me. But I'll be back, so don't you fret none," he whispered. Reluctantly, he released his hold on her, and before she could say a word, he slipped out the door.

Henrietta stood where he'd left her, frozen as if in a tableau. He'd kissed her. She'd been kissed for the first time in she couldn't remember how long. His tender touch had shivered through her, thawing the feelings she'd kept frozen for so many years. She stroked her cheek to ease the tingling, but it didn't go away.

She wanted to be angry. She should rail that he had taken advantage of her. She should swoon because he had crossed the boundaries of acceptable behavior. But she couldn't.

Instead, she found herself succumbing to schoolgirl giddiness, the almost-forgotten urge to sort through her clothes for the prettiest dress to wear the next time he came to call, the desire to curl her hair in a different way. But that was ridiculous. She forced herself to snap out of this fatuous spell Beauregard—Dr. Jackson—had cast upon her.

She hustled around the kitchen, concentrating on her chores, trying to ignore the lightness in her step, the tuneless melody she could not stop humming. She resolved to be stronger the next time he came, to be prepared for him to attempt to take advantage of her. But deep in the back of her mind, she toyed with the idea of not showing her outrage until after he kissed her again.

In a few minutes, Dr. Jackson was rumbling down the road in his buggy, flicking the reins to hurry his horse. He could not believe he'd been audacious enough to kiss Henrietta Talbot. Not that he hadn't wanted to do it for a long time. He should be encouraged that she hadn't screamed like a stuck pig when he touched her.

He couldn't ignore his feelings for her; she made him feel like a man again, not a dried up, crusty old shell. His blood pounded in his ears when Henrietta walked by with those subtly rustling silk skirts, and her light perfume intoxicated him. Winfield was fortunate she hadn't affected his doctoring.

Dr. Jackson wouldn't wish ill on anyone, but he thanked providence that Winfield's injuries confined him to the Talbot house, giving a prudent doctor the justification to stop by and spend time with the best-looking woman he'd ever seen. He considered how he should approach Henrietta the next time he went to the house, but before he reached any conclusions, he spotted a cloud of dust coming toward him, a sure sign someone was driving a wagon quickly down the road. He pulled over to the side and waited, waving when he saw Guin driving.

She pulled on the reins to slow her horse, and stopped next to him. Dr. Jackson saw the spitfire anger in her eyes. He doffed his hat. "Hello, Miss Guin. Seems like you're in a mighty big hurry."

"I'm getting as far away as I can from that stupid man," she said.

Dr. Jackson leaned back, surprised by her vehemence. He could think of only one stupid man she might refer to. "Your trip to town was a mixed success, I take it."

"I got the supplies, but that man—that man had the nerve to suggest—"

"Why don't we walk a spell," Dr. Jackson suggested. He climbed from his buggy and extended his hand to Guin. In a swift movement, he secured the horses and took her arm.

"Now why don't you tell me what this is all about," he said, walking her down the road as if they were taking a casual stroll.

"I don't know where to begin," she said, shaking her head. "I went to the store, and Mrs. Bennett showed me the latest edition of *The Sentinel*. Mr. Eldridge has written a terrible editorial, claiming that Winfield wasn't in an accident and suggesting that Kellen's resort will ruin the town."

"Isn't that what you've believed all along?"

"Yes, but . . ." She hesitated a moment before continuing. "I met Kellen in town and showed him the editorial because I thought he'd want to know people might not believe Winfield had an accident. He had the nerve to suggest I was pleased by the editorial and would do anything I could to stop his resort from being built. After my grandmother and I have put ourselves at risk if Winfield's attacker came looking for him, he thinks of me like that."

Her story weighed heavily on Dr. Jackson's mind. He'd watched Guin and Kellen circling each other, wary and aware, and he'd hoped something might come of it. He'd thought all along that someone like Kellen would be good for Guin, and the more he'd come to know the young man, the more impressed he was. But this . . . this wasn't good. No sir.

"I'm sure he didn't mean nothing by it, Miss Guin."

"Oh, he meant it, all right," she argued. "He had his whole conspiracy all worked out."

"How did you resolve it?"

"I told him he was an ungrateful, miserable man."

Dr. Jackson winced. "Them's powerful words. It might could be awkward the next time you sees him, what with Winfield convalescing at your place."

"He's a clever fellow. He'll know to come while I'm working away from the house."

He heard the bruised feelings behind her stoic tone, and wished he could find the right words to comfort her. She was too angry to be reasoned with or placated now.

Dr. Jackson wasn't sure how, but he had to campaign to get these two back together again, or at least back on civil terms. He sighed in frustration. With Guin unhappy, his courting of Henrietta would be awkward. He'd have a talk with young O'Roarke. At his age, he didn't have time to wait for those two young'uns to figure things out for themselves.

Chapter 13

Still uneasy about being in Jonathan Clarke's house, Kellen laid his fork on the plate and glanced across the gleaming mahogany table at Julia as she toyed with her wine glass. So far, this evening had produced nothing but a good meal. Jonathan's absence, a quick trip to Sacramento, Julia had said, had surprised him, but he quickly realized Julia could be as determined to get what she wanted as her father. It hadn't taken long to figure out that what she wanted was him.

So, what did he want? Information. What was Jonathan up to? Was Julia part of the plan?

"Let's sit in the parlor, shall we?" Julia suggested. She patted her lips with a fine linen napkin, then rang the little crystal bell resting on the table.

An older woman dressed in a simple gray muslin dress appeared in the doorway. "Yes, miss?"

"We're finished here."

"Yes, miss." The woman disappeared again.

Kellen rose from his seat and went around to the other end of the table where he pulled Julia's chair out and offered her his hand. "That was a delicious dinner. My compliments to your cook."

"She does all right for a country woman. Of course, we had a European chef in San Francisco. He made wonderful dishes. His stuffed rabbit was exquisite."

Kellen watched her theatrical sigh and her pout—not too much, just enough to be noticed. He struggled not to laugh, and finally coughed to hide his amusement. He had to admit that she was a fine little actress. Her mannerisms were rehearsed to perfection.

He had tried to steer the dinner conversation in directions that would reveal information about Jonathan's plans. Julia had waltzed away from those topics with grace and charm, asking instead about his plans. So far, he hadn't been able to tell if she was fishing for information, or was simply an accomplished coquette. Perhaps he would stay here until he found out.

Kellen followed Julia to the parlor and took the seat she offered next to her on the settee. He would have preferred the wing-backed chair opposite so he could watch her. He leaned against the high, curved arm of the settee and rested his arm along the back while he studied her in the light of two kerosene lamps.

As he had each time he encountered her, Kellen acknowledged Julia was a beauty. With her blond hair and bright blue eyes framed by long sooty lashes, any man with blood coursing through his veins would take a second look. She knew how to dress too, using flounces and lace to accentuate her feminine curves. Her manners were exceptional; she had been well trained in the skills of a society lady.

So different from Guin Talbot, who disliked formal social gatherings. Whose direct gaze left a man feeling awkward and discomfited.

Whose kiss left a man breathless and wanting more.

Kellen brushed away his troublesome reflections and forced his attention back to Julia. Although she tried to hide it, he sensed she was intelligent, and quite enterprising when it came to getting what she wanted. He realized she was everything he had always thought he would want in a wife, someone who would be an asset in business. Now that the time to seriously consider a wife was approaching, he found himself full of doubts about what he really wanted.

"I'm so glad we had a chance to be together this evening," Julia said, breaking into Kellen's thoughts.

"It's been very different," he said with a smile. "Much quieter than the other times I've seen you."

Julia sighed. "I do so enjoy a party. That's what I miss most about home."

"You mean San Francisco?"

"Of course."

"I thought you had moved here permanently."

Julia laughed and reached for Kellen's hand, toying with his fingers for only a moment before dropping her hand back into her lap. "Good heavens, no. My father insisted we move here, although he promised we wouldn't stay longer than the end of summer. Even that is much too long."

"Besides the lack of parties, why don't you like Spring Valley?"

"This hamlet?" Julia shook her head, and artfully fluffed her curls with shapely fingers. "I can't imagine being stuck here. No one but farmers to talk to, and no real stores to shop in. No theaters, no exhibitions. I might just wither away and die unless I get back to the city." She leaned forward, her eyes wide with innocent pleading.

Kellen moved his hand off the back of the settee. "Surely your father would take you back to San Francisco if you really insisted."

Julia laughed, but it sounded bitter to Kellen. "I've already begged him, and he's said not until his business is finished here. Everything is work to him. If there's no wheeling and dealing involved, he's not interested."

This was the first indication she'd given that Jonathan might be up to something more than running for state legislator. Wary, Kellen wondered how far he could probe without risking suspicion. "He is running for office, and I suppose it would be natural for him to want to be involved in local business."

"I don't know. He mentioned something about running for some office." Julia shrugged. "He doesn't tell me anything, says I'm not to interfere in men's business."

This time her bitterness came through clearly, and Kellen's wariness eased. She sounded as if she wasn't acting on Jonathan's behalf. Maybe her father's presence in Spring Valley had nothing to do with Kellen or the resort, maybe it really was a coincidence.

Still, he couldn't afford to let down his guard. The problems at the resort and Winfield's accident were too coincidental to be random events.

Julia brushed his hand with hers, regaining his attention. "I don't want to talk about my father when there are so many other things we could talk about. Tell me about your resort." For the first time, she sounded sincerely interested.

Kellen eyed her cautiously. He could tell her things that were common knowledge, things he would share with any potential guest. Then, he realized that telling her about the resort might actually help his plans. She could notify her friends and acquaintances, stirring their interest. With her participation, the resort could be a success quickly. That would probably infuriate Jonathan, which was fine with Kellen. Still, did he want to use Julia that way? Would that make him as selfish as Clarke? Would it make him one of the people he most detested?

He glanced around the parlor and contrasted its ornate decor with Guin's parlor. As soon as he'd walked in Guin's front door, he'd felt warmth and hominess, even though she had coldly escorted him out at gunpoint.

Eating dinner in Julia's dining room seemed so formal compared to catching a meal in Guin's kitchen. He missed the companionable familiarity that had developed between them since Winfield's accident, when he sat at the table and talked to her as she fixed the evening meal. For a few short days, he'd felt as if he belonged there. A deep sadness settled over him that he had never belonged anywhere, only laying his head in one temporary place after another. Julia's parlor was like those places. It lacked the personal touches of pictures and treasured mementos, leaving it as cold as a hotel lobby.

He tried to shake off the sense of loss as he rose from the settee. "It's late, Julia, and I should be going." He stifled a yawn, then grinned sheepishly.

"You poor man, you look exhausted."

"I've been going to the resort before dawn every day, and it's late when I get back to the hotel."

"Surely you aren't working out there when it's dark."

"Not all my work is at the site." Kellen didn't want to tell Julia he spent every minute possible with Winfield. After the way she'd maneuvered the box social, he sensed that if Julia thought it would bring her closer to him, then she'd camp on Guin's doorstep until she gained access inside on the pretense of helping to care for Winfield.

"Why are you working such long hours?"

"There's always a lot to do," he hedged. Finally he shrugged. "I guess I just like being there."

Julia looked skeptical. "In the dark? Sounds creepy," she said with a delicate shiver.

Kellen laughed at her amusing affectations. "It's not creepy at all." He glanced at the ornate grandfather's clock as it gonged somberly in the corner. "I should be going."

"Don't leave. I'm all by myself, and it gets so lonely."

"Your housekeeper is here," he reminded her.

"Housekeepers don't count," Julia said disdainfully.

Kellen winced at how arrogantly she discounted the person who took care of all the chores and duties in this house so she could practice her pout and be bored.

He could not imagine Guin reacting that way; she found something to like in everyone. Even him. No, he corrected, she had let him think she liked him, lulled him into a false sense of security. "I have to go."

Julia heaved a sigh. "If you must." She stood and led the way to the entry.

Kellen opened the door and stepped to the porch. He turned to face Julia. She stood in the doorway, the light behind her creating a halo around her tousled curls. Her eyes were almost level with his, and it seemed to him that she bent forward ever so slightly.

"Thank you for dinner, Julia. I enjoyed this evening."

"I'm so glad you came," she said, her voice wispy soft.

He knew she wanted him to kiss her, but he couldn't do it. She was attractive, she was poised, she had the social contacts he needed, but he still couldn't do it. He looked away.

"Kellen?"

He glanced back at her, and she took his head between her hands and leaned close enough for her lips to graze against his. Even when they touched, he felt nothing. He kissed her, a token kiss that would not offend, but didn't promise more than he was prepared to offer. Then, he grasped her wrists and gently pulled her hands from his face.

"Come again, Kellen."

He heard the wistful hopefulness in her voice and almost felt sorry for her.

Almost.

"Goodnight, Julia." Kellen turned and walked away.

Through the darkness he felt her penetrating stare. He hoped he hadn't angered her. The last thing he needed was another problem. But he wouldn't feel right leading her on. Because he wasn't interested.

Guin strolled between two walls of hop vines. Holding onto her broad-brimmed hat, she looked up. Braced on their support poles, the twining plants grew high above her head, the broad leaves sheltering green burrs that would soon plump up and ripen. She took a deep ragged breath. This year, she was on her own. She was the one who would hire the pickers, she would talk to each one, and supervise the drying and bagging of the burrs. Her survival depended on her ability to remember what her father's steps had been. She had done everything possible with the field to grow a bountiful crop.

Her feet kicked at the dry ground. She tried to remember if her father had ever had problems with the irrigation before. This year, the furrow walls collapsed with annoying regularity, blocking the water from reaching the plants. Each morning she checked the irrigation flow, and every few days, she found the system shut down. With the hot July days, she worried about the plants at the far end of her field. The leaves on several plants looked wilted, the burrs not as plump as the others.

She left the field and made her way to the gentle rise that separated the fields from the rest of her farm. She turned to look at the straight, even rows of green swaying in the gentle breeze. The plants appeared healthy, but still she worried something would go wrong and she would lose her crop. There were only a few weeks left before harvest. She prayed the irrigation system would not fail, that she found enough pickers, that the bottom didn't fall out of the hop market, that. . . .

She stopped. It tempted fate to pray for too much all at once, better to concentrate on one thing at a time. Leaving the field behind, she went to the hop kiln, a two-story wooden structure used to dry and bag the hop burrs for market. She paused and looked at the building, remembering harvests in the past, when pickers brought their overflowing bags to the kiln to be weighed and tallied, the burrs spread evenly along the floor of the second story to dry, then swept through the trap door to the next level where they were bagged and loaded onto wagons to be sent to the brewers.

She had always helped her father. Sitting quietly at a table set at the edge of the field, she had tallied the number of bags picked by each worker. She watched as her father spoke to them, friendly with all, turning stern only with those who handled the burrs so roughly they fell apart or who tried to slip twigs and leaves into the bags to add weight.

She rubbed the back of her neck as worry tightened into a familiar ache. Closing her eyes, she breathed deeply, evenly, until the tension eased, and she relaxed enough to know she had averted another headache.

Once harvest began, she could have only one thought on her mind. Those few weeks allowed no room for error, no room for distraction or negligence. Whether she saved her farm or lost it depended on that short interval. From her memories of how her father scheduled his time, she knew this was her chance to patch and mend the pickers' bags, clean the dust and cobwebs from the kiln, and check the hinges and the trap doors.

Coming around the corner of the kiln, Guin stopped. A strange horse was tied to a hitch near the rear loading dock. She hurried forward and saw the large double doors were un-locked. She swung open the doors and walked inside the building, hesitating as her eyes adjusted to the dark after the brilliant daylight outside.

"Hello," she called. "Anyone here?"

"Miss Guin, what a surprise." Lawrence Gaspard, the banker, stepped out of the shadows.

"Mr. Gaspard!" Guin frowned. "Can I help you with something?"

"No, no." He pulled out a large linen handkerchief and mopped his face. "Warm in here this time of year."

"Yes, it is." Guin eyed him. What on earth was he doing here? "It's rather dirty too." Worried that he'd take that as a sign of incompetence, she reached for a long handled broom and beat down some nearby spider webs.

"I don't want to interfere with your work, but I'd like to talk to you for a few minutes." Gaspard moved away and brushed at his clothes. "Perhaps we could step outside."

Guin leaned the broom against the wall and nervously dusted her hands. "Ah, all right."

She followed him to a nearby white oak tree and stood in the shade. Gaspard took a few steps toward his horse, then stopped.

She watched him curiously. "Is there something you want?"

"Well, I was in the area and thought I'd stop and see how things were going."

Guin bristled at the banker's implied doubt. "I'm doing very well, Mr. Gaspard. I'll be able to make my loan payment."

"Guin, my dear," Gaspard said, patting her shoulder lightly. "I have every confidence in you. I've heard nothing but good things about your work. When I've ridden by, I've seen for myself that your fields are flourishing."

She smiled. "Yes, I'm hoping for a bumper crop this year."

"Have you heard what the prices will be?"

She shook her head. "Nothing yet. It's still too early. But I'm sure I'll have enough to pay off the loan completely."

"I wanted to talk to you about that."

Alarm bells clanged in her mind, and she struggled to remain calm. Tension clawed at the back of her neck, pulling her scalp painfully taut. "Is there a problem?"

"Not at all."

"If I can't pay the loan off in full, I know I'll be able to pay most of it," she said with rising panic.

"Guin, I'm—"

"You aren't going to foreclose on me, are you?"

Gaspard's eyes widened with surprise. "Mercy, no. I wanted to tell you that if you make the interest payment after the harvest, I'd be happy to let the principal ride until next year."

"What? I don't understand. Why wouldn't I pay off the loan when I have the money."

Gaspard shrugged. "You may want to replace some equipment. Or buy some new stock. Several of the folks down river are adding fruit trees, and others are looking to raise sheep."

"I don't know," Guin said, shaking her head. "I've got my hands full with the hops. Besides, that's all I know."

"You're a smart girl, Guin. You need to think about the future. Times are changing in Spring Valley. There's new investment coming into our community, new opportunities. We need to change, keep up with progress."

"Are you referring to Kellen O'Roarke's resort?"

Gaspard started, then quickly recovered, but not before Guin saw him blanch at her words.

"Does your offer have anything to do with Kellen's resort?" she asked again.

"N-no. Of course not. It's just good banking to help customers with their businesses. It's good for the bank if you invest in new ventures. You'll make more money, which means the bank has more money to lend to others."

That didn't make sense to her. If she didn't repay the principal, then that money wouldn't be available for someone else to borrow. At last, a thought came to her, sickening in its simplicity and its cleverness. "Did Kellen tell you to come out here?"

"Heavens, no! Why would you ask that?"

"If he thinks he's going to sweet-talk his way across my land by meddling with my loan, then he's got another think coming. You can tell him that for me," Guin said.

"I assure you, Guin, Mr. O'Roarke knows nothing about this. I'm here—"

"I will pay my loan in full, Mr. Gaspard. I don't want to owe anyone anything." Looking down, Guin took a deep breath and eased it out.

She removed her hat and fanned her face before turning to Gaspard again. "My father always told me not to go in debt unless I couldn't find any other way. Nothing against you, Mr. Gaspard, but I don't feel right having that loan hanging over me like a thunder cloud, threatening to wash away everything I've worked for."

She saw an odd look cross Gaspard's face. Then it disappeared, replaced by his usual jovial demeanor. "I quite understand how you feel, Guin. Maybe after a season or two, you won't be so concerned. My offer to extend your loan still stands. Think about it. I'll let you get back to your chores."

Guin nodded and watched Mr. Gaspard walk to his horse. He hesitated a moment before taking the reins and swinging into the saddle. He touched the brim of his hat in farewell and then ambled toward the road.

Still bothered by his unexpected visit, she watched until he disappeared, then went into the kiln. Why was Mr. Gaspard in her kiln? What was he looking for? The whole thing was so odd, so unlike him. If he'd had questions about the farm and her crop, he should have come by the house in the evening, or talked to her during the day when she could take him for a tour through the field to see first hand how well she was doing. Instead, his words made it sound as though he watched her secretly. As if he thought she had something to hide. Stirring dust with every step, she climbed the stairs to the second floor and pushed the heavy window coverings open. Fresh air and sunlight swirled into the closed-in space, blowing out the musty air and illuminating the darkness. Dust motes floated in the room, and Guin sneezed three times in rapid succession. Maybe she'd have Joel and Pedro clean these rooms and check the kiln.

She looked around the empty space before descending the stairs again. Wearing heavy gloves, Guin pulled the canvas bags from a storage bin and held them carefully with out-stretched arms as she carried them outside. Spreading the last of the bags on the ground, she shook her head, still unable to come up with a logical purpose to explain Mr. Gaspard's comments or his skulking around.

Unless, regardless of what he'd said, he was working on Kellen's behalf. But she could not think why Kellen cared one way or another about her loan. If she forfeited on the loan, it would be too late for him to gain control of the property and build the spur line in time for the resort to open.

Mr. Gaspard had suggested paying the interest only, so the bank still would hold the note. As long as she met the terms of the loan, no one could take her farm away from her. It just didn't make any sense.

Guin glanced at the late afternoon sky. The air lay hot and heavy against the land, and she felt weary from her long day.

She'd leave the kiln's upper windows open overnight, then come back tomorrow to start cleaning it out. Soledad would mend the pickers' bags as she did every year, so that was one task Guin didn't need to worry about.

Harvest was only a few weeks away, and Guin felt a shiver of anticipation for her favorite time of year. She needed to speak to Joel about lining up pickers. During her next trip to town, she would talk to some of the other growers and find out what arrangements had been made for delivering the hops.

But despite her increasing excitement, she couldn't shake the uneasiness that something was going on that threatened her farm.

Chapter 14

Guin pushed the bedroom door open with her hip and carried in the breakfast tray. "Good morning, Winfield."

"Good morning, Miss Guin. It appears my memory has commenced its return."

He spoke so calmly, Guin almost missed his words. "What did you say?" She set the tray on the dresser and hurried to him.

"I said I believe my memory is returning. It suddenly came to me that I have contracts to renegotiate with farmers who have not kept their word."

Stunned, she sank down on the edge of the bed and took his hand. "Oh, Winfield, it is coming back."

"I must say, I am quite pleased. Not remembering anything was becoming rather tedious."

Guin felt his forehead for fever and searched his face for any paleness, but Winfield appeared quite healthy. "You certainly gave us a bad scare."

"I appreciate your concern over my predicament, as I felt much the same. I regret any inconvenience this may have caused you."

Guin waved aside his apology. "It's no problem. Grandmother and I were more than happy to help. Do you remember anything about the accident?"

Winfield thought for a moment, then winced. "No. It appears I have not yet regained that bit of memory."

"Don't worry about it. I'm sure it'll all come back to you."

She glanced behind her. "I almost forgot; I brought your breakfast."

"Do you think I might be allowed to eat in the kitchen today?"

Hearing the wistfulness in Winfield's voice, Guin smiled. "You'd better eat here. When Dr. Jackson comes, he'll tell us if you can get up."

Winfield mumbled under his breath as he shifted his position and straightened the blankets, but his face brightened when he saw the food she set before him. "Your cuisine is exemplary, Miss Guin. I am greatly indebted to you and your fine grandmother for all the kindnesses you have shown me."

"I'm just glad we could help. Eat your breakfast and Dr. Jackson will be here soon."

"What about Mr. O'Roarke? When will he be here?"

Guin scowled. "I'm sure he'll be here soon too." She saw Winfield's raised eyebrow, a sign she had not done a very good job of hiding her personal feelings about Kellen. "I'll be in the kitchen."

She excused herself quickly, reluctant to be questioned by Winfield. Since their argument in town a week ago, she had caught only glimpses of Kellen. He timed his arrivals and departures from the house so as to spend as much time with Winfield, yet avoid coming in contact with her.

In a way, she was glad Kellen avoided her. She did not want to face him after he'd accused her of supporting the newspaper editorial against his resort. The memory of their argument refueled her anger, reaffirming her resolve to have nothing to do with him. And yet. . . .

And yet, she missed him. She missed his easy smile, the quick way he laughed. With a shiver, she realized she missed the way he looked at her, up and down, making her feel desirable. She missed the way he'd kissed her, and the way he'd confided in her after Winfield's accident. Guin took a deep breath and sighed heavily. As much as he distracted and bothered her, as much as she hated to admit it, Kellen O'Roarke had become a part of her life, and she did not like the empty hole created by his absence.

She burst through the kitchen door. "Has Dr. Jackson arrived? Winfield's regaining his memory."

"That's wonderful," Henrietta said. "The doctor should be here soon."

Guin glanced at her grandmother, and noticed the bright pink spots on her cheeks and the nervous way she plucked at invisible wrinkles in the tablecloth. She frowned, wondering what was agitating her grandmother. Through the open back door, she heard the gentle clop-clop of a horse.

"He's here," Henrietta whispered. She smoothed her hair and her apron with fluttery, ineffectual gestures, then busied herself stirring a pot of soup Guin had started that morning, a pot that wouldn't need stirring for a very long time.

There was a tap-tap on the door before it opened and Dr. Jackson walked in. He removed his hat and bowed slightly toward Henrietta.

"Good morning, Miz Talbot. How are you on this fine morning?"

Henrietta blushed. "I'm quite well, Dr. Jackson. Thank you for asking. How are you?"

"Dr. Jackson, Winfield has regained his memory," Guin said before Dr. Jackson could answer.

The doctor slowly turned toward her, as if reluctant to look away from Henrietta. "He what? Oh, that's mighty fine. I should see him now." He turned back to Henrietta and gazed down at her.

A broad grin spread across Guin's face as she considered

the quaint courtship style between the two older people. She found it sweet, even touching that they could express their interest in each other as if they were young and falling in love for the first time. In a way, they reminded Guin of her parents, having eyes only for each other.

A yearning seared through her, a yearning to share that same feeling of breathless anticipation. But here she was, twenty-five years old, and kissed only once in her life.

Determined not to think about what she would never have, Guin quickly gathered her things and left by the front door, reluctant to interrupt what was going on in the kitchen. Dr. Jackson would check on Winfield soon enough.

She walked across the yard toward the path that would take her to the fields and saw a cloud of dust on the road. She sighed. It was probably Kellen. He was the last thing she needed this morning, but she felt obliged to wait and intercept him before he blundered into the kitchen and embarrassed everyone. She returned to the front porch and waited, steeling herself for their first confrontation since their meeting in town. Kellen rode directly toward her and quickly reined in his horse.

"What's wrong?" he demanded as he slid from his saddle.

The harshness of his tone took her aback. "Nothing's wrong. I just wanted to tell you to go in the front door instead of the kitchen."

"Why?"

"Because Grandmother and Dr. Jackson are talking in the kitchen," she said, irritated with his snappish attitude.

He threw the reins over the hitching post. "Are they talking about Winfield? I need to be there." He took several steps in the direction of the back porch.

"The whole world does not revolve around you and your problems, Mr. O'Roarke."

Her words brought him up short. He turned and glared at her.

"My grandmother and Dr. Jackson are chatting about themselves. Nothing they're saying has anything to do with you or me or Winfield," she said. "Oh, by the way, Winfield says he's getting his memory back."

Kellen sprang to her and grabbed her arms. "He . . . ? What'd he say? Tell me."

"I'll tell you when you stop biting my head off." She pulled away and wondered what had ever made her think she missed him. "This morning I brought him his breakfast tray and he told me he remembered he had some contracts to renegotiate. He doesn't remember anything about the fall."

Kellen frowned and rubbed his mouth. "That's better than before, but we still need to find out who's responsible for his 'accident.' "

"I'm sure the memory will come back with time. I have work to do at the kiln. I assume you'll be gone when I return," she finished, the words more a statement than a question. Something flashed through his eyes that she could not decipher. Regret? Anger? Whatever it was, it disappeared at once, and she shrugged it off.

"I have things to do too, Guin. With Winfield incapacitated, my workload's doubled. But then, I'm sure you understand all about that sort of thing, what with running your little farm." He took the front steps two at a time and quietly disappeared inside the house.

Guin swatted her side with her broad-brimmed hat. Drat the man! She hadn't meant to imply he hung around her house all day, only that she didn't want to see him when she came home. He had a way of twisting her words, making them an insult when she'd only been trying to make a statement of fact.

Arrogant, condescending, insufferable man.

The prickling at the back of her neck warned her of an impending headache, and she groaned. She didn't have time for one now. She had too much work to do, too many things needing attention, even if she only had a 'little farm.' The burst of irritation at Kellen's derisive comment ignited a flare of pain up the back of her head. Maybe if she ignored it, concentrated on something else, she could hold the headache off at least until evening when she could lie down in her darkened room and let her mind drift. Drift into that blissful state where she felt nothing. Right now, she had work to do, and it couldn't be put off.

Kellen shut the front door softly behind him. He heard the murmur of voices coming from the kitchen, then Dr. Jackson's deep chuckle and Henrietta's higher pitched laugh. Kellen shook his head in bemusement and made his way down the hall toward Winfield's room.

"How're you doing, Winfield?" he asked, searching his friend's face for the signs of the recovery Guin had told him about. The warm smile that flashed across Winfield's face reassured him that she'd told the truth.

"Good morning, sir! I am most pleased to see you again." Winfield finished the last of his toast and set the tray aside. "Come, sit here, and tell me how you are progressing with the resort."

Kellen sat on the edge of the bed and gave Winfield an update on the construction. "It's coming along," he concluded. "But I'm concerned about losing more workers. I lost three this week, so I'm down almost half. I have to tell you, Winfield, I'm really worried."

"You will find a solution, sir. I have every confidence in you."

"Do you remember me asking you before the accident to nose around and find out if these problems were a coincidence or if someone was behind them?"

Winfield shook his head slowly.

"Do you remember anything about your fall?"

"No, sir, I do not." Winfield winced. "It appears my brain is not ready to consider such matters yet, either. It still pains me to think on them. I am quite certain, however, that I have much work awaiting me. All your affairs are in a grievous mess, are they not?"

Kellen didn't want to say how disastrous they were. "I don't want you to strain yourself, Winfield. If this much of your memory's returned, I'm sure the rest will come back too. I only hope it's soon enough," he murmured quietly. He did not have much time before the damage from the delays would be irreversible.

"I certainly do not wish to be a nuisance, sir," Winfield said, interrupting Kellen's thoughts. "However, I would be most pleased if my confinement to this bed came to an end."

Kellen looked at his friend and smiled. "I'm sure you're more than ready to be up and about. Dr. Jackson's in the kitchen. I'll get him and he can make the final decision."

Winfield sighed. "I would be eternally grateful, sir, if you would do me that kindness."

Kellen headed for the kitchen and remembered Guin's comments about Dr. Jackson and Mrs. Talbot. He walked noisily so as not to surprise them, but even though he knocked on the kitchen door before opening it, he knew he had startled them. Henrietta snatched her hand from Dr. Jackson's. Her face crimson, she jumped from her chair and bustled around the kitchen, while Dr. Jackson smiled in that slow, easy way of his as he reclined in his chair and watched her.

Kellen glanced from one to the other. "Morning, Mrs.

Talbot," he said politely, nodding to her. Then he turned to Dr. Jackson. "Sorry to bother you, but Winfield is going stir-crazy in that room. Any chance he can come out?"

"I should be seeing to my patient. We'll just go take a look and see what we find. Miz Talbot? We'll continue our little chat after I see to Mr. Winfield."

Henrietta nodded. "I'll make some cake to go with our coffee."

"That'd be mighty fine, Miz Talbot, mighty fine, indeed. Come, son, let's go look at your friend."

Dr. Jackson's examination seemed unhurried and thorough to Kellen. Winfield's excitement about getting out of bed brought a smile of relief to Kellen's face. He'd worried so much about his friend, first fearing he would die, and then that he would never be the same. When Dr. Jackson turned and nodded his approval for Winfield to leave the room, Kellen released the breath he had not realized he'd been holding.

Kellen helped Winfield slip on a dressing gown. "Here, Winfield, take my arm. You're probably pretty weak after all this time in bed."

"It is rather embarrassing, sir, to be dependent on so many for one's daily functioning."

Kellen eased slowly down the hall, Winfield holding onto him with one hand while his other hand pressed the wall for balance. Kellen glanced over his shoulder at Dr. Jackson. "How're we doing?"

"Just fine, son. Just as I'd expect. Perhaps Mr. Winfield would like to sit on the porch? It's shady out there this morning. And Miz Talbot, she made some mighty fine lemonade that will liven Mr. Winfield's insides."

"That sounds delightful, Dr. Jackson," Winfield said.

Although Winfield tried to sound energetic, Kellen heard

the exhaustion in his friend's voice from even this short trip. Winfield still had a long way to go before he recovered his strength.

At last, they reached the porch, and Winfield sagged into the rocking chair with a sigh. He leaned his head back and closed his eyes, his skin pale. Alarmed, Kellen looked questioningly at Dr. Jackson, who shook his head.

"You rest a spell, my friend," Dr. Jackson said, patting Winfield's hand. "If you're needing anything, you holler. Don't be getting up on your own. One bad fall's all a man's allowed."

His eyes still closed, Winfield smiled weakly and nodded. "If you insist," he whispered.

Kellen perched on the porch railing. He desperately needed to be at the resort. God only knew what problems had developed in his absence this morning. But he couldn't bring himself to leave Winfield. He tried to stifle a yawn, then rubbed his face with both hands, realizing he was more fatigued than he'd thought. The long hours, the restless nights, the worry about Winfield, and the problems at the resort had taken their toll.

Winfield was going to be okay. Kellen breathed a deep sigh of thankfulness and relief. He didn't know what he would have done if his friend had not recovered. His driving need to return to work drained from him, and he leaned against the railing corner post. With his eyes closed, he relaxed for the first time in a very long while.

The banging of the back door startled him to full consciousness. Kellen shook the lingering traces of sleepiness from his mind and saw Henrietta step onto the porch carrying a tray. He hurried to her and took the heavy tray from her hands and set it on a small table next to Winfield's rocking chair.

"Did you make these cookies?"

Henrietta smiled with pride. "Guin made them last night."

Kellen swiped one before she could swat his hand away. "Mmm," he murmured as he chewed. "These are really good."

"I don't know what I'm going to do with her. She works hard all day in the heat, then comes home and cooks and cleans." Henrietta shook her head. "The girl's going to expire from working so hard."

Stricken with guilt, Kellen recoiled from taking another cookie. He'd promised to get help for Guin, then hadn't because he wanted to keep the extent of Winfield's injuries a secret. No, to be completely honest, he'd forgotten about his offer, carried away with his own worries, as well as his anger at Guin for supporting the editorial.

Tobias Eldridge had confessed that he'd written the column to build interest and stir up controversy. In his heart, Kellen had known she couldn't have joined in an attack on him like that. It simply wasn't in her to be malicious. She'd shown Winfield nothing but kindness, opening her home and caring for him as if she had no other burdens or responsibilities. Kellen had reciprocated with recriminations and rudeness. He owed her so much more than he could ever repay.

"Is she in the field now?" he asked.

Henrietta looked at him with a hard, speculative gaze before answering. "She's at the kiln, readying it for harvest."

"Thanks." He left the porch and struck out across the yard, not sure what to say when he found her.

Kellen approached the kiln and set aside his troubled thoughts. Their brief conversation earlier had not been pleasant. He wavered, then took a deep breath and stepped inside. Hearing a swishing sound, he walked to the middle of the cavernous room and looked around.

A billowing cloud of dust descended on him. "Hey!" he cried out, swinging his arms and moving away.

"Who's there?" Guin called.

Kellen swatted at the dust still floating in his face and looked up to see a trap door. "It's me. Kellen."

"I'm busy." The swishing sound resumed.

He raised an eyebrow. Not an auspicious beginning. "I want to talk to you."

"I don't have time." The sound of sweeping quickened, followed by another cloud of dust tumbling through the trap door. Kellen stepped back. "Please?" Silence answered him. "I'm sorry I was rude," he said.

More silence.

Kellen stood with his hands on his hips and stared at the floor, rocking back and forth on his heels. "I'm also sorry I said those things to you last week. I was angry, but that was no excuse to lash out at you."

"You had no right to accuse me."

"I know. I was wrong."

"I never said anything against your resort, you know."

He pursed his lips. "I know that. You're too fair."

He heard her walk across the floor overhead and watched her climb down the ladder and approach him, her expression rigid, her eyes full of suspicion. He also saw the hurt she tried to hide.

"I was only trying to help when I showed you the newspaper. I thought you'd want to know right away." She held herself stiffly, her hands clenched into fists.

"I did." He took a step toward her, then stopped when she backed away. "I'm sorry, Guin. The editorial caught me by surprise." He walked away from her, running a hand through his hair. He turned to face her and frowned. "My only excuse is that I was tired and scared, and you were standing there when I exploded."

"I may not agree with you, but I'd never deliberately hurt you. Or anyone." Her voice was filled with pain, and his stomach clenched with regret.

"I know that," he said. He went to her and took her hands, felt the strength in her fingers when she tried to pull away. He held her in his grasp. "I was wrong," he said again, gazing down at her. "You've done more for Winfield and me than anyone else ever has. Thank you."

She shrugged and slipped her hands from his, then stepped away. "It's no more than I would have done for anyone else."

"I still appreciate it."

She stood tall, holding onto her dignity, and he saw the wariness in her eyes.

"Is there anything else?"

"No. I just wanted to apologize." He wanted more, but he didn't want to say it.

"Fine. I have work to do."

She headed toward the ladder, but before she reached the second rung, he was beside her, pulling her to him.

"There is something more," he said, lowering his head to hers.

He kissed her softly at first, then more fiercely. Caught by surprise, she stiffened, then her lips softened, parted, and he plundered her mouth with his tongue. She tasted sweet and warm, like berries picked fresh in the hot summer sun. He felt her hands settle on his shoulders, then slip around his neck and hold him to her. His spirits soared as his hands roamed her back. A deep hunger filled him with the desire to feast on her softness, to taste more of her sweetness. He shuddered from his abiding need, and feared he would drown in the heated womanly scent of her. At length, he eased his lips from hers and cradled her head to the curve in his shoulder.

"I accept your apology."

He felt her smile against his chest and he chuckled. "That wasn't part of it."

"I thought it an ingenious atonement."

"My pound of flesh?"

"Something like that." The amusement in her voice mingled with a breathiness he found inviting.

"Truce?"

She nodded her acceptance, which pleased him.

"Leave your broom and come with me."

"But I—"

"I'll help you clean the kiln later."

"Very well," she agreed. "Where're we going?"

"To the oak tree near the house. To sit for a while. Your grandmother thinks you're working too hard."

Guin shook her head as she followed him to the tree and sat down next to him. "Farms take work. I keep telling her that."

Kellen shrugged. "That doesn't mean she can't worry."

Guin grimaced before turning serious. "Kellen, I want to ask you something, and I want you to answer me honestly."

"Sure," he said, alert to the edge that had crept into her voice. "What is it?"

"Mr. Gaspard came here the other day. The banker," she said in response to his questioning look.

"What did he want?"

Guin frowned and plucked at the grass next to her. "It was quite odd. I came here from the field, and I found him inside

212

the kiln. It was almost like . . ." She shook her head. "Like he was snooping around. But that doesn't make any sense, really."

"What did he say when you discovered him?"

"He said he was just looking to see that everything was going well. Then, he told me I didn't have to pay off the loan, that I could pay the interest and keep the capital to reinvest in the farm."

"That doesn't sound so odd," Kellen said with a shrug. "I'm sure banks do that sort of thing all the time."

"You may be right, but he seemed . . . nervous about the whole thing."

"Maybe he feels awkward about your having your father's loan."

"If he was so concerned, why hasn't he talked to me? Why hasn't he come to the field when I'm there, or to the house in the evening? Why is he snooping around my kiln?"

"Was anything moved or changed?"

"Not that I could find."

"It's probably nothing." Kellen leaned his head against the tree. He reached out and clasped her hand, felt the soft strength of her fingers entwined with his.

The sun felt warm on his face, and a gentle breeze stirred the heated scents of summer grass and dry earth. Such a peaceful place, he thought drowsily. A place where a man could set down roots. A place where a man could belong. . . .

He dozed, peripherally aware of sounds around him, bees droning amid the climbing roses that covered the porch, quiet conversation and low laughter filtering from inside the house. Worry about Guin's tale niggled at the back of his mind. He wanted to relax, to enjoy the companionable silence. He tried to tell himself she was overreacting to Mr. Gaspard's visit. He couldn't quite convince himself.

Chapter 15

Guin hurried down the stairs to the kitchen. Her stomach churned and the all-to-familiar tension tightened her shoulders. She paused at the foot of the stairs.

Today was the day. The start of harvest. All her months of work and worry would culminate in a frenzy of activity over the next two weeks. This would decide if she kept her farm, or. . . .

She refused even to consider that possibility. Not at this point, not when she was so close.

She entered the kitchen and jumped in surprise at the sight of Winfield hovering over the stove. "Winfield! What are you doing here so early?"

"I intend to be of assistance to you, Miss Guin."

She looked at him closely. His skin was pale and he moved stiffly, but she saw determination in his eyes and the way he stood up from the table, straight and tall. "You don't have to. I have plenty of workers lined up."

"Picking was not what I had in mind," he said with a dry smile. "The good Dr. Jackson has relayed to me that in the past you contributed to the harvest by serving as bookkeeper for your father."

"That's true, I did." Her heart sank as she realized she had been so worried about finding enough pickers that she'd forgotten the task of tallying the bags.

"From what I have heard, you have no one to fill that auspicious position. I believe my credentials are more than sufficient to meet the challenge."

She took his hands in hers. "Winfield, I would be truly grateful. Are you sure you're up to it? You haven't left the house to do more than walk from here to the barn and back."

"Believe me, Miss Guin, if I do not take advantage of this opportunity to make myself useful, and to escape the confines of my convalescence, I will surely go mad."

Amused by his dire description, his offer to help filled Guin with the conviction that with Winfield by her side, she could only succeed. After all, he was Kellen's talented assistant, and Kellen had come far in the world.

"I accept your offer, Winfield. We'll go as soon as you finish eating." She started toward the door.

Winfield moved away from the table and joined her. "If you would be so kind as to instruct me as to your expectations, I am ready to begin now."

In the early rosy glow of dawn, they walked slowly across the yard to the hop field on the other side of the small rise, Winfield leaning heavily on Guin. They topped the crest of the hill and looked at the activity below.

"My word," Winfield said, his eyes wide in amazement.

"It's really something, isn't it?" Guin gazed at the busy scene before her, a smile tugging the corners of her mouth. "This is the best time of all," she whispered. It happened every year, yet she still felt the thrill of excitement and antici- pation as if it was her first harvest, and in a way, it was. Hers alone.

In the last several days, pickers had arrived in droves to set up camp along the river. Indians, Chinese, and poor whites from San Francisco; each had established their own little communities of campfires, lean-tos, and tents. Guin caught the aromas of coffee and bacon and fried pan bread.

Children laughed and played, dodging around the temporary shelters. Women drew water from the river and chattered with each other, renewing old acquaintances and making new friends. Men gathered in small clusters near campfires and swapped stories.

She spotted Joel supervising the delivery of the pickers' bags from the kiln to the edge of the field. "Ready to start?" she asked Winfield.

"Whenever you are, Miss Guin," he replied. "This will make a grand adventure to include in my memoirs."

Guin looked at him in amusement, then led him toward Joel.

"Do we have enough bags?" she asked.

"I think so. Leastwise I got all the ones in the kiln." Joel brushed his arm across his forehead, already beginning to sweat from his exertions. "I don't know, though. This year's crop 'pears bigger than last year's."

"What about the scale?"

"The wagon's coming back with it, along with the table and chair."

"Good," Guin said. "Joel, you remember Winfield Somerset."

"Pleased to see you up and around, sir." Joel shook Winfield's hand.

"He's going to tally the bags for us this year," Guin said.

"I'm glad you got some help, Miss Guin. I was worried you'd be trying to do it all by yourself."

"So was Winfield," she said. "Here's Pedro with the wagon."

The three men quickly set up the scale, and Guin acquainted Winfield with the ledger book. Each picker's name would be entered the first time a numbered bag was brought to the scales. After it was weighed, Winfield would start the running tally of the bags' numbers and their weights. At the end of the day, Guin would pay each worker based on the number of pounds of hops picked.

Once the scales were set up, pickers drifted toward the table to get their bags. Most knew Guin from previous years. They greeted her warmly and offered condolences on the loss of her parents.

All morning Guin had tried not to think about her parents, but the pickers' kind words, the memories they shared with her, brought tears to her eyes. She swallowed hard, willing herself to smile and thank the workers. Now was not the time to fall apart. Maybe later tonight, in the dark of her room, she would again grieve for her loss.

Pedro stayed with Winfield to distribute more bags, and Guin went with Joel to get the pickers situated. They started on the lower part of the vines first, picking from the ground up as high as they could. Guin walked slowly between the poled vines, encouraging the workers to pick only the ripest ones, to be gentle with the burrs and keep them whole, to leave twigs and leaves on the ground.

The field, which had been a quiet solitary place for so many months, now vibrated with chatter and laughter and singing. Young children played at their mothers' feet while older ones helped with the picking and toted water for their parents.

Guin noted with amusement the way married women focused intently on their task while the single women's eyes strayed frequently to the handsome young men working on nearby vines. The Indians worked quietly while the Chinese hummed in a high-pitched singsong way. Those who'd traveled from San Francisco looked weary at the start, and Guin wondered if they would survive the grueling heat of day.

She returned to Winfield as the first pickers arrived with

their full bags. As her father had done in the past, she greeted each one and praised his or her work while quickly scanning the bag to be sure it wasn't weighted down with twigs and leaves. She knew from previous years which workers were most likely to pad their bags. And she knew getting angry would not change them.

Instead, she pretended the additional weight was an accident, an oversight on the picker's part, but the weight was adjusted in the tally book, and a mark placed by the picker's name. She knew that for some it was a game, a challenge to see if they could get away with it. Once they learned she could not be fooled, the problem usually resolved itself.

Back and forth she went, from the field to the wagon. Finally she was confident Joel and Pedro could handle the pickers while she stayed with Winfield. Despite his protests, she worried he would push himself too hard.

She finished talking to a picker and weighing his bag, then realized no other pickers waited behind him. "Where. . . ."

Startled, she looked around and saw the field had emptied and the pickers had returned to their camps. "Is it noon already?" she asked Winfield.

"It would appear so," he said, closing his ledger book with a thump.

Guin's stomach growled in agreement. "I guess we should get something to eat too."

"That's a marvelous idea," said a voice from behind her.

Guin jumped and turned to see Kellen approach. He carried two hampers that looked very familiar. "I see you've been visiting my grandmother," she said.

"Sure have." He hefted the baskets. "She filled these with all kinds of goodies."

The scent of fried chicken and fresh baked bread wafted through the air. Guin glanced at Winfield and could tell from his appreciative sigh that he smelled it too. "Let's sit under that tree," she said, pointing to a tall white oak.

"That, Miss Guin, is one of the best suggestions I have heard you make all day," Winfield said.

Kellen led the way, and they were soon seated on a blanket with full plates. Guin hadn't realized she was so hungry until she took the first bite of chicken. There was little conversation as the three of them ate.

Replete, she set her plate to one side and leaned against the tree with a heavy sigh.

"Full?" Kellen asked.

"Mmm," she answered, her eyes closed.

"I think I will take a brief stroll before we must return to our duties," Winfield said.

Guin heard the crackle of dry leaves as he left. Despite the shade, the heat lay heavy, sapping her energy. Or maybe it was eating so much, or perhaps she had consumed all her nervous energy in the morning's frenzied activity. A nap would be nice. She sighed with contentment.

She sensed Kellen before he actually touched her, caught his musky masculine scent a moment before his lips brushed hers. She kissed him back languidly, enjoying the feel of him, but too sleepy to put any effort into it.

His quiet laugh rumbled against her mouth, then he eased away. "I see I have competition for your attention."

"No. Not really."

"You're almost asleep, Guin Talbot. That doesn't bode well for me."

She opened one eye for a moment, then closed it again. "Timing is important."

He chuckled again and lay down beside her. "I can see that." He took her hand and stroked the pad of her thumb. "Your hand is so soft. Always wondered how you did that."

Sleepiness faded, and she opened her eyes to look at him. He was stretched out next to her, his head supported on one arm, his eyes closed. The sun peeking through the leaves fell on his face in a dappled pattern that shifted with the barest breath of a breeze. His black hair had almost a bluish cast where the sun hit it, and she could see the new growth on his chin.

When had she come to care for this man? This man who was all wrong for her, this man who dreamed very different dreams from her own? Somewhere along the line she'd succumbed to his charms, found herself waiting with breathless anticipation for his arrival. Her soul found warmth only when his smile turned to her.

Shifting her position against the tree, she looked at Kellen's hand, large and square, holding her hand, making it appear small, almost delicate, by comparison. His thumb moving across her palm excited her, made her want to lie next to him, feel the length of him. She wanted the touch of his lips against hers again, his hands following her curves, caressing her—

"Miss Guin!"

She looked up and shaded her eyes. "Yes, Joel?"

"The pickers're going back to the field."

"I'll be right there." She squeezed Kellen's hand and tried to pull her hand away. He held it fast.

"Where do you think you're going?" he growled.

"Back to work."

He sighed. "I suppose I should get back to work too. Resort won't build itself."

"Are you still having trouble?"

"Yeah." His voice was filled with a worry he couldn't hide. He frowned and ran his hand through his hair. "I'm down to a quarter of the original crew. Of course, I knew I'd lose a lot of them around now with the harvests, but I'd hoped to be further along than this."

"Maybe it'll pick up when harvests are over."

"I guess. Keep an eye on Winfield, will you? This is the first time he's been seen away from the house, and I don't want to spook anyone from town who might come around, in case they mean to harm him again."

She nodded. "I'll stay by him. He's been a great help."

"I know." Kellen started toward the house with the hampers in his hands. "How late are you working tonight?"

"Until the pickers quit."

"I probably won't see you then."

Hiding her disappointment, Guin watched him walk away. "Thanks for coming by," she called after him. She found herself mesmerized by the way his shirt fit his broad shoulders, the way it rippled when he moved, the muscles in his bare forearms as he swung the hampers in rhythm with his stride. The way his denim pants hugged his narrow hips and waist.

And she reminded herself to breathe.

She wished he could stay, but knew it wasn't possible. She had work to do; he had work to do. Even though he hadn't talked about it, she knew he still wanted her property.

The harvest days flew by for Guin, blurring together while settling into an exhausting routine dictated by the rapidly ripening hops. Picking, weighing, counting, supervising the pickers, settling the squabbles that naturally arose when large groups of strangers were confined together for long periods of time. All the things her father had done when he was alive. All the things she was doing in his place. After the long months of worry and hard work, it was coming together, and it was everything she'd hoped for.

It had taken the pickers a week to strip ripe burrs from the lower branches of the hop vines. Earlier this week, some of the men had lifted the towering redwood poles from the ground and laid them gently on the ground. The pickers had swarmed over the vines, gleaning burrs from the previously unreachable upper branches as well as the now ripening burrs from the lower branches. Guin could stand at the edge of her field, and for the first time in months could see all the way to the river on the other side.

In the kiln, Joel oversaw a team of men who kept the first floor furnaces burning at an even temperature to dry the burrs spread out on the floor above.

Winfield had taken well to his assignment. He'd even assumed responsibility for the payoff at the end of each day, freeing Guin to ramble through the field and the town of tents, to look after these people while they worked for her.

Now the work was almost over and it was time to celebrate. Guin had returned home early this afternoon, to bathe and put on a clean dress—not a fancy one like the one she'd worn to town, but a pretty muslin. She washed her hair and rolled it loosely, allowing a few tendrils to curl down the side of her face.

As the sun settled behind the distant foothills, leaving the opposite hills glowing in a bronze light, Guin turned away from the empty field and approached the kiln. She breathed in the sulphur-laden air from the furnaces, the sweet smell of success.

The last of today's load had been carted to town in overloaded wagons and transferred to the agent who would see that the bags of dried hops reached the city. More than half of her crop still covered the upper floor, needing another week of drying before being bagged and shipped by railroad car.

After today, the workers would start drifting away, looking

for other crops to harvest. A few would remain to help Joel and Pedro keep the fires stoked and the hops turned for proper drying. Guin was almost sorry harvest was over. It had been exhausting, but gratifying.

She looked toward the campsites. Nearby, the sound of axes chopping firewood split the calm, and katydids piped their evening song. Usually the camp town quieted after dark, but tonight Guin felt the special sizzle in the air.

Pushing the main door wide to let cool fresh air in, Guin entered the kiln. Heat still radiated from the furnaces inside and from the sun beating down during the day. That did not seem to slow the men who scurried around the building. She watched them gently sweep the hop burrs into high piles at the edge of the large drying room that took up most of the second floor. Wooden shutters had been opened wide to let the heat escape.

Guin climbed the stairs to the top floor and looked out. She heard the excited chatter of voices float across the air from the campsites, and knew the workers and their families were preparing for tonight's dance.

From the time she was a child, Guin had always looked forward to coming with her parents to watch the Saturday night dance held in the kiln at the end of the harvest. The pickers' children played in the corners under their parents' gaze, the older girls and boys flirted openly, and anyone who understood the steps followed the caller's directions as the dancers whirled around the room. She smiled in anticipation. The fiddlers were tuning up in the drying room. In only a short time, strains of music drew people, laughing and talking, from the camp.

Guin waited until most of the workers and their families had arrived before entering the drying room. The chatter quieted as she made her way to the corner where the musicians sat. In the past, she'd participated in the harvest in small ways. But mostly she'd watched from the sidelines.

This year, she'd immersed herself, worked beside these people, talked to them, learned about their lives. She'd become a part of them, and now she thought of them as a large extended family. She felt suddenly shy, overwhelmed by emotion. She glanced at the faces nearest her. Smiles and warm expressions reassured her.

"Good evening." Her voice cracked with nervousness. She clasped her hands, hoping the tremors of anxiety would not show. "I'm glad you all came tonight."

Someone set a stool in front of her. At first, she hesitated, then she took a deep breath and stepped onto it. She smiled shyly, and was startled when those in front started clapping. Then others clapped, until the room reverberated with the sound of applause.

Finally Joel stepped forward and lifted his hands to signal for quiet. "Miss Guin, everyone knows this season was hard for you. Some didn't think you could do it. Now everyone says you are the nicest to work for. And the prettiest," he said.

Stunned, Guin blushed and looked around questioningly at the nods and smiles that confirmed what Joel said. "Thank you, Joel, everyone. I don't know what to say. I remember my father always thanked everyone for their hard work, and encouraged you to come back the next year. He loved this land, and he was proud of the hops we grew."

She heard her father's words echo in her head, and she faltered. "This was a hard year for me. I thank each of you for helping with the harvest. I wish my father could be here to see our best year ever. Thank you so much. And please, please come back next year," she said with a heartfelt smile. "Now, let's start the music!"

Her final words were met with whoops and cheers. Guin

jumped from the stool and moved away from the couples forming up. The fiddlers took a few practice strokes, then the caller started clapping and stamping his feet to set the rhythm of the music. He shouted the first steps and the dancers glided across the floor.

Guin stood across from the door and watched, clapping her hands and tapping her feet in time with the music. The women wore their colorful dresses, and skirts flew as they moved around the circles. Men shouted and whistled as they followed the caller's lead. The music would play until midnight, when everyone returned to camp.

Guin leaned against the wall and relaxed, thoroughly enjoying herself. She remembered another dance; it seemed so long ago when she'd danced for the first time with Kellen, yet only a few months had passed.

As if conjured from her fantasies, Kellen stepped through the door. He looked swiftly around the crowded dance floor; his gaze passed Guin, then returned to her. The heat in his eyes warmed her in a way the hot, crowded room never could. He inched toward her, and she watched his progress.

"Quite a crowd," he yelled in her ear. Kellen grabbed her hand and led her down the stairs and outside. "Whew, it's noisy in there." He slung his arm around her shoulder and they strolled toward the nearby oak tree.

She smiled broadly, her ears still ringing from the noise. "It should be noisy. We're celebrating the best harvest this farm has ever seen. I'll be able to pay off my bank loan and have plenty to live on for the next year."

Kellen gave her a quick hug. "That's great."

Guin wished he hadn't released her so fast. She liked the feel of his strong arms surrounding her, the feel of his hard chest against her.

"How's the resort doing?" she asked.

His expression was bleak. "I'm afraid I'm not doing as well as you. If I can't finish the buildings in the next month, I'm ruined."

She was torn between relief and dismay. He wouldn't be pressuring her for her land, but she had come to care for him and didn't want to see him fail.

"What about after harvest? Some of the local people could help you then."

He shook his head. "A bunch of them started working for me last spring, then came up with flimsy excuses for why they couldn't continue. They made it clear they weren't coming back, but never gave us a good reason why not. That was all before Winfield's accident."

"Kellen, what if . . . I mean, I'm done with my harvest, except for needing a few men to finish the drying and bagging. Some of my pickers might be willing to stay on."

"That's a thought." He tapped his finger against his mouth. "Can they stay here?"

Guin shrugged. "I don't see any reason why not. The weather's good for a while yet, and I can ask Mrs. Bennett to keep sending a supply wagon every day."

"If I get the men I need, I can finish the construction in two, maybe three weeks, and still have time for the finishing work." Kellen broke into a radiant smile. "Guinevere Talbot, you're brilliant."

He picked her up by the waist and swung her around. She squealed at the easy way he handled her, and then her breath caught at the heated look in his eyes as he slid her down the length of him until her toes barely touched the ground.

Kellen clutched her to him, searching her face before he made his decision. He must have seen the fire smoldering in her eyes; he lowered his head and claimed her mouth in a searing kiss.

Chapter 16

Guin's spirit soared in Kellen's embrace. Her lips softened as his tongue plundered her mouth, and her heart ignited under the heat of his hands as they drew her hips hard to him. She felt his urgency as he pressed her against the tree, his body molded against hers. She heard a moan that she distantly recognized as her own yearning. He covered her cheeks, her eyes with kisses, trailing down her neck, returning to the spot by her ear that made her tingle.

Kellen leaned his forehead against hers. "Guinevere Talbot, what am I going to do with you?"

She heard the frustration in his voice, and she laughed, a deep throaty laugh she did not recognize. "You could kiss me again."

He did, a softer kiss this time, tender rather than urgent and demanding. She sighed against his lips, wishing she could stay here in the moonlight with this man for a very long time.

Nearby voices and muffled giggles brought them back to earth. Kellen raised his head and she lay her cheek against his warm, solid chest.

"It's just kids," she whispered. "The older ones sneak away from their parents."

"I suppose it wouldn't do for the landowner to be discovered under the bushes by some lusty adolescents."

Guin smiled at the image. "Probably not. We should go back."

"I'd rather stand here and look at the stars. And hold you."

Even in the dark she could see the smoldering light in his eyes. The possessive clamp of his arms around her waist urged her to stay. "I'd like that too."

Still, they slowly made their way to the kiln. Guin wished she did not have to be responsible, that for just one night she could be as unrestrained as the unmarried pickers. What would it be like to lie with Kellen under the stars? She shook her head. That would never happen to her.

The clamor inside the kiln seemed deafening after the relative quiet outside. She and Kellen would not be able to talk, which might not be all bad, she decided. Her feelings about him were too jumbled.

Before she could dwell on them, Kellen caught her hand and drew her into a newly formed circle for the next dance. The music started, and she found herself caught up in the fervor. Following the caller's commands, she moved from partner to partner, twirling and circling with the people she had worked so closely with the last two weeks.

She partnered briefly with Joel, and as he swirled her around the circle, he said, "It's good to see you happy."

"I am," she said with a light-hearted smile.

"You work too hard," he yelled over the noise. "You worry too much."

As he passed her on to her next partner, Guin smiled chidingly at him. It was nice of Joel to care about her, but this was her farm. She was responsible for supporting herself with her crops. She was responsible for keeping her land, and that meant she could pretend only for rare, precious moments that she was carefree.

At midnight, the fiddlers stopped, and tired dancers began to drift away toward their campsites, laughing and chattering as they went. With a gentle swooshing sound, several men swept the hop burrs away from the walls and spread them evenly across the floor to begin the drying process again.

Guin spotted Kellen across the room. He glanced toward her and stopped, a slow smile spreading across his face. She felt herself flush, and knew the heat had nothing to do with the temperature of the room. Then Joel approached and she turned away, following him down the stairs.

"How much fuel do you think we should put in the furnace to get started?" Guin asked. Before Joel could answer, she heard footsteps on the stairs.

Guin looked up. "Kellen! What are you doing here?"

He shrugged. "Just thought I'd see if you needed any help."

"No, thanks. Joel and I can handle it." When he didn't leave, she asked, "Is . . . is there something else?"

"No. I just . . . I thought I'd walk you back to the house."

"Oh, that's not necessary. I'm staying to watch the furnace tonight."

"You can't—"

"Miss Guin," Joel interrupted. "I'll go see that everything is in place." He glanced from Guin to Kellen, then ducked out of the room.

"Now see," Guin said. "You've scared poor Joel off."

"Good. It's his job to watch the furnace, not yours."

Her eyes narrowed. "What do you mean?"

"Guin, you're a woman. You can't stay here all night."

"I may be a woman, but this is my kiln, and my crop. My job is to watch over it."

"It isn't . . . safe," he finally said.

"Safe? What can possibly happen? We've used this kiln for weeks, and every year in the past. We stand watch at night, every night, to keep the fire burning."

"We still don't know who attacked Winfield. Someone could hurt you."

"It's not as if I'll be alone. Joel will be here too." She crossed her arms over her chest.

He stiffened with frustration. "So you're staying."

"Yes. Go home, Kellen. Stop worrying over nothing."

"All right." He raised his hands. "It's none of my business. You've made that abundantly clear."

Guin watched him turn on his heel and stride from the building. She wanted to shake him. Why was he spoiling a wonderful evening? She kicked a piece of kindling to the side of the room.

"Miss Guin?"

She turned around. "Oh, Joel. I'm glad you're back. I'll change my clothes and we'll get started."

Guin ducked into a small storeroom and replaced her pretty dress with work clothes. She rejoined Joel and together they loaded the furnace and started the fire. Hands on her hips, Guin watch the flames catch. The heat soon warmed her face. "How much time have we lost tonight?"

"Only a few hours. The burrs held some of their heat when we pushed them into piles, and they warm back up fast." Joel frowned and shifted his feet. "Miss Guin, you can go home. I'll keep the furnace stoked until the men arrive in the morning."

"No, Joel. I'm staying," Guin said firmly. Here was another man with misconceptions about what she could and could not do. "My father always did it, and I'm not going to start shirking now."

She helped Joel load the furnace and together they watched the thermometer rise. Once the flames settled to glowing coals, Guin looked around. "Sounds like everyone's gone."

Joel grinned. "They worked hard all day to bring in the last of the hops, and tonight, they danced to celebrate. They're too tired to linger."

"I'm exhausted too, but I don't dare sit down."

"I know." Joel yawned. "I'll get some more wood for the furnace. It shouldn't take me long."

"Fine." Guin followed him to the door, then pulled it to, leaving a small opening for air to flow.

Alone at last, she squared her shoulders and returned to the furnace room. The furnace radiated its heat upward. Guin went upstairs to the second floor and picked her way through the hop cones spread evenly across the drying room. The thermometer indicated the heat was rising to the level they wanted.

She was amazed that only a short time ago this had been the scene of gay revelry. What a grand night it had been. Now the quiet was almost deafening.

She climbed the ladder to the tiny tower that also housed the flue and looked out. In the distance, the campsites lay quietly below, most of the fires extinguished. Off to the side lay the remains of her field, the leaves golden brown and vines lying on the ground.

In the opposite direction, she spotted her house, and she frowned to see a light glowing in the kitchen window. She'd told her grandmother not to wait up for her, and leaving a lantern burning was a waste of money. Guin smiled. She wouldn't have to worry about money, at least not for a while. When the last of the crop was delivered to Mr. Johnston, she would pay off the loan and have enough left to live comfortably until next year.

Yet what about next season? Hops did so well here, but perhaps she was being shortsighted to stick to one thing. Should she think about growing other crops too? Maybe she should plant a fruit orchard and buy a few sheep. She rested her chin on her arms as she leaned on the sill. She had come a long way from the isolated young woman she'd been last spring. It was heartening to know that now she had choices.

And then there was Kellen. He made her think about things that only a few months ago would have made her blush and die of embarrassment. She'd never dreamed a man's kiss could ignite a fire deep in her belly the way Kellen's did. Even now, the thought of his touch kindled a yearning so strong she wondered how she had lived all these years without being aware of it. Perhaps that was because she'd never met a man like Kellen before.

Even though she'd been annoyed with him for his ridiculous notions about her "place," she sensed his demands were sparked by a fondness that must have surprised him as much as it did her. She knew she played with fire every time she was around him. He still wanted her land, even if he did not mention it. The subject would come up again; it had to. But for a little while, she wanted to ignore the bells that clanged a warning whenever Kellen stepped into view.

A noise broke through her musings, and Guin straightened, listening hard. It was nothing, she decided. The wind maybe. She stretched and yawned, then started toward the drying floor. Despite the overriding odor of sulphur, she caught a whiff of something different as she climbed down the ladder. Pushing her way gingerly through the hops piled on the floor, she checked the thermometer and noticed the temperature was down.

That was odd. Joel should have returned by now with more wood and be watching the temperature from the furnace room. She went down the stairs and coughed, realizing there was more in the air than the heavy sulphur smoke.

"Joel?" The furnace room was smoky, much smokier than

it should be. Joel had not returned with more fuel. The embers she'd left earlier were still glowing. She looked around and spotted thin trails of smoke and the flickering flames seeping in between the floor and the outside walls of the kiln.

Fire.

Her heart pounded. "Joel!" She grabbed some canvas bags lying in a corner and started to beat the flames. "Joel! Where are you?"

Fire. A farmer's worst nightmare.

Joel wasn't responding to her calls. Where was he? The smoke was getting worse. Guin ran to the main door and pushed, but the door wouldn't budge. She pushed again, harder this time. The door still would not open.

Guin raced up the stairs, ignoring the hops she squashed as she darted across the drying room. A hose was there, as were the buckets of water used to wet the burrs at the beginning of the drying process. The water was also kept in case of emergency. This was an emergency, she thought through gritted teeth. She'd be damned if she would lose her crop at this stage.

Kicking the burrs out of her path, she dragged a barrel to the opposite wall and heaved it onto its side, letting the water whoosh across the burr-covered floor. She tipped over a second barrel and a third. Smoke billowed up through the cracks. She was losing.

She scrambled up the ladder to the tower. "Help! Fire!" she called toward the campsite. She dared to look down, then wished she hadn't. Flames licked at three sides of the wooden kiln. Only the back of the building was not yet involved. She suddenly realized that more than her crop was in danger, and terror surged through her.

"Fire! Fire!" she screamed.

Answering shouts echoed from the campsite. If they could

only reach her in time. She slithered down the ladder to the drying area and poured more water on the hops, praying they would become so waterlogged they wouldn't burn. Tears streamed from her eyes as the smoke swirled around her.

Refusing to give up, she forced herself to go down the stairs to the first floor. She stepped back in horror when she saw the door and surrounding walls enveloped in flames. Dashing into the furnace room, she closed the vents, hoping to shut down some of the heat, then she fled to the second floor.

Smaller containers of water were stored in the rafters, and she scurried to get them, pouring as much water as she could on the floor; the last one she poured over herself. Covering her mouth with her skirt, she backed away from the heat she could now feel through the floor.

God help me.

By the time Kellen had ridden halfway to town, he realized he was being unreasonable and pig-headed. Of course Guin would want to spend the night at the kiln. He'd do the same if his future were riding on it.

He should leave and not come back, leave her to her fertile fields and blossoming friendships with the townspeople. He had nothing to offer her but friendship. And some incredible kisses. Maybe that was why he couldn't go without clearing the air with her, perhaps even apologizing. But he didn't want to return to the kiln right now, not in front of an audience.

He'd wait for her at the house, let her do her job, then he'd talk to her when she wasn't distracted. He put his horse in the barn, and as he crossed the yard, he hoped Winfield and Henrietta were still awake. The company would be nice. But the only light came from the kitchen.

Kellen stealthily climbed the steps and knocked softly. A

low growl greeted him. He eased the door open. "Colonel, it's okay. It's just me. Everyone else gone to bed?"

Colonel woofed quietly, then his claws clacked across the plank floor. "Easy boy, it's just me. Your old friend, Kellen."

Kellen extended his hand cautiously and hoped Colonel wouldn't chew on it. Instead, the dog licked his fingers and Kellen grimaced. God, he hated dogs, especially big, slobbery dogs. At least Colonel was letting him inside without biting his head off. He gently closed the door and patted Colonel on the head. "Good dog." He listened but heard nothing. Winfield and Henrietta must be asleep.

"Well, now, Colonel. Let's see if there's anything left to eat." The dog's ears perked up, and Kellen laughed softly. "So you're hungry too, are you?" Colonel promptly sat at attention and watched Kellen's every move. Maybe the dog wasn't so bad after all.

Kellen glanced around the kitchen. The room was immaculate, nothing sitting out that he could nibble on. Normally he would have shied away from prowling through someone else's cupboards, but his stomach growled so loudly that even Colonel cocked his head to one side.

Besides, Guin wouldn't object to him helping himself, he rationalized. He proceeded to search and soon had the table spread with cold roast chicken, fresh baked bread, and even some wine. By the time he finished and had shared some with Colonel, Kellen realized how tired he was. He poured himself another glass of wine and sipped it slowly.

Looking at the dog, he said, "Wish your mistress would come home so I could talk to her."

In response, the dog lay next to Kellen and heaved a big sigh. Kellen nodded. "My feelings exactly."

He thought about how much Guin had changed, from the remote grieving girl he'd met at the town meeting, to a vibrant young woman who tackled any obstacle to reach her dream. The farm was secure. She had succeeded.

He drained his glass. If only he could be as confident about his resort. Tomorrow, he would talk to the pickers again. He'd take anyone with some experience. He might even take some who didn't have any if they showed potential. Which meant he'd have to supervise their work very carefully.

Kellen frowned. Guin should be home. He didn't want to leave without seeing her, but he didn't want to return to the kiln too soon and have a fight. All he wanted was to apologize. Maybe even kiss her again. Smiling at the thought, Kellen tipped his chair against the wall and closed his eyes.

It was Colonel's tongue slobbering in his ear that finally roused Kellen. His eyes still closed, he swatted at the dog. "Go away, Colonel." Kellen wiped his face with a napkin. "That's the thanks I get for sharing my dinner with you?"

Colonel whined and went to the door. He scratched at it, then turned back to Kellen, whining and barking.

"Okay, okay. I'll let you out. What time is it anyway?" Kellen ran a hand through his tousled hair and stumbled for the door. He pulled it open, intending to let Colonel slip through the narrow space, when an odd glow caught his eye. He stepped onto the porch, and stopped.

"Jesus, Mary, and Joseph!" Something was burning. The kiln?

Kellen raced across the yard, Colonel leading the way. They reached the rise that separated the fields from the house, and Kellen stopped. Fire surrounded the building. "Oh, Guin," he whispered in anguish at the loss of her crop.

"Mr. O'Roarke! Mr. O'Roarke!"

Kellen saw Pedro lumbering toward him. A new fear paralyzed him. He gripped Pedro's arms. "Where is she?"

"Inside. She called the alarm. Joel was unconscious out-side, and the doors were locked." The words spilled from the usually taciturn man.

Pickers threw buckets of water at the burning walls as fast as they could, but Kellen feared it was useless. Still, he had to hope—he ran to the backside of the building where the fire was just starting.

"Guin! Can you hear me?"

The silence froze his heart.

Chapter 17

"Get a long rope! And a wagon," Kellen yelled. Those around him raced to comply.

He grabbed the rope Pedro brought and climbed onto the back of the wagon. Tying a loop on the end of the rope, he threw it over the iron pulley extending from the second floor window. The rope fell slack. *Too short.* His heart raced.

God save her, he prayed, watching the flames lick the building. He tried again. This time the rope hooked over the pulley apparatus.

"Pedro, let this end out as far as you can."

Pedro quickly ran the rope through the pulley while Kellen jumped to catch the looped end and stuck his foot through it. "Take me up."

Several men leaped in to help Pedro. Kellen gripped the rope and rose jerkily toward the second floor window. Thick smoke swirled around him, and flames licked at the bottom of the kiln. All he thought about was Guin. He had to find her.

When he reached the window, he waved to the men to stop. "Hold it," he called out.

Smoke was already seeping through the cracks. Praying he wasn't too late, he clung to the rope with one arm and beat on the wooden shutters with his free hand until they opened. Smoke billowed out, blinding him and burning his eyes. He grabbed the ledge and hoisted himself inside.

"Guin!" The smoke was so thick. He couldn't see anything. "Guin!"

He scrambled to his feet and felt his way across the floor. He had to find her; he couldn't leave without her because . . . because he loved her. The truth seared through him like the fire that was enveloping the kiln. He couldn't let her die. She was here, somewhere. He wouldn't leave without her.

Heat from below burned through his shoes. He moved faster, fearing that neither of them would survive. Then he found her, slumped over a barrel. Steam rose from her wet clothing.

"Guin!" He inhaled smoke and coughed, unable to clear his lungs. Kellen swung her over his shoulder. He prayed he'd found her in time.

He hesitated. Oh, God, which way was the window? Panic swept through him. He couldn't have come this far only to let both of them die. Clutching Guin's wet skirt, he put it over his mouth.

The blanket of smoke parted for an instant, just long enough for Kellen to see the window. He carried Guin toward it. Flames licked between cracks in the floor. If only the floor didn't collapse before they got out. Finally they reached the window.

"Pedro! I've got her!" He grabbed the rope and shoved his foot through the loop, then stepped out the window.

Pedro and the others leaned against the weight and slowly released the rope.

"It's breaking!" someone called.

Kellen felt the rope jerk as the pulley separated from the burning wall and fell. He hit the ground hard, twisting to land beneath Guin. Hands grabbed them, and he scrambled to his feet, still holding Guin.

"Run!" he croaked. "Get away!"

Cradling Guin against him, Kellen ran with the other men as far as he could, then set her down. He turned to see flames engulf the window where he'd stood only moments before. Groans and cries rose from those around him. He gripped Guin tighter. The front of the kiln collapsed in a shower of sparks, followed by large sections of the two side-walls. Kellen flinched as Pedro ordered the pickers to continue throwing water on the flames, more to keep the fire from spreading to the dry grass than from any hope to save the kiln.

Guin started coughing. Kellen held her so she could breath.

She sat there, a dazed look in her eyes. "What . . . what happened?"

"You were in a fire."

"I . . . I thought—" she looked up at him. "I almost—" She clung to him and cried.

"Shh. It's okay." He stroked her hair, releasing the scent of burning wood and sulphur.

What if he hadn't returned? What if he hadn't found her in time? What if. . . . He shuddered as he clutched her to him. "I'll take you home."

Guin pushed away from him and shoved her hair back from her smudged face. Kellen saw anguish reflected in her eyes and wished he had the power to spare her.

"I can't go yet." She turned and stumbled toward the pickers who now kept a silent deathwatch over the kiln, the smoldering funeral pyre of her dreams.

His heart ached for her. She'd done nothing wrong. She'd been fair and good to everyone. This shouldn't happen to her. If God hadn't answered his prayers to find Guin, he might have railed at the injustice of it all. But she was alive, and no one else had been seriously hurt. That was what mattered most.

He signaled Pedro to join him. The man looked as grim as

Kellen felt. Kellen spotted some burns mixed with soot on Pedro's face. "I'm going for Dr. Jackson."

Pedro nodded. "Joel has bad bump on his head."

Kellen frowned. "Watch her, will you? Don't leave her side. As soon as you can, bring her and Joel to the house. I want to get to the bottom of this."

She felt . . . nothing. Her mind raced, but her body and her emotions were numb. Did that mean she was in shock? A timber shifted, spraying the air with more sparks.

She swallowed hard. *Pride goeth before destruction, and a haughty spirit before a fall.* The words echoed in her mind. How cocky she'd been. How she'd flaunted everything her father had taught her about not wishing too far ahead. She had spent and re-spent the money from these hops over and over in her head with plans and schemes. And now?

She'd lost more than half her crop. She didn't want to begin to refigure what that meant. Maybe she had enough to pay the interest on the loan. Maybe.

She had nothing with which to pay down the principal, and certainly nothing to live on for the coming year. The hop vines would come back in the spring, and she could reuse the poles. The other hop growers had their own crops to harvest and dry at the same time. So without her own kiln, her crop was useless. Even the simplest kiln would cost more than she could hope to raise. No one would loan her more money or extend her credit.

Overwhelmed, she groaned, then caught herself. *Be strong,* she told herself. Don't let them see your desperation. She took a quivering breath and slowly made her way through the crowd. She thanked the pickers for coming to her aid, and understood the relief in their eyes that they'd already been paid. When some asked if they should return next year, she hedged.

She realized Joel and Pedro were behind her, and had been following like her shadow. She turned to face them and saw their mouths grim, their shoulders slumped in defeat. Guin searched Joel's face. "What happened?"

"I don't know, Miss Guin. I went to get wood, and that's the last I remember." Joel turned toward the kiln and shook his head.

"He has a large bump on his head," Pedro said. "Somebody hit him."

She glanced sharply at the people congregated around them. "We'll talk later at the house," she said in a hushed voice.

"We take you home, Miss Guin," Pedro said.

She eyed him sharply. His tone held a hint of an order, just like— "But—"

"Men are watching so the fire doesn't spread," Joel said.

"Mr. Kellen, he went for doctor," Pedro added.

So, Kellen was behind her shadows.

Taking another painful look at the smoldering ruins, all that remained of her kiln and her crop, Guin turned and headed for home. She walked slowly, fighting to keep her shoulders from slumping, fighting to keep the threatening tears at bay. This was worse than an accident. Someone had attacked Joel. Someone had almost killed her.

They reached the house and found all the lights on. Henrietta and Winfield were awake and waiting, everyone talking at once; Kellen had roused them before leaving to fetch Dr. Jackson.

Henrietta swooped down on Guin and hustled her toward the hall. "Come, dear, let's clean you up a bit. You'll feel better then."

Guin doubted she'd ever feel better. Her throat hurt from

the smoke and she had coughing spasms that left her breath-less and sore. Although Henrietta soon had the soot off her face and arms and dressed her in a clean gown, Guin wanted nothing more than to escape, to take a bath and wash her hair, to sleep . . . and to forget what had happened.

Instead, she returned to the kitchen. Dr. Jackson was there, examining the lump on Joel's head. Then she saw Kellen leaning back in his chair, his arms crossed, his pene-trating gaze watching her every movement. There was some-thing different about him. He radiated an intensity that both reassured Guin and scared her.

She approached him slowly. "You saved my life," she said simply. "Thank you." There was so much more she should say, but didn't know how. Maybe she didn't need to tell him how scared she'd been, how frantic to first save the hops, and then to save herself.

She gasped. "Kellen, you're hurt!"

Dr. Jackson looked over from Joel. "What's that?"

"He's been burned," Guin said.

Dr. Jackson shook his head. "Fool boy. Shoulda told me in the first place." He came over to examine Kellen's arm. "Hmm. Not too bad. I'll clean it up first. Miz Talbot, you got any grease?"

Guin sank into a chair, knowing she'd just be in the way if she tried to help. Between Dr. Jackson, her grandmother, and Winfield, they seemed to have everything under con-trol.

In a few minutes, Dr. Jackson came to her. "How're you doing?"

She gave him a sad smile and a shrug. "Okay, I guess."

He nodded. "Drink up that soup your grandmother fixed."

"We need to talk about tonight." Kellen seemed surprised

how all conversation stopped. Everyone looked nervously at each other.

"I left the kiln for a few minutes to get wood." Joel rubbed the back of his head. "I remember nothing until Pedro found me. Someone hit me."

"I knew something was wrong when you didn't answer me." Guin pushed her hair aside. The acrid smell of smoke once more hovered around her. "Everything was going the way it should. Then, Joel left for more wood. When I discovered the fire, I called for him. I tried to put the fire out, but it was burning too strongly. It seemed to be everywhere at once." She shuddered at how close she had come to—

Kellen turned to Guin. "Why didn't you get out when the fire first started?"

Guin looked at him. "Because the door was blocked."

Kellen's chair hit the floor as he sprang to his feet. "What the hell?"

"When I came downstairs to find Joel, the fire was burning the full length of the wall. I tried to push the door open, but it wouldn't move. Something blocked it from the outside."

"Jesus—" Kellen said. "That means someone knew you were inside and. . . ."

He didn't have to finish. Everyone knew the ending. The only sound in the room was the click of Colonel's claws as he pattered across the room to Guin and nudged her hand with his nose. She stroked his head, her gaze still locked with Kellen's until he began to pace the room, his finger tapping against his lips.

"So the question is, who did this? Who started the fire?" He turned to the others. "Any ideas?"

Wide-eyed, Joel and Pedro looked questioningly at each other and shrugged their shoulders. Henrietta, Dr. Jackson, and Winfield shook their heads.

"Who benefits from you losing your crop?" Kellen asked Guin.

She thought for a moment. "No one really. Mr. Johnston said there's already a shortage in other parts, so the price for our valley's crop is high. The only one who's hurt is me. I can't pay off my loan and I won't have enough money to support myself for the next year."

"Damn. This makes no sense at all."

"Of course, it doesn't." Guin sighed and wearily rubbed the back of her neck. "But then, neither did Winfield's accident."

"Do you think the two are related?"

"Who knows?" Guin slumped in her chair, the weight of her loss more draining than her exhaustion. "At this point, there's nothing more we can do. Except wait for the fire to cool."

Henrietta approached Guin, tears in her eyes. "My poor girl," she said gently clasping Guin's face between her hands.

Guin felt tears well up in her own eyes. "What am I going to do, Grandmother?" she whispered. "What am I going to do?"

She let Henrietta guide her upstairs and tuck her into bed before going to her own temporary room.

Alone, lying in the early dawn light, Guin could still hear the deafening roar of the flames, the crackling as it devoured the dry wood and hops. Thick smoke was still in every breath she took, the smell of destruction that had overpowered the sulphuric fragrance of her drying crop.

She had been fortunate not to be burned. Her hands and face had been protected by the barrel she'd been lying on. If she'd slumped to the floor, she'd be living in pain and disfigured by scars for the rest of her life. As it was, the scars were inside and didn't show. Images of her kiln, of its black and smoldering remains, would haunt her forever.

She feared she wouldn't be able to sleep, that her mind would relive the fire until she went crazy. Her body's need for rest was stronger than her anxiety, and soon she fell into a deep slumber.

In the kitchen, Kellen sent Joel and Pedro to the kiln to keep watch. He stared grimly at the two who remained with him.

"Miss Guin is certainly stalwart under the circumstances," Winfield said. "Most females would have fallen to pieces after such a grueling ordeal."

Dr. Jackson nodded. "Miss Guin, now she's made of fine stuff. Don't come any better than her. But this . . . this is a mighty terrible thing that's happened."

"It is quite clear that someone set the fire on purpose," Winfield said. "Would it be prudent to alert the sheriff?"

Dr. Jackson nodded. "Might not be a bad idea."

Restless, Kellen paced the floor. "I want to catch this guy myself, and smash his face in. If we acted as if we thought it was an accident, we could wait for the guilty party to relax and make a mistake."

"You mean like to leave out some honey in the open so as to catch us some flies?" Dr. Jackson asked.

"Yeah." He stopped and frowned at Winfield. "But then again, we tried that after Winfield's accident, and it hasn't helped at all."

Kellen looked from one to the other. They each cared about Guin, each was concerned about her welfare. At last he nodded. "Dr. Jackson, you go back to town and report our suspicions to the sheriff, but ask him to keep it quiet. Someone almost murdered Guin tonight, and we're not going to give him another chance. We'll set a schedule for watching the house and Guin. One of us, or Joel, or Pedro must be with her at all times."

From the porch, Kellen watched Dr. Jackson leave as the sun was beginning to lighten the sky. He returned to the kitchen to find Winfield cleaning up.

"Can't that wait until morning?"

"No, sir. It would drive me batty knowing it is here. Mrs. Talbot has gone to bed. You take my room. I will nap later."

"No, Winfield. I'm too angry."

"I understand, sir. Still, perhaps some quiet time in the parlor would help. I will watch Miss Guin for now and explain to Mrs. Talbot our plans to keep both ladies safe."

With a weary nod, Kellen left him and checked to be sure the doors were secure. Colonel followed behind him, a reassuring presence. Kellen settled into a chair in the parlor and rubbed the dog's ears as he leaned his own head against the wall. "We have to keep her safe, Colonel."

Kellen awoke, disoriented at first until he realized he was lying on the settee in Guin's parlor. A quick glance out the window told him it was late afternoon; it was his turn to follow Guin. Stiff from sleeping on the cramped sofa, he rolled to a sitting position and stretched.

Henrietta would grumble about turning the parlor into a temporary guest room, but with Winfield still at the house, there were no other options. Unless, of course, Henrietta wanted Kellen to sleep in Guin's room. As he made his way to the kitchen, he imagined Henrietta's apoplectic expression if he had voiced that idea.

He glanced out the window and saw Dr. Jackson sitting with Henrietta on the porch. They were gazing into each other's eyes as if they'd newly discovered each other. Did he now have to worry they were so engrossed with each other that they'd forget to keep an eye on Guin?

His thoughts turned grim again while he sluiced water on his face and through his hair. He should be so lucky when it came to staying with Guin. She was so damned independent, she'd probably resist a guard following her around. Even though she'd almost been murdered last night.

He mopped his face, pausing to hold the towel to his cheeks. Who was behind the fire? Who could have done this to her? From everything he'd seen and heard since he arrived in Spring Valley, Guin Talbot had no enemies. No one wanted her to fail. Even Jonathan Clarke had nothing to gain by Guin's loss.

After changing into a clean shirt, Kellen left the house. "Where is she?" he asked Dr. Jackson.

The doctor pointed across the field. "At the kiln."

Kellen grimaced and walked swiftly in that direction. Joel stood by Guin, and Kellen nodded at him to leave. Kellen stood quietly while Guin circled the perimeter of what was once the kiln, reduced now to smoldering rubble.

He watched as she poked dispiritedly at the charred remains with a long stick. Her shoulders were hunched, her chin drooped. She sighed heavily, coughed a little, then straightened, as if refusing to be defeated by this setback. In that moment, his admiration for her strength overwhelmed him. He'd never met a woman like her before. He felt humbled by her certainty that she would survive.

"Doesn't look any better in the daylight, does it?" he asked.

She turned at his words, and he caught the anguish in her eyes, the despair she fought so hard to hide before she steeled herself and once again cloaked her feelings.

"You don't have to pretend with me," he said.

Guin nodded, but said nothing. Instead, she turned to the kiln and continued poking at the remains. "I'd hoped that if I flooded the burrs they'd somehow survive," she said finally.

He came up behind her and placed a hand on her shoulder. "Nothing could have survived that blaze." He felt her shudder and cursed his thoughtlessness.

"I suppose you're behind my watchdogs?"

He didn't need to see her face to know she was scowling. "You mean someone staying within sight of you? Yes, I'm responsible. Everyone agreed."

"Everything is gone. I have nothing more to lose."

"Guin, someone burned down your kiln last night. You were inside. It's better to think they knew you were inside, and take steps to keep them from getting a second chance. I don't want to assume you're right . . . and find out the hard way that you were wrong."

She shrugged. "I suppose. But I don't want to live this way."

"It won't be for long." He saw the aimless way she walked, the pain that pinched her face as she studied the charred ruins of her life.

She stopped and her expression took on that resilient look he'd come to admire. "I have to stop doing this. It's not going to change anything."

He nodded. "Shall we go back to the house? Your grandmother probably has some lemonade, or you could take a nap," he suggested.

"No, Kellen. I need to get away."

"Away?" He panicked for a minute. Where would she go?

"Not far. I just need to get away from the farm for a little while." She looked at him for a moment as if assessing what she was about to say. "I'd like to see your resort."

"You what?" That was the last thing he'd expected to hear from her.

"I want to see your resort. At least one of us has dreams that . . ." she waved her stick toward the ruins. "That haven't gone up in flames. The harvest is over for me. All I can do is wait until I know how much money I'll get for the hops I've already delivered. Show me your resort," she repeated.

"Well. Okay." Not knowing what else to say, Kellen followed behind her as she walked to the barn. He helped her saddle the horses, then held out his hands to give her a boost.

"I should tell Grandmother I'm leaving," Guin said.

He nodded. "We will." He led the horses to the porch where Dr. Jackson and Henrietta were still sitting. "I'm taking Guin for a ride."

Dr. Jackson nodded "That's a fine idea. Fill her head with something besides the . . ." He waved his hand in the general direction of the kiln.

"Be careful, dear. Don't stay out too long."

"Yes, Grandmother."

Kellen found it interesting that Henrietta wasn't insisting she go along as a chaperone for propriety's sake. "I'll bring her back safely, ma'am."

Kellen motioned for Guin to follow him to the road, and soon they were galloping toward the foothills.

He didn't know if he should take her to the resort now. Was this the right time to show her the project he had everything tied up in, a dream he could lose so easily, just as she had lost her dream?

Kellen was relieved, actually, that Guin hadn't asked to go somewhere else. Until they knew who was responsible for the kiln, he didn't want to take her to town, or take her too far from home. The resort should be safe. Hell, he couldn't even get a full crew of workers up there.

The closer they got, the more excited he was. He couldn't explain why it was suddenly so important to share his dream with Guin; to show her what he had already accomplished and what he hoped to attain. Except, perhaps, because he loved her.

She understood about dreams. She knew what it meant to want something so fiercely you'd do anything to get it. She knew the bitter taste of failure.

They turned down a long lane, finally approaching his property, which was marked by a split-rail fence. They slowed as they approached the gate. It hung open, and all Kellen could hear were the sounds of twittering birds and rustling leaves.

Guin gasped as the main building came into view. "Oh, my! I had no idea." Her eyes widened as she took it all in. For a moment, she seemed to have forgotten her own worries. Kellen hoped his dream would captivate and draw her into the enchantment he was trying to create.

"I'll show you around," Kellen said. He led the horses to a nearby tree and tied them off, then helped Guin dismount.

His hands around her waist, he let her slide down the length of him, felt her little gasp as her breasts rubbed against his chest. As he set her on the ground, he looked into her brown eyes, smoldering with the beginnings of awareness. She felt light in his arms, light but strong. Her curves were subtle, and he found them much more intriguing than obvious voluptuousness.

Confusion filled her eyes and she stepped back, putting some distance between them. Kellen released her, reluctant to lose the spark of heat that had flared between them. The loud squawking of a jay startled him. He glanced over his shoulder and saw the workmen had left for the day, and the sun had started its descent.

251

"I'll show you around," he said again as he took Guin's elbow. He suddenly felt shy about showing her what he'd done. Her approval seemed so very important, more important than he would ever have imagined. He took a deep breath to steady himself, then guided her inside the largest building. The walls were up and the roof was on, but it still lacked doors and windows.

"This is the main lodge. We're standing in the lobby right now, and that's where the guests will register," he said pointing across the room.

Guin nodded, but said nothing, and the little boy in Kellen shriveled. Maybe this hadn't been such a good idea after all. Trying to ignore his rising misgivings, he led her into another room.

"This is the tea room."

Her eyes widened as she stared at the stone fireplace rising to the distant ceiling. "That's the biggest fireplace I've ever seen."

Relieved that she liked it, Kellen smiled. "I want this room to be inviting, even in winter. I don't want this to be just a summer resort."

"That's a good idea."

Encouraged, Kellen led her through the other rooms, including the common dining area and huge kitchen, which was almost finished. He smiled at the covetous look on her face when she saw all the equipment.

Guin sighed. "Makes my kitchen look pretty pathetic."

"It's not what's in the kitchen that counts, but what comes out of it." Kellen smiled at the blush rising to Guin's cheeks.

"I'd still like to try some of these utensils," she said as her hand caressed the large sausage stuffer.

"That one would be a little big for you and your grandmother's needs."

Guin shrugged as she removed her hand. "It'd still be fun."

"Let's go outside," Kellen suggested, afraid that if he watched her wistful expression much longer he'd end up giving her everything.

He took a gravel path across the yard and up a slight rise. "These are the cabins," he said, gesturing at the half dozen finished buildings.

"They look nice from the outside," she said.

"Wait until you see the inside." Kellen took Guin's hand and led her into the first cottage. "This one's for a family. There are bedrooms on that side of the main room for the children and the governess or nurse. The parents have two rooms, with a dressing area in between."

"You seem to have thought of everything," Guin said lightly. Kellen caught a tightness around her eyes, and he worried she was beginning to think about the loss of her kiln again.

"It'll look better once the furniture arrives. And the silk draperies. And . . . and I've ordered books for the shelves and there'll be games stacked in the corners that families can play together." He stopped and glanced around the room. Could she see it the way he did? Could she see his dream?

"I'll show you another cabin," he said when she only nodded. He led her up the path, past several more family-sized cottages, and into a much smaller one that was already furnished.

"This one is for single people or couples." He watched her enter the two-room cabin and walk through it.

Her hands touched lightly on the bookcase. She disappeared into the bedroom, and he followed her to the doorway. He saw her approach the window and gaze out.

And he saw the grim line that was her mouth, the hard

253

look in her eyes. "What's wrong?" he asked, full of disappointment.

"Nothing. I like it all very much. Everything's beautiful. Your guests should be very pleased."

He heard the words, but there was a flatness in her tone. "But?"

"Hmm?" She seemed distracted.

"There's something you don't like."

"I like everything, Kellen. I just told you it's beautiful," she said, impatience creeping into her voice.

"Then what's wrong?"

"Nothing's wrong," she snapped. She sighed and in a quieter voice said, "Nothing to do with you."

She turned away, but not before he saw her rub her forehead. She seemed smaller somehow, not the strong Guin he'd come to love. It was as if she was trying to shrink into herself.

He stepped up behind her and settled his hands gently on her shoulders. She flinched, then stood stiffly when he turned her around to face him. "Please tell me, Guin. What's wrong?"

Chapter 18

She sighed heavily. "It's nothing, Kellen. Just one of my headaches. Lord knows, I'm entitled after everything that's happened."

He led her back to the sitting room and sat her down on the window seat. Gently he massaged her shoulders, feeling the tightness, the tension that radiated from her, and he wished he could help her.

"Do you get these headaches often?" She nodded, her eyes closed, her breathing deep but ragged. "What do you usually do when you get them?"

"Depends. If I'm working, I try to ignore it and keep going."

He grimaced. That sounded like something she'd do, all right, Kellen thought. Pretend it isn't there, and it will go away. As she'd probably hoped on occasion that he would.

"And the other times?"

"Sometimes if I lie down in a dark room it goes away. If it's really bad, I take some powders that Dr. Jackson's given me."

"How bad is it now?"

"Pretty bad."

"Do you want to lie down here?"

"No. I don't think it'd help. The room's too bright."

Kellen thought for a moment while he continued to gently rub Guin's shoulders. His fingers eased along her neck, and caught in her hair, which she had tied up in its usual knot. Without thinking, he tugged at the ribbon holding it in place.

Her hair tumbled around her shoulders.

"Kellen!"

"Shush. Your hair's so tight that's probably what's giving you the headaches," he chided.

She shook her head in disagreement, but didn't argue. While he enjoyed the respite from her arguing, he missed her pointed retorts.

"I have an idea. Come with me," he said.

"I'd rather stay here."

He shook his head. "My idea's better."

She grumbled, but followed him outside, shading her eyes from the glare of the late afternoon sun. He took the path up the hill, turning every few yards to make sure she was still behind him. At length, they reached the springs.

He took her into the grotto. The rock walls and ceiling shielded most of the summer sun. Bubbling water gurgled in the natural rock pool.

"Take your clothes off," he ordered.

"I beg your pardon?" Guin said.

"Don't be silly, Guin. I'm going to leave you here. Take off your clothes and get in the water. It'll feel wonderful, and you'll be better in no time."

She looked skeptically from him to the pool. "What's in there?"

He smiled. "Nothing but mineral water. I think you'll be surprised. If you need anything, holler. I won't be too far. Just far enough to give you privacy."

"How considerate of you," she said irreverently.

"I keep telling you that I'm a nice fellow, but you don't believe me," Kellen said, feigning wounded feelings.

Despite the pain in her head, Guin smiled. "All right, I won't fight you. Now go so I can try this miracle cure of yours."

"You won't be disappointed," Kellen said. "I'll be outside if you need me."

Guin waved him away, then stood quietly for a moment, breathing deeply to counter the rhythmic pounding in her head. She sat on a flat dry rock and slowly rolled her stockings down. The simple act of unbuttoning her high-necked, long-sleeved blouse was liberating. The air, churned by the water's movement, swept across her arms and her chest.

The pounding in her head intensified. Still hesitant, but desperate for anything that promised relief, she shed the remainder of her clothes and slid into the water. The warmth enveloped her, and the buoyancy surprised her. Eyes closed, Guin leaned her head against the edge of the pool, and let herself float in the water. The gentle bobbing motion soothed her, and the tightness in her body loosened as her fears and doubts ebbed away.

Kellen was right. The water was wonderful, almost miraculous. When people heard about it, they would flock to the resort. Kellen would succeed.

She had come around to believing Kellen was not the snake-oil peddler she'd first thought. He had a deeper side. He obviously cared for Winfield, and treated him more like family than a servant. He had a sense of humor and was quick to laugh at himself. He'd even risked his own life to save her from the fire. She'd also seen the dark, passionate man who lay beneath a veneer of charm and sophistication, the man who made her forget the rules and the obstacles between them.

She sighed and languidly moved her arms back and forth in the water. This was not the time to worry about obstacles. She kicked her legs gently, savoring the ability to stretch full length in the water.

Opening her eyes, she looked around the grotto. The opening faced away from the bright sun, allowing only subdued lighting inside. The rock walls glistened with moisture, reflecting shimmers of light that angled off the pool. She took a deep breath and felt lethargy take over. The tension, the tightness, and the resistance were gone. Completely gone.

She had Kellen to thank for that, and she would do so when she rejoined him. Climbing unsteadily from the pool, Guin realized she had nothing to dry off with except her clothes. No matter. Surprised that she was relaxed enough not to be bothered, she used her skirt to pat herself dry, then eased into her drawers and chemise.

"I brought you a tow—" Kellen stopped at the grotto entrance. "Sorry. I didn't know you'd gotten out."

She could have reached for some clothes to hold before her, but she didn't. He could have tossed the towel to her and stepped outside. But he didn't. She knew the damp cotton fabric clung to her legs, her breasts, revealing her feminine curves.

Swallowing hard, she saw the questioning in his eyes. If he took a step toward her, she would melt into his arms, share the kisses he offered. If he took a step forward, she'd forget all the reasons why she shouldn't.

He stepped forward.

Reluctant to leave the bower where he'd found such happiness, Kellen pushed himself up on one elbow and leaned over Guin. He picked up her hand and trailed kisses across the palm and smiled when she shivered.

"Cold?"

"What do you think?"

"I think you're beautiful." She blushed and he bent to kiss the spot behind her ear he now knew was sensitive.

She squealed, clapping her hands over her mouth. "I need to go. Grandmother will be getting worried if I don't show up soon."

Kellen stood and pulled her to her feet, then handed her one piece of clothing at a time, enjoying his view of her body in the daylight. All too soon she was ready, and he dressed quickly. She started toward the path and he stopped her.

"What?"

"Your hair is beautiful in the sunlight." Kellen ran his fingers through the long tresses one more time before she smiled and stepped away. He watched with regret as she twisted her hair into a long coil, then rolled it into its usual knot. He sighed at the loss of her luxuriant hair draped over her shoulders.

Silently, he led the way to the horses and helped her mount. What with the turmoil last night and sleeping most of the day, he'd lost an entire day. Somehow it didn't bother him as it would have any other time. He couldn't think of a better way to spend his hours than with Guin in his arms.

Maybe they could become partners. He'd proposed it before, but Guin had adamantly objected. Now that she'd had a chance to see the resort, see his dream coming to life, she had to view it in a different light. She would want to help him, especially after her own dreams had gone up in flames; she better than anyone understood how important this was to him. When the resort succeeded, she'd share in the profits, which would cushion the financial loss of the fire.

He'd wait, though. Give her a little more time to think about the resort.

When they reached the bottom of the foothills and started down the road, Guin could still feel the languorous sense of well-being from the springs. From her time with Kellen. She'd never dreamed being with a man would be like that.

She took a deep breath, savoring the sights and sounds and smells of a sunny fall day.

Kellen moved his horse closer to Guin. "We should talk about the spur."

"What about the spur?" Guin brought her horse to an abrupt halt. All sense of well-being evaporated.

"You saw the resort, and all I've put into it. And you can see how important the spur line is to the whole project. I was thinking that after last night—"

"Was that what this afternoon was all about? Your spur line?" Her mouth twisted in anger. She could not believe she had been so stupid, so easily beguiled into thinking Kellen might really care about her. She thought of how she'd opened her heart, given herself to him, all the time believing they were sharing something special. "This afternoon was just a ploy to soften me up, wasn't it?"

Kellen didn't answer. His silence was as condemning as a confession. "It wasn't a ploy, Guin," he said at last.

But the denial came too late. She felt used and dirty, and wanted nothing more than to escape from him and hide her shame.

"I thought you'd change your mind about the spur line after you saw what I was building. Our being together just happened."

"Of course, it did." She scowled at him. "You don't do anything without a reason, without a plan for how it's going to work for you. That's the kind of person you are. You don't care who gets hurt along the way, as long as you get what you want."

"That's not true," Kellen objected.

"It certainly is. Look at poor Winfield. You sent him out to do some dirty work for you, and what happened? He almost got himself killed. And this afternoon? I thought it meant something," she said, tears brimming in her eyes. She refused to blink, refused to push the tears over the edge to stream down her cheeks.

"I'm never going to change my mind about the spur line, Kellen O'Roarke. Don't ever set foot on my land again." Guin tugged on the reins, wheeling her horse around, then nudged the mare sharply with her heels and galloped across the fields toward home.

The farm was where she belonged. She knew who she was there, she knew what she was supposed to do. Sure she had problems, but they were her problems to solve. Alone.

How had she ever dared think she was something else? For a time, Kellen had made her believe she was desirable, had made her want to wear pretty dresses and curl her hair.

How many times had he looked at her with those smoldering blue eyes of his, making her pulse quicken? Every time he touched her hand and sent shivers along her spine. He stole kisses under the moonlight and made her yearn for more. Then today, he had shown her what that more was, and she knew she would never be the same.

Now she knew what it was she had hungered for all these weeks. Now she knew she would live the rest of her life without it. She had trusted him, had given him her heart, and he had tried to use it to his advantage. She'd never trust again, not like that.

She'd been wrong to change her opinion of him; her first impression had been correct. He was a charismatic snake-oil peddler. She had been suckered along with everyone else in Spring Valley who thought Kellen O'Roarke was so wonderful. She would never forgive his betrayal.

Beauregard Jackson sat on the porch glider and glanced at the woman sitting next to him. She sat straight, but didn't seem as stiff as before. He smiled to himself. Yessir, Miz Talbot was might prickly on the outside, but he'd bided his time and slowly worked his way through the thicket of thorns to find the soft rose hiding within. He moved his foot to start the glider moving again and caught the momentary tightness around Henrietta's lips as she kept her balance. She was such a tiny thing, her feet didn't quite meet up with the porch deck.

"It's a mighty nice day, Miz Talbot," he said slowly.

"Hmph. It's warmer than I'd like." Henrietta waved her fan, setting loose wisps of white hair floating around her head. "At least it's not as humid as home."

Beauregard chuckled. "I don't know what it's like up north, but you got nothing on the south for hot and humid."

Henrietta sighed. "I suppose. Something has to make your crops grow so well."

"That's it exactly, Miz Talbot. Heat and wet air and rich, red soil. Nothing can beat it."

Henrietta rolled her eyes, but did not respond to the challenge. "Would you like more lemonade?"

"In time. Right now, I'm just enjoying sitting here in the shade with a pretty girl."

Henrietta threw him a disgusted look. "You don't give up, do you, Dr. Jackson?"

He smiled broadly. "No, ma'am, I don't. But . . ."

He hesitated. He knew what he wanted to say. He just wasn't sure what reception he'd get. He'd made progress the last few months. At least she sat next to him and talked to him, which was a far sight better than when she'd first come to town. Was he rushing things? Well, he wasn't getting any younger, and at their age, who knew how long they had left.

He took a deep breath for courage. Carpe diem! Seize the day! "I was thinking, Miz Talbot, that our times together are mighty pleasant."

Henrietta gave a half shrug. "I guess."

That wasn't the enthusiastic reception he'd hoped for, but at least she hadn't contradicted him. Encouraged, he continued. "We've been spending a fair bit of time together too, wouldn't you say?"

"If you count all the times you've come to see Mr. Somerset and stayed for dinner, I guess you could say so."

"Winfield's situation, that was a terrible thing that happened, but I like to see the good that comes out of those trials."

Henrietta looked at him sharply. "Is all this going somewhere or is this just you making conversation to pass the time?"

Beau sighed. He hated the northern way of rushing into things. He preferred to sidle up next to something and get a feel for it before he made a damned fool of himself. Feeling suddenly very hot, he mopped his forehead with a giant handkerchief.

"Are you all right, Dr. Jackson? You look a little pale. Stay here and I'll get you something cold to drink." Henrietta stood and started to leave.

"Wait!" Without thinking, Beau grabbed her hand and tugged. She tumbled into his lap and would have sprung up if he hadn't held her fast. "I better say this quick 'fore I lose my nerve. Miz Talbot, I think you're one fine woman and I'd be most honored if you'd be my wife."

There. He'd said it. He couldn't breathe, though, not until she answered. Her mouth opened, but nothing came out. Her eyes searched his and he felt her resistance seep away as she ever so gently leaned against him.

"Why, Dr. Jackson . . . Beau, that's very nice of you."

"Oh, it's more than nice, Miz Talbot. I mean it. I'd be mighty proud to have you on my arm for the rest of our lives."

Henrietta's lashes fluttered down and a shy smile lit her face. "I see. Well. That's a big step for a woman to take."

"It is that."

"I wouldn't be coming to you totally empty-handed, you know."

"I don't care if you're rich or poor. We'd be comfortable in my house in town, but it's not too far so as to be a problem to see Guin," Beau said in a rush, afraid Henrietta would turn him down because she felt obligated to Guin.

Relieved that Henrietta hadn't refused him outright, Beau watched as she stared off into the distance. He didn't want to break the spell for fear she'd reject his offer. Better to wait, to give her time to work her way through whatever objections she put up for herself to consider. Patience. That's what he needed.

Finally she looked back at him and said, "It's not as if I have much waiting for me when I return home."

Lukewarm, but better than a rejection. Beau felt his heart begin to pound. He said nothing, only nodded.

"When I first met you, I wasn't very nice," Henrietta said in a quiet voice.

"Well, now, I wouldn't fret about that."

"It was the war, and what it did to my Daniel."

"How long's it been since you lost him?" Beau asked gently. Even though he knew the answer, he sensed talking about it would help bring Henrietta to the decision he wanted.

She sighed. "Ten years since I buried him, but he hadn't been the same for much longer than that."

"That's a long time for a woman to love a man. And be without him."

Henrietta looked at him with a thoughtful expression. "Do you think so?"

"Yes, ma'am, I do. I think Mr. Talbot, he was a right lucky fellow to have a good woman like you standing by him." Beau paused a moment to let his words sink in. "But I don't think he would have wanted you to be alone for the rest of your life. I think he'd expect you to grieve and then move on, like we do with everything else that comes along in life. The good and the bad. Keep him in a special place in your heart. I'd like to think your heart's big enough to hold a special place for me too."

Henrietta smiled. "Oh, Beau, you do have a way with words."

"So do you, if they's the right ones."

Her smile broadened. "Yes, Beau, I accept your proposal."

He let out a whoop and kissed her hard, surprising himself, and her, if her startled expression was any indication. "Miz Talbot . . . may I call you Henrietta? Henrietta, you've made me the happiest man in the valley. Maybe even in all of California."

She laughed, really laughed, and she seemed transformed before his eyes. He saw how she must have been before the war and the loss of her husband. He smiled, knowing he'd brought her back. "I'm thinking we don't need us a long engagement."

"I suppose you're right," Henrietta said. "We could marry after New Year's."

"Damnation, woman. I'm not waiting that long. I was thinking October."

"That seems so hasty. What will people think—"

Beau roared with laughter and held Henrietta tight so she wouldn't fall off his lap. "At our age, I don't think folks'll think anything of it, least whys, not anyone in the valley. If'n you want family from New York, we'll telegraph tomorrow. If they want to come, they can get themselves here in time."

"Oh. Well." The blush that spread across her cheeks was most becoming. "I guess you're right about not waiting. I don't think there's anyone who would make the trip just to see an old lady make a fool of herself."

"Henrietta Talbot, when I look at you, I don't see an old lady. I see a warm, caring, vibrant female. I see the woman I love."

Before he could say more, he heard rapid hoof beats heading toward the barn. One horse. That was not a good sign. From the quick turn of Henrietta's head, she'd heard it too.

She slid off Beau's lap in spite of his protestations. "No, Beau, I'm not going to have my granddaughter find me in a compromising position."

He groaned. "But—"

"We'll tell her, but after all my preaching to her about her behavior, I can't let her see me—us—this way."

"Fine, but let me do the talking, all right?" He sat on the glider with Henrietta, forcing himself to appear calm. Inside, he wanted to scoop up this little lady and have her all to himself.

At last, Guin came around the corner of the house, glowering like a thundercloud. She faltered when she spotted them, and Beau wasn't sure this was the best time to share his good news.

"Afternoon, Miss Guin," he said when she reached the steps.

"Dr. Jackson. Grandmother." She continued up the steps and across the porch toward the door.

"Guin—"

Beau tried to signal Henrietta to wait, to not share their

news yet, but it was too late. Guin had already stopped and was looking expectantly at her grandmother. He sensed the tension radiating from the girl and hoped nothing anyone said now would change Henrietta's mind.

"Guin, dear, Beau—Dr. Jackson and I have something to tell you."

"What is it?" Guin rubbed her forehead in that absent way Beau had seen her do when her headaches came on.

"Maybe we should wait until Guin's feeling better. Can I help your headache?" Beau asked.

Guin waved him off. "No. I'll be all right. What is it, Grandmother?"

Beau didn't like the impatience in Guin's voice, a tone that told him this was not the time to share good news. But there was no stopping Henrietta.

"Guin, the good doctor has asked me to marry him, and I have accepted."

Guin paled, and for a moment Beau thought she would faint. He glanced at Henrietta and saw that she had finally noticed something was wrong with Guin.

"That's very nice. I'm pleased for both of you. If you don't mind, I need to go lie down." Guin turned and went into the house.

"Oh, dear," Henrietta said. "That wasn't at all the reaction I'd expected."

Beau shook his head. "I don't think she really heard what you told her. Something's upset her something fierce."

"Well, of course, with the fire—"

"No, I think it's something more than that. I think I know what, or who, is at the bottom of it."

Beau refused to say more, but he'd find that Kellen O'Roarke and throttle him for hurting the girl. Then he'd figure out how to fix things between those two young people, because he had a sinking feeling that Henrietta would not leave Guin if she thought her granddaughter was miserable. Beau had worked too long to bring Henrietta to this point to lose her over some foolish squabble between two pig-headed young'uns.

Chapter 19

Kellen leaned against a wall, distancing himself from the others who crowded the lavishly decorated ballroom. The party was a gala San Francisco affair, another in a long string of social gatherings he'd attended in the past week. The small orchestra performed flawlessly. The food was rich and the liquor smooth. The women were beautifully dressed, the men handsome in their evening attire.

He polished off his drink. Here it was, everything he'd dreamed of having, everything he'd worked so hard for was within his grasp.

But he didn't want it anymore. Disgusted with himself, he pushed away from the wall, then spotted a woman with a cloud of blond hair working her way through the crowd toward him. Julia Clarke. Kellen smiled to himself at how she'd changed from the pouty girl he'd met in Spring Valley. She was definitely up to something, but Kellen sensed she was up to something that went far beyond him. In spite of that, for some unfathomable reason, Julia had appointed herself his promoter.

Defiantly ignoring her father's reproachful looks, every evening she had introduced Kellen to important people, people who'd expressed great interest in the resort. When could they buy shares of the resort? Could they be the first guests? They wanted to invest in the project. These were shrewd businessmen. It heartened Kellen to know they thought the resort would be a good investment.

Yet, he didn't care any more. Guin's expression when he'd asked her about the spur line was seared into his memory, filling his every waking moment with guilt. How could he have done that to her? How could he have made love to her, and then been so stupid?

He replaced his drink with one from a passing waiter's tray and took a healthy swig. Damnation. What was he going to do? He'd fallen in love with a farm girl, a girl who would be totally out of place at this ball, but who had more sincerity and integrity in her little finger than all these people combined. He'd been more comfortable, more at peace with himself, sitting under a shade tree with her than at any of the social gatherings he'd attended since returning to the city.

He'd won, if response to his resort was any indication. He'd open for business and be wildly successful. But somewhere along the line, he'd lost his soul. He'd become like these people, viewing others only as opportunities to climb higher, never as friends. Since his return to the city, it hadn't taken long for him to realize that exposing Jonathan Clarke's perfidy to this group would only make himself a laughing stock for his naiveté. Better to continue on his own path and open the resort. Succeeding, and knowing that Clarke knew he'd succeeded, was revenge enough. The sweet taste of success was like ashes in his mouth.

"Kellen, darling!" Julia said when she finally reached him. She slid her arm through his and squeezed him close to her. "Smile, darling. Daddy's watching," she said with a bright smile that did not carry to her calculating eyes.

Kellen smiled for her. "When will you tell me why should I care if Daddy is watching?"

She glanced in her father's direction. A satisfied gleam crept into her eyes. "I can tell you now. It's because, darling, you are my hero. My salvation."

Kellen frowned and looked at her. Perhaps Julia had consumed too much champagne punch tonight. "You still haven't answered my question."

"Put your head close to mine, as if we're having a tête-à-tête." She gave him a winsome smile and this time she looked sincerely happy.

In spite of himself, Kellen did as she asked. "Now that we're having our tête-à-tête, tell me what you're up to. Why put on this act for your father?"

"Oh, Kellen." She laughed as if he'd just said the most outrageous thing and rapped his arm lightly with her fan. "Such an amusing man you are."

Kellen jerked away. "Wha—"

She pulled him back to her. "Now, don't go getting all huffy. Smile," she whispered through clenched teeth.

Only because she'd helped him so much since his return to the city, Kellen forced himself to comply. "Is this better?"

"Much better, yes. So, you'd like to know why you are my hero and salvation?"

"I admit, I'm intrigued," Kellen said, hoping Julia would finally explain what she was up to.

"Oh, oh. Daddy's coming this way. I'll have to hurry this. Daddy found out you came to dinner that night in Spring Valley, and he was so upset that he ordered me back to San Francisco. Which is exactly where I wanted to be in the first place. No offense, but that dreary little village was going to be the death of me if I had to stay much longer." Julia scanned the crowd again and grimaced. "Now where did he go? Anyway, I've met a wonderful man. He's handsome, though not as handsome as you, but terribly rich, and as much as you've come to mean to me, a girl has to pay attention to those things."

"I still don't understand." Kellen couldn't believe he was having this conversation. "How am I your salvation?"

"Well, Daddy's so afraid I'll marry you that he'll be ecstatic when Richard asks for my hand. So my happy future is all because of you, Kellen. That's why I've introduced you to people who can help you." She stood on tiptoes and frowned. "Come with me. I have to tell you one more thing."

Kellen followed her from the ballroom, even more surprised when she led him into the garden. She continued walking until she reached a small gazebo, well lighted under the full moon.

She glanced toward the house, then said, "I'm not a very nice person, Kellen. I'm selfish and spoiled. But I'm not cruel. I heard Daddy talking to his assistant, and he's up to something in Spring Valley. I don't know what it is. I'm telling you because even though I despise the dreary little place, the people were nice. I don't want them hurt. Oh, oh. Here he comes. Kiss me."

Julia threw her arms around Kellen, and he instinctively wrapped his arms around her and kissed her back.

"Julia!"

Kellen froze at the sound of Clarke's voice, even though he'd been expecting it. He eased his grip on Julia and turned to face her father. Kellen almost laughed at the older man's apoplectic expression, but forced himself to look serious.

"Julia, get back to the party. We'll talk later. You, young man, leave my daughter alone. I forbid you to have any contact with her. Do you understand?"

Kellen looked at Julia with what he hoped was a longing expression, then back at Clarke. "I don't—"

"Do you understand?" Clarke spat out the words, his hands clenched at his sides.

Kellen nodded, and Julia swept past him, turning to give

him a wink and a saucy smile before looking at her father with a contrite expression. He raised his hand in farewell as Clarke whisked Julia inside.

As they disappeared into the crowd, dread consumed Kellen. He considered Julia's last words to him. She wasn't cruel. Jonathan was up to something. Kellen had thought as much the instant he'd heard Clarke was in Spring Valley. Now he knew for sure. From here, he could only wonder and worry what it was. Julia had implied that everyone in town was in trouble. He didn't care about everyone.

Guin was in trouble. The woman he loved, the woman he had hurt, was in trouble. All his schemes were worthless if anything happened to her.

He'd do whatever he had to do to protect her. He'd go back inside to the party and do what he'd vowed not to do—he'd offer shares in his resort to investors. That would give him the money to build the spur line around Guin's farm. He'd have the money to finish the resort and open it on time. His success would be Spring Valley's success. Together, they would thwart Jonathan Clarke and his plans to hurt the valley. To hurt Guin.

In the morning, he'd telegraph Winfield first thing, and get himself back to Spring Valley, back to Guin, as quickly as he could.

It took Kellen longer than he'd anticipated to close deals with the investors. The same men who'd told him what a wonderful idea his resort was and how they wanted to be the first guests were a bit more restrained when it came to actually parting with their money. It took several days, and some smooth talking, but he had the letters of credit to give to the Spring Valley bank.

He'd telegraphed Winfield to find an alternate route for

the spur line, but he hadn't mentioned Julia's warning. That was not something he wanted made public until he'd returned and assessed the situation for himself. Now, with the letters of credit in his pocket, he rode his horse as fast as he could back to Spring Valley. Back to Guin.

Guin sat on her horse and gazed forlornly at the burned-out ruin that had been the kiln. Everything was gone. The kiln, the rest of the harvest, the bags, the poles. Everything except the roots in the ground for next year's hops. If there was a next year.

She'd added and subtracted the numbers over and over again in the past two weeks. The results always came out the same. If she paid nothing to the bank, she could make it through until next year, barring any emergencies. If she paid the bank, she wouldn't have enough left to live on. Either way, she had nothing to pay Pedro and Joel, and nothing with which to replace the kiln and supplies.

Even with disaster staring her in the face, the loss of Kellen hurt more. He had betrayed her, used her in the worst possible way, and she hadn't even seen it coming. She should hate him, but she didn't. She was angry and she was hurt, but it was worse than that. Now that he was gone, she felt his absence more keenly than she ever would have believed. She hadn't realized how much she'd looked forward to his visits, how much she'd enjoyed talking to him about anything that came to mind.

She hadn't realized she'd fallen in love with him. With him by her side, she could withstand whatever came her way. Alone, she found she'd lost the will to fight.

Maybe she'd sell Kellen his right-of-way. She knew from conversations with Winfield that the spur line was the only significant obstacle they faced. She'd seen the resort and knew it would be a success. She laughed, but there was no humor in it. Yes, she'd sell him the right-of-way for the spur line, and she would find someplace else to live.

Guin turned her horse toward home. At least she didn't have to worry about her grandmother. In fact, her grandmother falling in love with Dr. Jackson was the only good thing that had happened all year. Guin slowed her horse's pace as she approached the house. Dr. Jackson's buggy was not parked out front. Guin sighed with relief that he was out with her grandmother. She was in no mood to be pleasant. All she wanted was to be left alone for a while.

She rode her horse to the barn and took her time caring for the mare. Colonel joined her, and Guin found some comfort in his cold, wet nose nudging her hand until she gave him her full attention. As they crossed the yard to the house, Guin heard a horse and buggy coming down the road. She scowled that her time alone had been so short, then her heart sank as she recognized Mr. Gaspard, the banker. Of all the people she didn't want to see. . . .

She shaded her eyes against the sun. "Hello, Mr. Gaspard."

"Miss Guin," he said as he pulled the horse to a stop and climbed from his buggy. "I trust you are well?"

"As well as can be expected."

"Ah, yes. These are difficult times for some."

The back of her neck prickled with tension. "I suppose you're here to talk about the loan."

Gaspard laughed heartily. "Oh, it won't be as bad as you think. In fact, I may even have some good news for you."

Her curiosity piqued, Guin said, "Really? I can't imagine what you could say that would be good news. Would you like something to drink?"

"I'd like that. It's still hot and dry around here."

Guin led the way to the house and shooed Colonel to stay outside. "You can rest a minute in the parlor while I get something."

"Oh, that's just fine." Gaspard laughed, but not as heartily as before.

Guin wondered what he was up to, but she was tired and thirsty, and didn't argue. She went to the kitchen and pulled a pitcher of lemonade from the cooler and sliced the cake she'd made the night before. Given her finances, she wouldn't be making those any more. Sugar was dear, and so were spices. She'd have to limit herself to biscuits and homemade jam.

After she'd served the banker, she sat across from him and waited for the news she was sure had to be bad, despite Gaspard's reassurances.

"Mm-mm. That lemonade sure clears a dusty throat."

"Thank you." She still couldn't bring herself to ask.

After he'd finished the cake and another glass of lemonade, Gaspard settled comfortably in his chair. "I suppose you're wondering why I'm here."

Guin smiled wanly. "I think you're here to find out how I'm going to pay my loan."

"Well, now, not exactly."

"What do you mean?"

"I know about what's happened here. A body would have to live across the country to not know that losing your kiln like that was a real set-back."

"That's putting it mildly, Mr. Gaspard. I lost the kiln, most of my harvest, and all the equipment I need to grow and harvest the hops. In a nutshell, I'm ruined."

"Oh, Miss Guin, that sounds so harsh."

"Look, Mr. Gaspard. I appreciate your trying to sugar-coat the situation, but I know you'll foreclose on the farm and sell it to repay the loan. Before you do, please give me a chance to find a way to pay you. A couple of months, at least. If I can't do it, then I only ask that you sell it for a fair price so I have something to live on until I can find another place to live."

"Miss Guin! I wouldn't dream of turning you out of your home. No, ma'am. I have a proposition for you that'll take care of everything."

At Gaspard's feigned cheerfulness, Guin grew even more wary. "Oh?"

"Yes, indeed. I will let the loan stand as is, no payment due until next year's crop is harvested. I'll even loan you what you need to rebuild the kiln and replace your equipment. Nothing extravagant, mind you," he said with a phony chuckle.

"But . . . but, why? Why would you do this? How can you? I mean—"

Gaspard raised his hands for her to stop. "I understand, Miss Guin." He laughed again, and this time it really sounded false. "I can make this offer in good conscious because—"

"Hello! I say, is anyone at home?" Winfield's voice came from the kitchen.

"In here, Winfield," Guin called. She stood up to greet Winfield.

"Good afternoon, miss," Winfield said as he came into the room. "I say it's a good thing—You! What are you doing here?"

Guin frowned at Winfield's exclamation and turned to the banker. She gasped. Gaspard was now standing and holding a gun on them both.

"Get in here," Gaspard said, waving the gun to signal Guin and Winfield to cross the room.

"But—"

"Be quiet!" Gaspard pulled a handkerchief from his pocket and mopped his forehead. "Move those chairs and sit in the corner."

"But—"

"Will you shut up!" Gaspard shrieked at Guin.

"There is no reason to speak sharply to the young lady," Winfield said.

Afraid that Winfield might do something foolish, Guin put her hand on his arm. "It's all right, Winfield. But Mr. Gaspard, what's going on? Why are you waving a gun at us?"

"I can explain, Miss Guin," Winfield said. He pointed at the banker. "This is the man who left me for dead on the hillside."

Incredulous, Guin gaped at him. "What? What are you saying? Mr. Gaspard is our town's banker. He wouldn't . . . why would . . . I don't understand."

"Oh, it is very simple, my dear," Winfield said while he continued to glare at Gaspard. "The shock of seeing this man with you has returned the memory of my own unfortunate encounter. Your distinguished banker has a most wretched ability to choose investments, with disastrous results, I must say. The bank was in terrible financial straits up until a few months ago, when suddenly an abundance of money appeared in the vaults."

"How did you find out?" Gaspard demanded.

"It is quite astounding how much information one can gather if one knows the correct questions and asks the right people." Winfield seemed rather proud of himself as he stood taller and straightened his waistcoat.

"I still don't understand," Guin said with a nervous glance at Gaspard. "What does that have to do with me, and why is he holding a gun on us?"

Winfield sighed heavily. "Mr. Gaspard has made a pact

with the devil, my dear. Remember a few months ago, I reported that men who had agreed to build the resort had backed out? Others who had promised to provide produce and other necessities suddenly changed their minds. You can thank your banker for almost causing the ruin of my master."

"Mr. Gaspard? But why?"

"Because I sold the loans to someone else to cover my investment losses," Gaspard blurted.

"Quite considerable those losses were, I must say," Winfield murmured.

Gaspard looked even more desperate at that comment, and Guin nudged Winfield to be quiet. "So what happened?" she asked the banker.

Gaspard shook his head. "I was frantic, Miss Guin. I didn't want to hurt anyone, but I had no choice. I sold the loans, and went to each person and told them they didn't have to make payments if they promised not to help Mr. O'Roarke with his resort."

Guin shook her head. "I still don't understand."

"I will explain," Winfield said. "Jonathan Clarke wants the resort to fail. Or, if not fail, for Kellen to default on his loans so Clarke can take it over. It was a most devious scheme, I must say. It nearly worked."

"It is working!" Gaspard cried out. "This farm is the last hold-out."

"My farm?" The implication of the banker's words sunk in. "You? You ruined me?"

"I—I didn't want to Miss Guin, really I didn't. I didn't see any other way to stop you from letting O'Roarke build across your land."

"You set the fire," she said, horrified. "You burned my crop so I'd have no choice, but to accept your terms. You tried to murder me."

"No. No. I'd never do that. I didn't know you were inside. When Joel came outside for wood, I knocked him out and thought he was working alone. I never dreamt you'd be in there."

"The sheriff will not find the distinction significant when he puts you in jail," Winfield said.

"I'm not going to jail. You're the only ones who know."

"You plan to turn embezzlement into murder?" Winfield asked. "That does not sound like an intelligent decision to me. So many loose ends to deal with. Quite messy, besides."

Guin heard Colonel barking. Someone was coming, but she didn't want the banker to hurt anyone else. "Mr. Gaspard," she said in a loud voice. "Winfield has a point. We can work something out. In fact, I had refused to let Kellen build across my property, isn't that right, Winfield?"

"Yes," Winfield agreed. "Your refusal created a considerable amount of frustration for him."

"I explained it to Kellen a long time ago," Guin said. "If he put his spur line across my land, it would ruin my irrigation system. So you see, you burned my kiln for nothing." She couldn't stop bitterness from creeping into her voice. "You did it all for nothing. You ruined me for nothing."

Gaspard hung his head, but kept the gun pointed at her and Winfield. "Oh, Miss Guin, I am sorry. I—"

From around the corner, Kellen grabbed Gaspard's arm and aimed the gun toward the ceiling. Henrietta jumped from behind Kellen and swung a skillet at Gaspard's head. The banker's eyes widened for a moment, then he slumped to the floor.

"Kellen!"

"Guin, are you all right?"

Before she could answer, Guin found herself in Kellen's

arms. He squeezed her so tight she could hardly breathe, but it didn't matter. He was back.

Kellen loosened his grip and she felt lost, but then he kissed her soundly.

"What the devil happened here?" Dr. Jackson said from the entry.

Guin eased herself from Kellen, but stayed in the circle of his arms. "Mr. Gaspard set the fire, Dr. Jackson."

Winfield and Guin quickly told the others what had happened.

"I saw your note at the hotel, Winfield. When I stopped at the bank with my letters of credit, the teller told me Gaspard was coming this way. I got here as quickly as I could."

"We was just returning from our ride when this boy comes galloping down the lane like his tail's on fire," Dr. Jackson said. "We was concerned when we saw Gaspard's buggy out front. Figured we better sneak in quiet like. I kept Colonel in the barn," he said with a harrumph that told Guin he was not at all pleased with dog duty.

"I whacked him on the head," Henrietta said, looking quite pleased.

"I will take this scoundrel into town," Winfield said. "The sooner he's in the hands of the local constable, the better I shall feel."

"We need to do something about Gaspard's embezzlement and Clarke. Everyone in the valley has been victimized," Kellen said.

"I will contact the judge to begin a discussion as to what should be done about Mr. Clarke's perfidy," Winfield replied.

The three men carried Gaspard outside and tied him to the back of the banker's buggy. Winfield tied his horse's reins to the buggy, then climbed inside to ride to town.

"Well, don't that beat all," Dr. Jackson said as he watched Winfield drive away. "Miz Henrietta, I sure could do with some of your cool lemonade."

Henrietta looked from him to Guin and Kellen, then smiled. "Yes, I think that's a wonderful idea."

Guin knew they were leaving on purpose, and she watched their departure before turning to Kellen. "Well."

"Yes. Well."

She saw the pain and regret in his eyes, and despite the embrace and kisses he'd given her, she knew he wasn't here to stay. She couldn't stop the tears that welled up in her eyes. "When are you leaving?"

"Leaving?" A stricken expression crossed Kellen's face. "You want me to leave?"

"I—"

"You have every reason for never wanting to see me again, Guin. I know that. I'm so sorry about what I said last time. I never meant to hurt you. I . . . I love you," he said.

"You do?" Guin blinked and a tear trickled down her cheek. When he nodded, she whispered, "I love you too."

"I found a way, Guin. I sold shares in the resort, and Winfield found another route for the spur line. I don't need your land, Guin. I need you. I want you with me for the rest of my life."

"So do I, Kellen." She reached up to kiss him.

From the kitchen, Beau and Henrietta watched the younger couple. Henrietta sniffled and dabbed at her eyes.

"Tarnation, woman, what are you weeping about?"

"I'm happy for them."

"Harrumph. 'Bout time, if you asked me. Now will you stop worrying about that girl long enough so's we can get hitched?"

"Oh, Beau, you have such a charming way with words." Henrietta kissed him on the cheek, then returned to watching her granddaughter and her handsome young man.

Author's Note

The setting for this story is the Sanel Valley in Mendocino County, California. Hop farms flourished in the late 1800's, until Prohibition. The description of the harvest was drawn from an article in *The Cosmopolitan: An Illustrated Monthly Magazine*, published November, 1893. The railroad did not arrive until the late 1800's. The Vichy Hot Springs was built in the mid-1800's and was a popular resort for wealthy San Franciscans. Visitors still come to experience the "champagne" waters. Today, the landscape is dotted with vineyards, most with tasting rooms. All the characters and events portrayed in this story are figments of the author's imagination.

About the Author

Bridget Kraft lives in Western Washington with her husband and Brittany spaniel. When she's not writing, she loves to travel to Ireland and Germany, tracing her ancestors and finding ideas for new stories. At home, she haunts nurseries for new plants for her garden, bookstores for new research books, and office supply stores to fill the endless demand for paper and ink cartridges.